WHIS

LAST GOODBYE

KAREN WOODS

EMPIRE
PUBLICATIONS

EMPIRE PUBLICATIONS
1 Newton Street, Manchester M1 1HW
© Karen Woods 2017

ISBN: 978-1-909360-47-1

Printed in Great Britain.

Although my heart is broken,
It keeps breaking every day...
You, took my days with you...
You, took my nights with you.

In Memory of Darren Anthony Woods
My Brother My friend, My Angel in the sky.
I love you always.

ACKNOWLEDGEMENTS

THANK YOU SO MUCH to all my readers, your support is endless. Thank you to all my Facebook friends and Twitter, Instagram friends too.

This year has been so challenging for me. When you lose someone you love I don't think your heart ever fully repairs. My brother Darren will never be far from my side and I know he will only be a whisper away. He will always be my baby brother and I know he will be shining bright where ever he is. I love you our kid.

Thank you to all my friends and family for supporting me during these last few months.

Thank you to my children; Ashley, Blake, Declan and Darcy I love you always.

A big thank you to Rebecca Ryder for all her hard work. Thank you as always to Ashley Shaw and John Ireland for always believing in me.

My last thank you goes to Craig McDaid for making me smile again. Thank you so much for always being there and making me believe in love again. You're my fate, my destiny, my Prince Charming.

Big Kisses to my son Dale in heaven, your Uncle Darren is with you now and I know he will watch over you.

Always

Karen Woods
www.karenwoods.net
@karenwoods69

ACKNOWLEDGMENTS

CHAPTER ONE

THE CEMETERY WAS QUIET today and just a few people were about, huddled near graves; they were loved ones, the people who couldn't bear to say goodbye. There were parents begging for their children to come back to life and friends who couldn't believe their mate had died. This place was so depressing and there was so much sadness there. It was a dreary setting for anyone to spend time in, for sure. Who, in their right mind, would spend hours here talking to dead people? They must be off their heads. The dead can't hear you, they can't answer back; it was pointless. Dark clouds hung low in the sky above, they seemed angry with the world. Dead flowers had been chucked in the bin nearby, this place was pure misery. The graveyard was full of people who were gone too soon; loved ones who'd suffered; infants who'd never seen their adult life; such tragedies all held inside this one place. Everybody who walked through the large black metal gates had lost someone they loved or cared for and the heartbreak was visible across their faces. It was such a sad place to visit, morbid.

Harpur Murray zipped her coat up high and made her way to the grave she had visited nearly every week since the death of her younger brother. A bunch of red carnations held tightly in her grip, she held on to them as if her life depended on it as she trudged down the grey gravel path leading to his resting place. Taking a few deep breaths, she edged closer to his grave, nervously twitching. Scared she would break down crying again. This walk never got any easier, no matter how many times she came here. Taking a deep breath, she held a flat palm over her aching heart and moved closer through the thick brown mud, feet sinking low with every step she took. The weather had been bad lately and rain had fallen here for the last few days. Large puddles of brown, muddy, water trickled past her feet. Manchester had never had the best weather in the country and today was no different. They say it's grim up north – and they're probably right. The sunshine was never seen here for months on end. There was an eerie silence and nothing but a small gust of wind could be heard whispering past her ears. The fine blonde hairs on the back of her neck stood on end, goose pimples ran down her arm. She rubbed them quickly and tucked a long strand of hair behind her ears so she could see properly. Harpur swallowed hard and bent down low. Her eyes clouded over and it took a few seconds for her to compose herself. She needed to pull herself together, to come and say what she had to. Her fingers gripped the brown, gritty soil at the side of her, squeezing at it, her knuckles turning white with the anger that stuck in her throat. She hated that her brother was lying buried beneath her. Licking her dry cracked lips, she glided her tongue across her cold lips.

"Are you alright our kid?" Her nostrils flared slightly as she continued. "Nothing really much to tell you today, just the usual boring stuff. But ay, I just thought I'd call anyway to see how you are." She brushed her fingertips along the shiny black headstone, touching every word engraved there. A single fat bulky tear trickled down the side of her cheek, just like it always did when she came here. Harpur's eyes focused on her sibling's photograph to the left of the headstone and she closed her eyes slowly, as if someone was stabbing a sharp blade deep into her heart. His face, his memory, it was all so raw. She sat down and dug deep into her coat pocket and pulled out a cigarette. With a quick flick of the lighter, she sucked hard on the fag, trying to calm herself. Her hands were trembling slightly. A thick cloud of grey smoke circled around her as her cheeks sank in at both sides. Her eyes focused on the brown soil at the side of her legs. Her palm resting softly on the top of it, she whispered in a soft, calming tone. "It's alright for you Brady isn't it, but what about us, what are we supposed to do without you? You're a selfish bastard, didn't you ever think what this would do to us?" A black jackdaw hopped near the graveside and just froze as if it was watching her. She turned her head slowly and gawped at it. Her head dipped slightly to one side, then the other. She whistled over to the bird to try and get it to come closer. "Is that you Brady? Have you come back as a bird? If it is, just do something so I know it's you. Squawk, bounce about, just do something?" Harpur watched the bird with eager eyes in the vain hope that it would talk back to her, to do something different to show her that her brother was still by her side. But the bird was silent. It didn't make a sound. Her feathered friend flew away and left her with a blank expression and a heavy heart.

Brady's death had hit Harpur Murray hard and no matter how much she tried, she just couldn't let go of the time they'd spent together. She kept reliving the memories, the time he'd spent on this earth. This was so hard, she'd known him from birth, he had always been in her life, from the cradle to the grave. Her fingers played with the petals from the flowers in the black pot near where she sat. She'd bought it a few weeks ago and the gold writing on the front of it read "My Dear Brother." Harpur checked around the surrounding area and made sure nobody was listening to her. This was her time, her heartfelt words. "My mam is heartbroken you know, our kid. She'll never get over this. Why did you leave her, she's lost without you." She swallowed hard and stretched her eyes open wide, trying to stop the tears from gushing from her eyes. "Our Pat had a cushion made out of your shirt and all my mam does is sit there holding the daft bleeding thing all day and all night long. You know which one it is?" She closed her eyes and she could see the garment right there in her memory bank. It was as clear as daylight. "It's the one I bought you for Christmas, the red checked one. You looked smart in it too, didn't you? You always scrubbed up well when you wanted to." Harpur was getting angry now. Her fingers tightened and the two round balls were resting on her lap, knuckles turning white. "We said it was me and you forever, how could you leave me, just like that. I would never have left you. I need you back here with me, please come back Brady. This time, things will be different I promise you. I just need to hold you. To tell you everything is going to be alright." Harpur smashed her fist into the ground and her nostrils flared as her eyes clouded over. "We could have worked this out, you could have got help. You know I'd never give up on you. You're a selfish bastard, nothing else. You left me when I needed you most. You left us all. Who am I going to talk to now? You understood me, you always knew when something was wrong. I'm alone now. I just want you to come back. Please, come back."

Harpur sat sobbing with her head held in her hands, her shoulders shaking. Anyone who was listening to her would have thought she'd lost the plot. Why on earth was she talking to a grave? Nobody was listening. Her tone changed and her voice was soft and gentle, animated. She dabbed the cuff from her jacket into the corner of her eyes, soaking up the tears. "Is heaven nice? Are you with people you know? I've asked you lots of times to show me you are still with me and all I keep finding is daft bleeding white feathers. I want something more Brady. I need to know you're alright, safe. I can't sleep since you've been gone and everything reminds me of you. Daft songs on the radio, things on the television. I even thought I saw you in the street the other day. I chased some bleeding man thinking it was you. I swear Brady, he was your double. He had a blue cap on like you and even the shape of him was you. It's doing my head in now, you need to help me. I can't do this anymore. People think I'm fine, but I'm not. I'm hurting brother. Please take the pain away. I can't cope. I just want to feel normal again."

This woman was heartbroken, the poor soul needed to go now. Why on earth was she putting herself through this misery every week? Harpur looked around her. There were still a few people about in the cemetery in the distance, changing flowers, washing headstones, sobbing. She lifted her head up slightly and shot a look over at a man who was sat nearby at a graveside. He too was sat down on the ground and by the looks of him, he was having a hard time just like she was. Death was so final; there was no second chance, no time to say goodbye. Harpur closed her eyes tightly and the life she'd shared with her brother started to come back. Quickly, shaking her head, she gripped the ground and stopped the visions she could see forming in her mind. It was too painful, heart wrenching. She couldn't face it, she needed to blank it out, let it go, walk away. Whatever had gone on in her life, she was trying to forget it, run away from it and never face it again. Harpur's windpipe tightened and her breathing was strained. The colour drained from her and she was as white as a sheet. Jumping up to her feet, she bent over and clutched her knees tightly, starting to suck in large mouthfuls of fresh air, stamping her feet, walking around in a circle. She was having a full-blown panic attack.

Breathe, breathe, relax, stop stressing. Do what the doctor told you to do.

She was calming down now, she was back in control. Harpur looked at her brother's resting place one last time and started to edge towards the footpath. She was in a bad way and needed to get some fresh air in her lungs. Her palms were hot and sweaty and small droplets of sweat had formed on her forehead. She needed to leave before she collapsed. With a quick sign of the cross across her body, she left the cemetery in a hurry.

CHAPTER TWO

"LET'S BE CLEAR HERE GIRLS. Marriage is like a piece of steak. I know we all love a bit of meat, but no matter how much you try to disguise it, it will always be the same piece of bleeding steak." Bridget was drunk and she was waffling. Her words were slurred as she continued. Her expression was serious as she held everyone's attention. "Why do you think I carted Gary Jacobs after all them years. Go on, tell me that girls!" she shot her eyes around the table looking at her friends, pointing her finger, waiting on any of them to make a comment. None of them dared, they all remained silent. They knew better than that, they all kept schtum. Bridget flicked her hair back over her shoulder and snarled over at them. "I'll tell you why shall I? Because, it was the same every bleeding night. I hated the guy in the end, that's no word of a lie, he made me cringe. It wasn't his fault, it was mine. I just needed something more that's all." Bridget was drunk and she was getting angry with herself, regretting the years she'd wasted with different men.

Harpur chuckled and swigged a mouthful of her wine. "You have a way with words you do Bridget. I just think me and Neil are just going through a bad patch that's all. We'll sort something out, we always do. Stop stressing me out about it all. I'm out tonight for a good time, not to listen to you moaning about stuff. Just change the record and let's have a laugh like we always do."

Bridget shook her head slowly and ran her finger

slowly around the top of her glass. She had a mischievous look and the corners of her mouth began to rise slowly. "You need a bit of fun you do. Someone to make you feel alive again. If I'm putting my cards on the table here, Neil's a boring old fart, he always has been. You know he never deserved you, don't you?" Harpur rolled her eyes and got herself ready for the lecture that was coming next. Friday night with the girls usually ended up like this and Bridget was always the same when she'd had a few too many drinks. She was always trying to put the world to rights. The other girls moved away from the table, aware that Bridget was on one. Doom and gloom was the last thing they needed tonight. They wanted to dance, snog a random stranger, get pissed. Anything but listen to the same old story about how they should all wait about for Mr Right. This was old news to them; same shit, different day.

Bridget held her head to the side and licked her bottom lip slowly. She knew what she was doing and didn't care who was listening. "Neil was a rebound love, nothing more and nothing less. He was there when you were low and needed fixing that's all. I've told you this a hundred times before, he was punching above his weight with you and you know it. Why do you think he couldn't wait to get a wedding ring on your finger?" She sucked hard on her gums and stared directly at Harpur. She hunched her shoulders and held her hands out in front of her. "Come on, am I the only one who's being totally honest here tonight? Let's face the facts and tell it like it is, cut the bullshit for once in your life and be honest. I'm your best friend. Don't even dare to try and lie to me. Neil is boring and never in a million years would you have looked at him if you weren't on the rebound from that bleeding lunatic you was with.

He was the safe card that's all. Come on, admit it."

This was a bit strong, over the top and none of her business really. Bridget bent forward and held her ear to the side waiting on an answer. Harpur was on the spot and had to say something quickly before this got out of hand. She knew how to handle her, she tried her best to shut her up. "Listen, I love Neil. Okay, he's not my usual type but he was there when I needed someone and, I owe it to him to be a good wife. I have to make him happy. You're forgetting he fixed me when I was broken. And," she raised her eyes and her expression was serious, "I was a mess. You know that more than anyone. So please, stop going on about the past for crying out loud and give me a break will you?"

Bridget let out a laboured breath and flicked invisible dust from her shoulder. "What! You owe him nothing! You'll be miserable for the rest of your life if you carry on like this. I can't believe you sometimes. You need to face the facts. He'll never be the one who makes you happy. You should just divorce the prick and find somebody who gives you butterflies. The one, the love of your life. You know, the man you always spoke about when we were growing up. The man who made your heart beat faster, took your breath away. Have you forgotten about him ay?"

Harpur was losing patience now. She was sick to the back teeth of listening to this bullshit. After all, this was her husband she was talking about, the man she married, for better or for worse, till death do us part. She had to fight her corner, stand up for herself. "Bridget, you need to look at your own life before you start going on about mine. I never tell you what to do or who to date, do I? No, I just let you plod on and say nothing. Perhaps I should start getting busy on your life too. You're not perfect you know, far from it if I'm being honest with you."

Bridget let out a sarcastic laugh as she started to fill both their glasses up with more wine. This was water off a duck's back to her. So what, she'd had a few men in her life. And she'd messed up big time but her point was she would never settle for second best. Here she was again, chipping away at her best friend. "I've made loads of mistakes love. Why do you think I'm still on my own? I'm like you. Or like you used to be when you were younger should I say. I want to find that special someone, the love of my life. The man of my dreams. He's out there somewhere. I just haven't found him yet. So, put that in your pipe and smoke it." Harpur knew she was fighting a losing battle and never in a million years would she ever win an argument with Bridget when she had a bee in her bonnet. This debate would go on for hours now if she didn't agree with her, she just wanted the conversation about her married life to end, she'd heard enough. Harpur sat twiddling her thumbs, there was nothing more to say, she was deflated. But the truth was there for everyone to see, her friend was right. She'd hit the nail right on the head. Harpur was unhappy, she was stuck in a rut. Bridget could see she'd upset her and she reached over and ran her fingers through her long dark hair, regretting that she'd been so harsh with her words. Harpur had such lovely blue eyes, enchanting they were. Bridget had seen these eyes so full of tears over the years and her heart went out to her. Okay, perhaps she'd been a bit too open with her opinions and she should have kept her mouth shut but sometimes she just couldn't help it. It was just the way she was. She was her own worst enemy. Bridget let out a laboured breath, aware now that she'd overstepped the mark. "I'm sorry love. It just frustrates me to see you just plodding on every day. I know you're not happy. I can see it in your eyes. I'm sorry alright. I just get a bit carried away sometimes. You know me, I'm a passionate woman. Shoot me for even caring about you."

Harpur hung her head and spoke quietly. "There is no need to say it in front of everyone else though. This is private stuff between us two. I don't want the world and his wife knowing my business. I'll sort myself out. I'm just a bit low at the moment. You know I always bounce back. Just give me time. It's just our Brady death, it's done me in. I can't focus anymore. Every bleeding day is as hard as the last. When will it ever get any better? Go on, tell me when will I ever feel normal again and stop crying all the time."

Bridget gripped Harpur in her arms and squeezed her with all her might. "Orr love, come on, don't be getting upset. Your Brady will always be in your heart and with every day that passes it will get easier, trust me, it will. You won't ever forget him and that's all that matters. You two were as thick as thieves and nobody will ever take that away from you. Brady loved you, he just got a bit lost that's all. He got in deeper than he could handle. Who knows what he was up against? All we know is that he was in a bad place."

Bridget had to change the subject and fast, she knew where this was heading and there was no way she wanted to see her friend break down in tears again. Because once she opened the flood gates there was no going back. "Listen love, all I want is for you to be happy. I'm just saying that's all. Don't ever settle for second best. Follow your heart and you won't go far wrong." These words were from the heart and Harpur knew she had some serious thinking to do. It was a big scary world out there and she didn't know if she was ready or even strong enough to face single life on her own. Harpur bit hard on her bottom lip and shook her head. She was hurting, ready to sob her heart out. "I just miss him so much you know, it's so hard. I feel like my heart has been ripped to shreds." Bridget patted the side of her arm and shook her head slowly. This was all so sad, such a crying shame. Harpur's life was in tatters and there was no way out, she'd hit a brick wall. She had to face facts. She could never leave Neil, not now, she needed him to keep her head together. Harpur had a story to tell and her past was something she struggled with each and every day. Bridget knew her friend inside out and even though her words were harsh tonight, she only had her best interests at heart.

Bridget necked the wine from her glass and stood up and dragged Harpur by the hands. "Come on love, drink up and let's go and have a boogie. Fuck our problems, they'll still be here in the morning."

CHAPTER THREE

HARPUR OPENED HER EYES as the morning light cracked inside the room. This was such a lovely bedroom; peaceful, pretty, everything neatly placed, tranquil. The stencil quotes on the wall showed this woman was a hopeless romantic, she believed in true love, the one. Every morning, she'd sing the words from the song she'd had stencilled on her bedroom wall. "Kiss me under the moon of a thousand stars." This woman had so much love in her heart and after years of domestic abuse in her past, she was at peace with herself now. Neil hated the wall designs and said there were much better things to display on their bedroom wall than some singer's lyrics, perhaps a wedding photograph... Memories of their time together, not words that meant nothing to him. He was like that Neil, he hated her being creative. Turning her head slowly, she looked at her husband asleep next to her. She reached over and stroked the side of his cheek slowly. His body was warm. She studied him, every crease on his face, every line, every wrinkle. Did she still love him? Was he her true love? She just didn't know anymore, her head was all over the place and she was so mixed up. Over the last year or so the couple had just drifted apart. Most nights Neil just stayed downstairs watching the TV and it was very rare they slept together anymore. I suppose most couples were like this after fifteen years of marriage, they'd just given up on each other and the romance had definitely gone. Neil was a lovely guy in his own way, he cooked and cleaned and worked a full-time job. So why was this woman still not happy? Was she searching for something that didn't really exist? Perhaps the fairy tales she'd read as a child had misled her, maybe there wasn't a Prince Charming, a man who would sweep her off her feet. The guy who would make her heart leap about inside her ribcage. She wasn't sure if true love even existed anymore. Neil began to stir, his eyes opening slowly. "What time is it sweetheart, is it time for work yet?"

Harpur smiled gently, her fingers still resting on his cheek. "It's half past six love. Your alarm will be going off soon." Harpur had been awake for ages now. She was lucky to get a few hours' sleep each night if she was lucky, her mind was always active and since the death of her brother she just couldn't really relax anymore. She had so many unanswered questions, so many things running around in her mind, tormenting her. Somebody knew more than they were letting on regarding her brother's death and by hook or by crook, she was going to uncover the truth and find out the real reason her brother was taken from her.

Neil stretched his arms above his head and pulled her over next to him. There she was lying on his chest and he had no idea she wasn't happy. He was oblivious to it all. He didn't make her feel safe anymore, she was drifting further and further away from him with every day that passed. Neil was a plain man and lived for work. He didn't like change and he would have stayed in the same clothes for years if his wife would have let him. A penny pincher he was, a tight arse, always watching his money and never letting a penny go by without it being accounted for. Neil kissed the top of her head and rolled out of the bed. She watched him carefully as he began to get ready. "Bridget and her new man are going away to a spa for the weekend if you fancy going?" She tucked the quilt neatly under her chin, waiting on his reply.

"No, I'm skint. And I can't be arsed spending time with her anyway, she has too much to say for herself. You know me and her don't see eye to eye, she's a trouble maker, she always has been."

Harpur kept her mouth shut but the disappointment was written all over her face. Why did she ever think he would say yes anyway? He never said yes to anything anymore, he was a misery. Old before his time. And if he was being honest with himself, he would have said the marriage was over years ago anyway, just like she would. Neil bent over and kissed the top of her head. Nothing special, just a peck. "See you later babes. The football's on tonight so don't be making any arrangements for me to go anywhere. I'm going to chill out with a few beers if you don't mind."

Harpur rolled on her side and watched him leave. She didn't care about him watching football on the TV anymore, she didn't care if he never came home at all. Neil left the bedroom. The front door slammed shut and she listened as he started the car. Staring at the walls around her, she was becoming restless. Reaching over, she picked up her phone and logged into Facebook. Everybody she knew was on this social network and it was her way of escaping her normal everyday life. It helped ease the boredom too, it excited her. Harpur smiled as she read some of the statuses people had written. Bridget was hilarious and some of the stuff she wrote on her timeline was so near the bone it was a wonder she wasn't banned from Facebook for life. Harpur scrolled through with a single finger. Her eyes were wide open and she was alert. She didn't start work for a few hours yet and she had some time to kill before she had to make a move. Her boss was understanding and told her to take as much time as she needed to help her get over the loss of her brother. Some weeks she only went in for a few hours. Harpur froze, eyes staring at the screen. She sat up in the bed and she was concentrating. Her fingers tapped at her phone rapidly. Grabbing her mobile phone, she dialled a number. Her voice was low as she chewed rapidly on her fingernails nervously. "Hello Bridget, it's me. You never guess what?" The voice at the end of the phone was sleepy and she had to speak up to make sure Bridget was listening. "Are you on Facebook? I know you're in bed but go on it please, I need to show you something." Harpur held the phone to the side of her head as she stared at her phone. Her heart was beating faster than normal and her cheeks were bright red. "Meet me before work, we can have a coffee. I'll explain when we meet up. What a turn up for the books, you'll never believe it in a million years. Move your arse and hurry up. I'll see you there." The call ended suddenly and Harpur just lay in the bed still looking at the screen, she never flinched. The bedroom door opened suddenly and made her panic. She stashed the phone away quickly and brushed her hair back to the side of her cheek.

"Nana, can I have a drink please?"

Harpur patted the bed next to her as a small boy stood looking at her. "Come and get in bed with me and let's have a special cuddle." The kid ran to the side of the bed as Harpur cupped him into her arms and put him in the bed next to her. "Just let's have a snuggle and I'll get up and make you some breakfast. Where is your mam, is she still asleep?"

Joseph nodded his head and smirked. "Yes, she told me to come and wake you up and to leave her alone." Harpur smiled and kissed the top of her grandson's head. His mother Joanne had been living with her for over ten months now. Well, since her son had been slammed into prison for the lifestyle he was leading. It was only supposed to be until she found a new house but as of yet there was no sign of them leaving any time soon. Harpur loved them being there anyway and she liked Joanne, she treated her like one of her own. This house was never empty and she liked it like that. She loved the company. Harpur had a son and a daughter. They were grown up now and had their own lives to lead. Sam was from a previous relationship and he was ten years old when Neil came into her life. The two of them had never really seen eye to eye and they had been nose to nose on quite a few occasions. Sam was like his dad; violent and unable to control his temper. Even from an early age she could see his father's traits in him. So for him to end up in prison came as little surprise to anyone in the family. It was sad to say but Harpur was at peace knowing where he was. No more police hammering at her front door, no more court appearances. Her son attracted trouble, he craved excitement, the usually stuff that landed him in the big house. He had a big heart though and loved his mother. He would have died for his family, spent life in jail to make sure they were alright.

Maddie was Neil's daughter and the apple of her father's eye. He always thought he could never have any children and after they set out to try for a child, his heart leapt when she told him she was carrying his baby. His world revolved around her and he thanked the Lord above every day for the child he'd sent him. Harpur reached down to the floor and shoved on a grey t-shirt. She was in a rush now and whatever she'd seen on the website had made her smile, she was all flustered, glowing even. Standing over the bed, she spoke in an animated voice to her grandson. "Joseph, you stay here and I'll make you some breakfast. I'll put the TV on for you and you can watch some cartoons while I'm making it." Joseph snuggled deep under the duvet and smiled over at his nana. He was so angelic and he could never do any wrong in her eyes.

Harpur leaned over the kitchen side and listened to the kettle boiling. She was just staring into space, she was unsettled. Tapping her fingers on the black kitchen worktop, she licked her lips slowly. The house phone started to ring and made her jump. "Hiya mam, yes, I'll call after work. Please stop crying, you're going to make yourself ill if you carry on like this." Harpur held her ear to the phone and swallowed hard as she ran her fingers through her hair. "Mam, I'm struggling too. We just need to help each other get through this. Brady wouldn't want us crying all the time. Please, just try and calm down. Go and make a cup of tea and sit down for a bit. Read a book and take your mind off it."

The conversation went on for a few more minutes and when the call finally ended, Harpur was upset herself. Joanne walked into the kitchen and walked up behind her slowly. She'd seen this woman on her hands and knees crying her heart out for weeks now and wished there was something she could do to help. She touched the top of her shoulder and pressed down slightly. "Come on, don't cry. It's going to get better. Your mam is just having a bad day that's all."

Harpur snivelled and her body melted over the kitchen

table before she finally sat down. "Every day is a bad day for her Joanne. When is it ever going to stop? Are we ever going to feel normal again? Brady has left a massive void in all our lives, don't you understand that. It will never get better?"

Joanne tried to console her. "Time's a good healer, or so they say. It doesn't help that the inquest report isn't back yet either. I bet your head's all over the place isn't it? It's the not knowing that would do me in. No wonder you can't settle."

Harpur stood up and carried on making the cups of tea. "I know something happened to make Brady take his own life, something tipped him over the edge. He wouldn't have just gone without speaking to me first. I know him inside out. It just doesn't make sense. The inquest will only tell us what we already know anyway, he was drugged up and he hung himself. It's as simple as that."

Joanne plonked herself down on the chair and played with her fingers. "It is weird, I get that. But, you know what Brady was like, he was depressed, he was always trying to top himself. He cared about nothing but the drugs." Joanne covered her mouth with her hand and her eyes were wide open. It just slipped out, she didn't mean to be so blunt. She was thinking out loud. Harpur's head twisted slowly, her teeth clenched tightly together. This wasn't good, how could she have been so thoughtless, blunt even. "Don't you ever judge my brother! He had problems, nobody knew the half of it. And as for 'always trying to top himself', as you so rudely put it. Yes, he was unstable, but don't you think that was a cry for help? He was reaching out, trying to find some peace somewhere. Do you know how hard it's been for me to watch my brother over these last few years?" Harpur was on one now and she was ready for snapping, punching Joanne's lights out.

Joanne hung her head low and sucked hard on her lips. It was her fault for being such a big mouth. Fancy making a comment like that when she knew the reaction she would get! Joseph ran into the kitchen and saved the day. He was singing and dancing and making them both laugh. Joanne was relieved, this could have got messy. There was silence. Harpur shot a look over at Joanne. This would keep, there was no way in this world she was getting away with the comment she'd just made. When they were alone again she was getting a mouthful, getting put in her place. Joanne sunk back in her chair, her and her big mouth had done it again.

CHAPTER FOUR

HARPUR WAITED EAGERLY in the coffee shop, sipping on her latte, twiddling her thumbs, watching the public through the window. Her eyes focused on the door; every time it opened she was on the edge of her seat. Something had rattled her for sure. She checked her wristwatch again, where the hell was she? Bridget was late, she should have been here over ten minutes ago. She let out a laboured breath and tapped her fingers on the table nervously. Harpur had to be in work soon and she didn't want to be late. Harpur Murray worked as a receptionist for a motoring company. She loved her job and met different people every day. There were always fit guys calling in the office, proper eye candy she called them. Many a time she'd been tempted to give her phone number out to a few of the good looking ones. She loved a good old flirt. Come on, what woman didn't? How nice was it to get attention from another man? Well, she wasn't getting any at home, so it was all fair in love and war she supposed. Neil used to always tell her how good she looked when they were dating, how sexy she was, how she was the only woman for him. But these days, he took her for granted and very rarely noticed anything about her. Even when she'd picked up a new dress, or tried a new hair style, he never made a comment. He was oblivious to anything she ever did. Well, until she pointed it out to him that was. How hard was it to give your partner a nice comment, it isn't rocket science is it? It's child's play really.

But that's what happens when two people take each other for granted, they just drift apart. They stop trying.

The coffee shop was busy today and lots of meetings were already taking place here. It was a cosy set up; dark red walls with cream trimming. It was the kind of venue you could have stayed in for hours, it felt like home. This was a meeting place where you could discuss secrets, guilty pleasures. Things that you were hiding away from the outside world. Looking around the coffee shop, she noticed laptops sitting on the tables nearby. There were two men sat there in deep conversation. She held her head to the side and tried to earwig, anything was better than just sitting there looking like a spare part. Bridget's timekeeping had never been good and all through their friendship, this woman had never been early for any meeting they arranged. She'd be late for her own funeral! Harpur was never one for being alone and often wondered how women her age coped when they were single and had no friends, no social life. No, she loved companionship and never planned anything unless she was meeting a friend. Harpur loved watching people too, she loved making up her own stories about them and the lives they led. She had a very creative mind and had always thought about taking it further. She'd discussed this idea with her husband on a few occasions and as always, he just pulled a sour face and put a dampener on it. Neil was so negative, Chief Black Cloud she'd nicknamed him. He hated that she wasn't just happy going to work and coming home like the rest of the world did. He loathed that she had dreams, goals to achieve, places to go, people to meet. Even the bucket list she'd created years before was laughed at by her husband. He was just a coach potato these days with no real ambition.

Suddenly, the shop door flew open like a hurricane had started outside. Here she was at last, about bleeding time too, she was over twenty minutes late. Bridget barged into the coffee shop and made her way straight to the counter. She smiled over at Harpur as she dragged her fingers through her hair and pulled a sour face. "It's bleeding freezing out there, look at the state of me, sorry I'm late." Bridget was out of breath and her bright red hair was like a big fur ball. This woman wasn't exactly pretty but there was something about her that was pleasing to the eye. She wasn't fat, but let's say she was carrying a bit of extra timber around. Bridget was always dieting, but never seemed to lose any weight. Probably due to her sweet tooth, she loved chocolate, she loved cakes. Harpur blushed and hung her head low as all the people looked over at her. Bridget had always been a motor mouth and the pair of them were like chalk and cheese really. They should never really have become friends but somehow, they just hit it off when they were children and their bond was so strong, nothing could ever come between them, not even Harpur's jealous husband. Bridget picked up her coffee from the counter and marched over to where her friend was sat near the window. She plonked down opposite her and started rooting around in her handbag in a panic. "This better be something good love. Look at the state of me. I've ran out of the house without any make-up on. I'll be arrested by the ugly police if anyone sees me. You better help me sort my hair out too." Bridget checked her surroundings and banged her hand onto the table. Go on spill then, while I start putting my face on." Bridget pulled out a small compact mirror from her bag and started to fan her eyelashes out with some black mascara, mouth open wide, concentrating.

Harpur spoke in an excited tone. She'd been waiting all morning to tell her this. "Did you look on Facebook then?"

Bridget was concentrating as she carried on doing her lashes. "For what? I don't know what I'm even looking for. You were like a woman possessed before. I haven't got the foggiest what you're going on about. You speak in riddles woman. How am I supposed to know if you've not told me?"

Harpur was excited, her eyes wide open, she licked her lips slowly and fanned her hand in front of her face. She was ready to unveil her gossip. "You never guess who is on Facebook? Go on, see if you can figure it out."

Bridget sighed heavily, she was in no mood for games today. She hated it when her friend did this to her. Patience wasn't one of her good points. She urged her to continue. "Just get to the point. We both have to be in work soon so hurry up and tell me. You're doing my head in now." Harpur edged forward and her voice was low as if she was about to uncover the world's biggest secret. She licked the corners of her lips slowly and sat twiddling her hair, cheeks blushing. Bridget shot a look at her and raised her eyes again. She was losing her rag for sure. "For crying out loud, are you going to tell me or what? You know I hate guessing games. And, as you already know I'm shite at them. So crack on with it, otherwise you'll be here all day."

Harpur smirked and dipped her eyes, she played with her gold wedding ring, twisting it slowly on her finger. "I was flicking through the statuses this morning on Facebook and there he was as one of the people I might know. You know when they give you a list of people who are friends of your friends so you can add them?"

Bridget was listening now, she closed the small mirror and tapped her finger on her front tooth with interest. She urged her to continue, she'd grabbed her full attention now. "Yeah, yeah, I always find old friends on there. So, come on, who's popped up? The suspense is killing me?"

Here it was, the moment she'd been waiting for all morning. Harpur looked around and reached over and touched Bridget's fingertips. "I couldn't believe it. A blast from the past. There he was, just there and my heart was like, is that really him?"

Bridget was chomping at the bit, she needed to know who she was going on about, her patience was wearing thin. "Bleeding hell, who was? You're doing my nut in now, just tell me for crying out loud before I lose all faith and keel over and die."

Harpur took a deep breath and even his name on her lips made her heart skip a beat. "Dessie Ryan." Harpur sniggered like a young school girl, cheeks getting brighter by the second.

Bridget's jaw dropped low and for a few seconds she was speechless. Whoever this man was, they both blushed thinking about him. Bridget shook her head slowly and swallowed hard as she continued. This wasn't good news. Dessie Ryan broke Harpur's heart many years ago when she was just a teenager and Bridget knew this was a code red, dangerous ground. Harpur kept her voice low and continued. "I'm as gobsmacked as you. I mean, I've not seen him for over thirty-odd years. I was seventeen when I last seen him. Anyway, he looks more or less the same as before, a bit rougher around the edges but I knew it was him the minute I seen his profile photograph."

Whoa, what on earth was going on here, this woman was heading for disaster, she needed to back off now before it was too late. Bridget gave her head a shake and her expression was serious. She focused on her best friend and made sure she heard what she was saying. "You two were like dynamite when you were together. How long did you go out with him for now?"

Harpur closed her eyes and tried to work it out. "I think it was about a year. And, as I remember, he was the feisty one not me. He just wound me up all the time."

Bridget sniggered and covered her mouth with her hand. "Bloody hell, what a turn up for the books. Dessie was an alright lad, a bit of a heartthrob if I remember rightly. What happened with you two anyway? As far as I remember, one minute you were together and the next you wouldn't even speak his name. What happened, refresh my memory?"

Harpur folded her arms tightly across her chest and her nostrils flared as she became defensive. She gritted her teeth tightly together. It was obvious she was getting angry. "He was a tosser, he cheated on me. Don't tell me you don't remember that? I hated the girl he cheated on me with too. Wendy O'Malley. See, I still remember her name." Bridget pulled herself straight and watched her friend with a close eye as she continued talking. "We could have been good together but I found out he was seeing someone else and…" she paused and started to rub at her arms as some goosebumps started to appear on them. "And to put it in a nutshell, I walked away and met that bastard who led me a dog's life. The rest is history."

Bridget reached over and patted her arm softly. "Sorry love, it was years ago. I just forgot that's all. You know what my memory is like. I have a memory span of a goldfish I do, sorry." Bridget hadn't forgot, she just pretended she had. How could she have forgotten something like this? Harpur had been heartbroken, Dessie had left her in a right state. Harpur closed her eyes and for a split second she looked like she was going to burst out crying. Taking a few deep breaths, she started to regain her composure. This wasn't the time or the place to discuss her past. It hurt too much, it ruined her day.

Bridget pulled her phone from her bag and logged into Facebook. She had to have a look for herself and see what all the fuss was about. She was a right nosy cow. "I better have a butcher's at him then and see what's got your head into a spin hadn't I? It's obvious you still fancy him otherwise why would you have me sat here talking about him."

Harpur growled and screwed her face up. There was no way she still had feelings for him, she just found it interesting that a guy she'd not spoken to for years was now on Facebook. Her tone changed and she was cocky. "Who said I fancy him? I just thought I'd tell you that's all. Dessie Ryan is a pain in the arse. He's full of himself. He always thought he was God's gift to women. I've been there and done that, got the t-shirt so to speak. He had his chance with me and blew it."

Bridget ignored her comment and started to search for Dessie on the social network. Once she found his profile picture, she sat back and gasped her breath. She examined the screen very carefully. "Oh, now I see what you mean. Is that really him?" Bridget sat gawping at the snap and enlarged it on her screen. She smirked over at her friend. "Yes, that's him alright, look at his blue eyes, bloody hell he's not lost his looks has he?"

Harpur snarled over at her friend. "And, what? I have!
That man was always punching above his weight when he
was dating me and he knew it."

Bridget just spoke out of turn and said whatever was on
her tongue. "If that was the case why did he cheat on you?
You couldn't have been all that if he had to go elsewhere.
Did you have sex with him or what?"

Harpur checked around her and kept her voice low,
she was embarrassed. "No, I bleeding didn't. I was only
young. We just played about, nothing more. What do you
take me for some kind of a slapper?"

Bridget sniggered and remembered her own childhood
with a cheeky grin. "No wonder he pissed you off then.
Didn't I always tell you, you was frigid. Everyone in school
was having a bit of slap and tickle. Come on, you must have
had a touch of it?" Harpur was beetroot and Bridget knew
exactly what she was doing to her. Harpur was always
a private person and to discuss her sexual activities was
something she rarely did. Well, until she was pissed and
then she'd tell her everything. All the nitty gritty stuff too,
she left nothing to the imagination. When she'd met Neil
she never shut up about sex with him. Let's just say he
wasn't the best in the bedroom and she had to put a big
amount of work into that department to make him reach
any kind of standard. Her mates had laughed long and
hard over this subject and after years of training Neil was
finally hitting the bar, or at least trying to. Bridget could
see Harpur was interested in this bloke and she did a bit
of her own groundwork to see if her gut feeling was right.
"Anyway, he's old news now isn't he? He had a shot at the
title with you and messed it up, so why would you even

give him the time of day anymore? His loss not yours."

Oh, this girl was clever, she just knew how to set the ball in motion and find out exactly what was going on in her friend's head. She watched her from the corner of her eye as she started to log out of the social media site. "Yes you're right. He messed up with me and I deserved better. Thanks for reminding me about that, love. It's just what I needed to hear."

Bridget was going for gold here and she was dangling the carrot right in front of her friend's nose, testing her. "Add him, there is no harm in that is there? I mean, you were friends years ago so at least you can chat about the days gone by. It's not like you two will ever run away together is it?"

Harpur drained the last bit of coffee from her cup and changed the subject quickly. "I've got to go around to my mam's later. She was in a right state this morning when she rang me. I can't cope with my own grief and hers on top of it as well. Every time I go there, it's like I have to relive our Brady's death all over again. I swear Bridget, all she does is talk about him and the things he used to do. She makes him out like he was a saint. Has she forgotten the misery he brought to her door? The endless nights of no sleep worrying about him?"

Bridget nodded her head and sighed. "He was the apple of her eye love, what do you expect?"

"I know, but please agree with me on this one. Our Brady has always been a handful, you know that more than anyone, right? Even growing up he was a little swine. My mother was never away from the police station with him."

"It's just all so sad that's all. I'm not agreeing with anything she does. But, I could never imagine losing a child. How do you ever get over something like that? My heart goes out to her."

Harpur rubbed at her arms and the hairs on the back of her neck stood on end. "If anything happened to my kids, touch wood," Harpur placed her hand quickly on the wooden table as a good luck gesture. "I'd never get over it. But it just keeps playing on my mind what happened to Brady. You know as well as me what our kid was into but to do what he'd done? It just doesn't make sense. It just doesn't add up. There is more to it, I just know it," Harpur closed her eyes slightly but carried on speaking. "My mam has told me to let sleeping dogs lie but I have my own suspicions about what happened. And you know me once I get a bee in my bonnet, I won't let it go until I find out the truth."

There was an eerie silence and Harpur clenched her teeth tightly together. Bridget started to click her fingers in front of her face and brought her back to the moment. "Right, I better move this fat arse of mine to work. Are we still meeting up later? You can come to my house. The football is on so Neil won't even know you're missing will he?"

Harpur raised her eyebrows high. "You can say that again. I could walk around the room completely naked and that man wouldn't move a muscle if the football was on. I'm sure he's turned on by it. I swear to you, it's the only time he's happy when he's watching a ball being kicked about. I would rather stick hot pins in my eyes than watch a load of men chasing a ball around for ninety minutes," her eyes were wide open. "And he has the cheek to call me boring," she played with her hands and let out her breath. "Yes, I'll be round at your house later. I'll bring some wine, we can get pissed and put the world to rights like we always do on a football night."

Bridget grabbed her handbag and pecked Harpur on the cheek. Just before she left her she sniggered. "Add Dessie, go on I dare you. Do it for a laugh. Let's see what he's up to. He might be the excitement you need in your life to keep you going with that fossil you married."

Harpur burst out laughing and all the other café folk sat there staring over at her. What was so funny? Had they missed something or what? Blushing, she hurried out of the coffee shop behind Bridget. "Bleeding hell, shoot us for laughing. Did you see their faces in there, have they never heard laughter before? Miserable gets they are." The women left the coffee shop together.

Bridget headed off in the opposite direction to her friend. She shouted back over her shoulder. "Remember to add him. I want all the juicy gossip later on when you come around to my house. Live a little, ay."

Harpur waved as she watched Bridget waddle away in the distance. Perhaps she would add Dessie. It was only a bit of fun, what was the worst that could happen anyway? He was old news; an old flame that had dwindled years ago. Yes, she was going to send him a friend request, why the hell not.

CHAPTER FIVE

HARPUR LOCKED THE CAR and headed down the path towards her mother's house. Just before she reached the gate she twisted her head back to see a black car in the distance parking up. Her blood was boiling and she stopped dead in her tracks. How dare he show his face around here after what had happened! He knew she was gunning for him. This lad had more front than Blackpool. There he was in his full glory. Paul Burton, the drug dealer. "Look at you, you smarmy bastard," she whispered under her breath. This man was the root of all evil in her eyes. He'd been supplying the local junkies for as long as she could remember. Yes, he had a nice car and all the top swag but did he have a clear conscience? How could this prick sleep at night knowing how much misery he was bringing into people's lives? Everybody knew what he was doing and not once had anyone shopped him for his seedy ways. The police must have been aware of his activities, he'd been doing it for years. This prick had supplied her brother with drugs too, she knew that for a fact because Brady was always caught talking with him. She hated him with a passion and in the past she'd had a right few run-ins with him. She wasn't scared of Paul and he knew it. Harpur stood still, observing his every move. She watched a man walk to the car and bend down slightly. Her neck stretched and she was waiting for the drugs to be exchanged for cash. She didn't have to wait long either. There it was, the switch had taken place. Her fist clenched tightly together at the side of her legs and she gritted her teeth hard. She was on the move. What the hell was she doing, she was heading straight for him, guns blazing. Her heels clipped along the pavement at speed. There was no stopping her now, she was on a mission. Harpur marched to the passenger side of the car and banged her flat palm on the window. Her voice was loud. "Oi! Fucking Charlie big spuds, fuck off from around here and go and sell drugs where you live. Don't you think you've caused enough misery around here! Go on, piss off before I ring the dibble on you myself." What had happened to Harpur? She never spoke like this, she was raging.

Paul's window slowly slid down and he lifted the peak of his cap up to get a better look at her. Once he'd clocked her face he shook his head and smirked. This guy had no respect for nobody. "Listen, you fucking do-gooder. Do one, before I run you over. I don't know what your problem is with me, just leave me alone. I've told you a hundred times before that your kid was a dirty smackhead that killed himself, so don't be looking to push the blame onto me because he topped himself. He was better off dead anyway if you ask me."

Harpur was raging, colour draining from her face. This guy was pushing her now. "Oh, you cheeky heartless prick. You know what my problem is and you know in time the truth will come out. You killed my brother. You give him the drugs and you supplied him with them anytime he wanted them. Don't you realise what you are doing to people's lives? You daft little ferret?"

The passenger in the car started to snigger, he covered his mouth with his hand quickly. Harpur was right, Paul did look like a ferret. He had two large teeth at the front of his mouth and his face looked as if someone had squashed it tightly together. Paul shot a look at the person riding shotgun and growled over at him. "Ay, bollock head, don't encourage her. She's a crank. Leave it out ay before I one bomb you?"

Harpur reached her hand inside the car and tried to grab at his neck. Her eyes were dancing with madness and by the looks of her she meant business. Paul tried to wriggle free and struggled to twist the key in the ignition. This woman was wild and she was out to damage him. Harpur was being dragged now as the car started to move off. Her head was still inside the window and her grip was strong on his windpipe. She wanted to end his life, to make sure he never breathed again. She was screaming at the top of her voice and the neighbours were out at their garden fences watching all the commotion from a distance. Her mother Sheila was there too, shaking like a leaf, head hung low. Nothing would stop these bastards. She had been at war with the drug dealers in the area for years and nothing ever changed. They were a law unto themselves and they would never listen to an old woman.

Sheila held the bottom of her back and staggered towards her daughter, screaming at the top of her voice. "Harpur, just walk away, let him go. They will get their comeuppance one day. Just leave it love, let them crawl back under the rock they came from. They're scum, dirty lowlife people who prey on others when they hit rock bottom."

The neighbours were up in arms and a few of them shouted abuse at the car as it went speeding off. They would never have said anything to their faces though. No way, their windows would have gone through if they got wind of their comments. Harpur stood shaking as she finally let her grip go on Paul. Adrenaline was pumping through her body, the vein at the side of her neck was beating like a speeding train. With every last breath she had left in her she screamed after them, hoping they heard her every word. "Go on, fuck off and don't come back around here again. The next time I see you here I'll smash that car up. Yes, you heard me, the car my brother probably paid for along with all the other junkies around here."

Sheila hurried to her daughter's side and gripped her in her arms. "Come on love, get inside, they're not worth your breath, they will all answer to God one day and I hope the lot of them will rot in hell."

Harpur was struggling to breathe, her windpipe had tightened and she was as white as a sheet, a panic attack had set in. "Mam, they killed him. I know it was something to do with them lot. Our Brady would be here with us now if it wasn't for them wankers. Why are they allowed to still be on the streets? My brother is dead because of them and no one gives a flying fuck. Why doesn't somebody do something about them?" The neighbours were whispering now, discussing the harrowing death of Brady. Everybody there had their own opinions on how he met his death but none of them would breathe a word about it. It was none of their business. It was just gossip, people putting two and two together and coming up with six. Sheila led her daughter back towards the house, away from prying eyes. She was such a frail woman and if a strong gust of wind had come along she would have been knocked from her feet and put on her arse. Sheila shook her head as she walked past the people gathered on the street. Her heart had been shattered since the death of her son and everyone there knew the heartbreak she was facing. It was such a crying shame for her, she used to be such a happy-go-lucky person, she loved life, but she loved her son unconditionally and in her eyes he could do no wrong. There was an uncanny silence when Harpur and Sheila walked past her next door neighbour. They'd heard so many arguments from inside her house, so many fights in the midnight hour, smashing, crashing, verbal abuse. They all knew the life she'd led. Not a word, silence.

Harpur sat down on the sofa and sucked in large mouthfuls of air. "I wish these panic attacks would leave me alone mam. I'm at my counselling session tomorrow and I'm going to see if there is anything he can do to help me. I swear to you, it feels like I'm going to have a heart attack."

Sheila came and sat on the arm of the sofa and reached over to touch her head with so much sadness in her eyes. "It's just the stress love, it will pass. You've been through a lot lately and it's just your body's way of telling you to calm down. And as for confronting drug dealers in the street? You're facing a losing battle. Look at me, how many times have I had words with them all? They just look at me as if I am daft. They have no heart, no morals. It's all about the money to them. They don't care that they are destroying families."

Harpur sipped on a cold glass of water that her mother passed her. "Mam, I'm just struggling every day with our Brady not being here. This house is where he lived. Look at his chair, he used to be always sat there. How will I ever get used to him not being here with us anymore? It's not right, it's all so messed up. I feel like pulling my hair out."

Sheila dropped her head low, something was wrong

with her. She stood up and walked to the living room window, messing about with the curtains, straightening the blinds, trying to occupy her mind. Her eyes clouded over and her bottom lip trembled. "My son is at peace now. I watched him fighting his drug habit for years and let me tell you something for nothing, I've seen him on his knees. I've witnessed him going to hell and back for the drugs he needed. You don't know the half of it, love. I would have given my right arm to see him clean but you know as well as me that was never going to happen. He'd done things love, bad things to feed his addiction. Stuff that would make your toes curl. You don't know the half of it." Sheila rubbed her arms vigorously and her eyes closed slowly. She walked back to Harpur and patted the top of her shoulder. "Come on love, pull yourself together. You have Neil and the kids to look about. They must be sick to death of seeing you upset. Come on, dry your eyes."

Harpur snivelled and dabbed the corner of the tissue into the corner of her eye. "Don't you think I know that, mam. I try my best you know but I just have bad days. Seeing that prick serving up druggies just made me see red." Harpur stood up and wrapped her arms around her mother. "I'll be alright. It's you I'm worried about. What you seen, what you had to do, God only knows how you are still breathing."

Sheila sat down on the sofa and pulled a cigarette out of her packet. Flicking her silver lighter, she popped her fag into the yellow flame. A thick cloud of grey smoke circled her face as she sucked hard on the cigarette. "I'll be fine love. Stop worrying about me. I'll get there just like you will."

Harpur walked to the mirror and straightened her hair.

"Bleeding hell, look at the state of me. I'm supposed to be going round to Bridget's tonight for a few drinks. I look like I've been dragged through a hedge backwards."

Sheila held a blank expression. "Why are you going round on a week day?"

Harpur rolled her eyes and let out a laboured breath. "Football's on television isn't it. You know what Neil's like when his team are playing. No one gets a look in. I'll tell you something for nothing mother, when Manchester United are playing no one can get a word out of him. The world could stop and still he wouldn't notice a single thing."

Sheila tried to make light of the matter. She could see her daughter was getting upset. "Oh, come on, Neil's not that bad. He works all the hours God sends and you could do a lot worse. Remember where you come from and the life you led before him. I'd count myself lucky and be grateful for all you have. It could have been a lot worse."

Harpur shot a look over at her mother. What? So she had to be grateful that her married life was a shambles and she was dead inside? Surely there had to be more to life than this? Could she open up to her mother and tell her about her problems at home? She studied her for a few seconds longer than she needed to. No, what good would that do? She wouldn't understand, she was old school and under the impression that once you made your bed you had to lie in it. Sheila had been married twice in her life and it was fair to say that she had got the shit end of the stick more than a few times. So in her eyes, Neil was a safe bet; no complications, just plain sailing, she could see no wrong in him whatsoever. Harpur decided to keep her problems to herself and she was probably right in her decision. Sheila didn't need to know how unhappy her daughter was, she already had enough problems of her own without adding to them. "Right mam, I'm sorry for being a headache. I just get angry don't I? I'll be fine, don't worry about me. I'm just having a bad day that's all."

Sheila watched her daughter from the corner of her eye and started to clean up. Harpur walked to her side and pecked her on the cheek. "I'll call after work tomorrow. I should be in a better mood by then. Why don't you sit down and relax? The cleaning can wait."

Sheila shot a look about the front room and nodded her head. "I know love. I'll just shift this last bit of washing and I'll get sat down. All day my back has been aching. It's just not getting any better either. Two hours' sleep I had last night, I'm drained I can tell you, absolutely knackered."

Harpur walked to the door and looked behind her one last time. Her eyes shot to her brother's chair and her chin began to shake. She had to go, she had to leave, she was ready to start crying again. "Night mam, love you, see you tomorrow." The front door slammed shut and Sheila was alone. She sat down in her chair and lifted her eyes up to the ceiling, whispering under her breath. Who was she talking to? There was nobody there.

★

Bridget had the tunes on in her house and she was singing her head off to a Take That track. She didn't hear the hammering at the front door. Harpur lifted the letterbox high and peeped inside it. She could see her singing and dancing and she couldn't help but laugh. This woman had moves and when she hit the dancefloor everybody knew about it. "Bridget, open the door!" Harpur shrieked through the tiny gap. She repeated this several times before her friend eventually heard her.

Bridget squeezed her eyes tightly together and hurried to answer the door. She was out of breath as she stood with her hands resting on the door frame. "Sorry love, once I'm in the zone I can't hear nothing but the beat of the music. Look at the state of me, I'm sweating like a camel's arsehole. I should be at least eight stone the way I move about. It's amazing that I'm still a porker."

Harpur sniggered and moved her away from the doorway with a quick arm movement. She held a bottle of red wine out towards her and turned her head back. "Dance your way into the kitchen then and fill me a large glass up with it. The day I've had, I need it." Bridget was still singing and shaking her body. Take That were her favourite band back in the day and both of them had been to see them in concert when they were younger. Gary Barlow was Bridget's guilty pleasure and even though he wasn't that tall, she always told everyone she would still ruin him given the chance. And this woman would have. She had no inhibitions and she always took what she wanted. Sometimes Harpur wished she was a bit more like her best friend. She just seemed to breeze through life and never really had any serious issues or problems, she oozed confidence. Of course, she'd had man troubles in the past, but what woman didn't? Bridget slammed the front door shut and danced with the bottle of wine into the kitchen, she was still singing her head off. Harpur sat down in the front room and kicked her shoes off. It was a lovely place to be, full of lots of memorabilia from Bridget's life. It was fair to say that this woman had had her share of lovers too. The longest lasted around five years, before she eventually told him it was over and just walked away. Yes, Bridget just marched in one night from her job as an estate agent and told the poor guy it was over. There were no warnings, no nothing, she just carted him and that was the end of the relationship, ruthless she was when she wasn't happy. Harpur was as shocked as anyone when she found out about the split and wondered if her best friend had even thought it through. But, that was that, he was gone and a week later, Bridget just carried on as if he never existed. That wasn't right was it? How could anyone just forget someone who had been in her life for as long as Jacob had, she was heartless. Even to this day she still said she never missed him. She just put on a happy face and didn't speak of him again. It must have been tough.

"Put track ten on love," Bridget shouted from inside the kitchen. "We can have a dance. Well, that's if you can still remember how to move your bony arse. I'm actually thinking of getting another dancing partner if you don't shape up. If truth be known, I think you've lost it over the years. I wasn't going to mention it but you know me, I say what I see."

Harpur smiled and took her coat off. She knew Bridget was winding her up and she was used to her sense of humour, she didn't reply. Harpur loved being here, it reminded her of when she was younger. These two shared some great memories here together. They'd done everything together back in the day; babysitting, Morris dancing and they even shared clothes, they were inseparable. Brady, Harpur's brother, had always tagged along with this crazy duo too and if they were ever a member short for their new band, he always stepped up and learned the dance routine with them. Brady was a good dancer and if he'd have taken that path of being creative, he could have succeeded. The guy could move. Bridget held two glasses in her hand as she walked into the room, they were filled to the brim. There was no measuring how many units they were drinking tonight, their aim was to get pissed as fast as they could. Both girls liked a drink and once they started it was hard for them to stop; party girls Bridget liked to call them both.

Harpur turned the music down and walked towards Bridget to get her drink. "You'll never guess what happened tonight?" Before she could answer, she sat down and began to fill her in. "I got a grip of that ginger bastard Paul Burton. There he was parked up near my mam's, serving junkies up just like he always does. The cheek of him. I swear to you Bridget, I would pay someone to end his life, the sweaty runt. Seriously, he makes my skin crawl the hard-faced fucker."

Bridget slurped a mouthful of her drink and sat down next to her. She was serious as she spoke. "I know some men who can wipe him from the face of the earth if you want, love. You just say the word and he will go on the missing list. I have connections you know; just one word and that prick will be in a body bag."

Harpur looked at her and studied her further. Was she being serious or just chatting shit? She wasn't sure. Either way it was good to know that if that was the route she wanted to go down, she had other options. Harpur folded her arms tightly in front of her and gasped her breath. "I'm going to get a grip of that Tony Wallis, you know who I mean don't you? He was a good friend of our Brady's. He knows more than he's letting on and I'm sure he's been avoiding me for some reason," she reached over and gulped a mouthful of her drink before she continued. "Since our kid has been gone he doesn't set foot near my mam's door anymore. I mean, he was there every day when Brady was alive so what's changed now? Something isn't right I just know it!"

Bridget held her head to the side and replied. "Perhaps he can't face your mam that's all. He's still in the same boat as Brady. Are you forgetting that he's still a heroin addict and nothing's changed in his life? So he probably doesn't want her seeing him wrecked out of his head does he?"

Harpur screwed her face up and slammed her drink back down on the table. "Are you for real? It never bothered him before. Come on, you've seen the state of him when he's been sat in my mam's house with our Brady. The both of them have been off their rockers, completely spaced out. They didn't care who saw them. It's not like he hid anything away from my mam is it?"

Bridget sighed. "You can say that again. I don't know how she coped with it all. I don't want to speak out of turn here love but she should have kicked them both out on their arses. Did he not have any respect for where he lived at all?"

"She just did anything in the end to make sure she knew where he was. Bridget, you don't know the half of it where he was concerned. I've had to hold a lot back because of my mam but when the time is right I'm going to tell her exactly how he disrespected her in her own home."

"I would love to know what he got up to. We only knew a few things about his life but come on, there must have been so much more to his story. He was out until the early hours nearly every night. Where the hell was he going, did he ever say?"

Harpur nibbled on the edge of her fingernail. She closed her eyes slightly and twisted her hair slowly. "My mam thought he had a girlfriend but I don't believe that for one second. He was off his napper twenty-four hours a day so how could he ever hold down a serious relationship? What kind of woman would put up with that?"

"It might have just been a shag. You know what men are like, a booty call it might have been."

"No, it just doesn't add up. I know I keep saying it but I'm going to find out what really went on. I owe it to our family. I don't want people talking behind our backs about what they think happened anymore. I want to put it to bed once and for all. They know nothing about what Brady was going through." There was an awkward silence and they both sat there thinking. Was Brady's life really such a big mystery to them both? Harpur rubbed her arms and shook her head. Her eyes started to cloud over. Not again, she was sick to death of breaking down and crying all the time. It just happened without her having any control over it whatsoever.

Control it girl, control it.

Harpur let out a laboured breath and spoke. "Let's change the subject, it just makes me angry when I think about it all."

Bridget opened her eyes wide and popped a cigarette from the packet. "Do you want one?"

Harpur declined, she'd smoked so much lately and she was trying to cut down. Bridget sucked hard on her fag. "So, did you add him or what?"

Harpur was still in a world of her own.

"Who?"

"Bleeding hell, and I thought it was me with the dickey

memory. Dishy Dessie of course, that's who."

Harpur smirked and dragged her feet up under her bum cheeks, making herself comfortable. "Oh, stop it. What are you like? What makes you think I'll add him anyway?"

Bridget tapped the side of her nose and sniggered. "Let's just say I know you. Come on, look at you, you're smitten already. Look at your eyes, you're blushing at just the mention of his name. He still rocks your world doesn't he?"

Harpur held a flat palm on the side of her cheek. Bridget was right, her cheeks were bright red. She had to admit defeat and smirked. "Alright, I'll do it now from my phone. I swear, if he starts winding me up I'm going to block him. I'm only doing this to prove a point to you, nothing more, nothing less. Me still fancying Dessie Ryan, are you having a laugh or what?"

Harpur logged into her account on her iPhone and searched for her old flame. Once she found his profile she sat looking at his photograph a bit longer than she needed to. Her finger hovered over the friend request button and her heart was racing. Bridget was eager to get this over with. "Have you done it, come on, we've got two bottles of wine to drink, just do it, hurry up. Stop wasting time, live a little." It was like being back in school and all Harpur could visualise was a gang of girls gathered around her shouting, "Do it, do it."

Boom! She pressed the button. There was no messing about thinking about it any more.

Harpur covered her face with her hands, she rubbed her skin vigorously and already she was regretting sending the friend request. Why had she just done that? What the hell was going on with her? She was a married woman, was she forgetting that?

"Oh my God, you've done it haven't you?"

Harpur nodded her head. She was still digesting her actions. "Yeah, it's a bit of fun isn't it? We're both adults now and like you said, it's not like we will run away together is it?"

The pair of them sat chatting for a few minutes when an alert was heard from her phone. Bridget picked her phone up and shrugged her shoulders. "It's not me, it must be you."

Harpur pulled her phone from her pocket and she studied the screen. Her jaw hung low and her eyes were wide open. "He's added me, he's accepted my friend request."

Bridget jumped up from her seat and sat next to Harpur, scanning the screen. "What a result! He did it so fast too. See, he's an eager beaver. Send him a message and see how he is. Go on, let's see what he has to say for himself."

This was all going way too fast and Harpur seemed to be caught up in the moment. She was alive and excited. "Send a message saying what?"

Bridget sat thinking for a few seconds. "I don't know, erm, just say 'how are you doing?'"

Harpur scowled. "No, that's so cheesy. Think of something else."

Bridget sniggered and sat back in her seat. "Well, say 'I still fancy you' then and cut to the chase. Let's see what he has to say to that."

Harpur giggled and held the bottom of her stomach. "I don't fancy him at all. Get that out of your head. You better stop saying stuff like that, you'll get me in trouble if anyone gets wind of it. I'm just interested to see how his life has turned out that's all."

"Oh, just write something, anything, just let's see what he has to say for now." Harpur licked her tongue across her front teeth and her fingers started to type. Bridget was peering over her shoulder, egging her on.

"Hi there Dessie, it's been years since we've spoken, how are you doing? Hope you're well Love Harpur x"

She pressed the send button and turned to face Bridget. "There you go. Who says I don't have any balls?"

God this was getting out of control. What next? A meeting? Sex? A broken marriage? Stories like this were all over the media, internet romance, blasts from the past, meeting over Facebook years later. Neil hated social media and said only people who had no lives went on it. Why would anyone want to get in touch with old school mates or old work colleagues? No, his view was final. Facebook was for sad, lonely, bored people. Harpur didn't seem to care anymore what her husband's thoughts were. She was actually laughing, she had colour in her cheeks, she was alive inside again. The two of them sat watching the phone for a few minutes, there was nothing, not a peep. Was he playing it cool? Had he even read the message? Harpur wasn't sure anymore. This had all gone pear-shaped and backfired on her. Perhaps he thought she was desperate, a stalker, someone he wanted to forget forever.

Bridget was aware she was a bit downhearted and patted the top of her shoulder. "Stop flapping, he'll reply to you just give him time. Trust me, if he doesn't I'll show my arse in the corner shop."

Harpur burst out laughing. "I don't know what I'd do without you. You're just always there to cheer me up when

I'm feeling a bit down. Come on then, put some tunes on and we can see if I've still got some kick-arse moves left in me before you recruit another dancing partner." Bridget didn't need to be asked twice. She jumped up from her seat and flicked the music back on. This was a girl's night in and nothing was going to spoil it.

Harpur had been in bed now for over twenty minutes. Neil was still downstairs watching the highlights from the football match he'd watched earlier. She could never get her head around his obsession with football and often asked him why he was so passionate about the sport. It was the same every time his teamed played. He'd watch the highlights and then tune into TalkSport on the radio to listen to the presenters talking about the same game he'd watched twice. Talk Shite she nicknamed it. It bored the life out of her, just as her husband did. In fairness she liked football until she married Neil. He just made her sick to the back teeth of it. He took the fun out of it. If his football team lost then the house would be up, he'd call his team every bastard name under the sun. He'd shout at the screen, launch stuff at the TV, and his language was horrific. Yes, Neil was a football fanatic. The moon was full tonight. A silver, enchanting ball of mystical light. Everything was so quiet in the bedroom and she was starting to unwind. Joanne had not long come to bed and she could hear her in the next bedroom rummaging about. Harpur closed her eyes, she could hear the TV being unplugged downstairs. That was all she needed, Neil waffling down her ear all night long about the football results. Turning on her side, she tucked the duvet tightly around her body. There would be no sex tonight, no hanky panky. She was pretending to be asleep. It was already late and she had to be up early tomorrow to the bins out. Sex was the last thing on her mind at that moment and something she could do without. It was just a chore for her these days, he didn't turn her on anymore. It was just two bodies banging together. No passion, no lust, no kissing, just laborious sex. Harpur listened carefully and heard Neil coming up the stairs. She knew every creak, every stair he stood on. The noise of his feet coming up the stairs stopped suddenly, nothing, complete silence. Harpur listened again but still not a sound. Eyes closing slowly, she started to drift off to sleep. Perhaps he'd changed his mind and decided to watch a film downstairs.

CHAPTER SIX

"MAM, HAVE YOU GOT some money for me please? I'm going to nip to town with a few of the girls. Just twenty quid will do. I'll pay you back when I get a job. I promise I've got an interview this week that could land me a great job. A fantastic career." Before Harpur could open her eyes, Maddie had opened her handbag and she was already locating her purse to hand over to her. "Can you hurry up mam, they'll be here in ten minutes and I've not even started my hair yet." Neil rolled over and smiled at his daughter. "I'll drop you off in town if you want princess, just give me five minutes to have a coffee and I'll be ready to go." Maddie nearly choked. There was no way in this world she was letting her old man drive her about in his shite car. Her friends would have made her a laughing stock. I mean who drove a Renault Clio anymore? They were family cars, for pensioners.

She had to tread carefully so as not to hurt his feelings. "No dad, you stay in bed. You need to stop being so protective over me. I'm old enough to look after myself now. It's just embarrassing you ringing my phone all the time and checking on me. Take a chill pill and relax. I'm streetwise, dad. I know the crack." Oh, this girl had attitude. Considering she was brought up in a loving household, she always seemed so angry and wanted more from life. It was like her parents weren't good enough for her. This girl loved money and power and it was common knowledge that she would never even consider going on a date with a guy unless he had a few quid. Yes, this girl was a gold digger and she wasn't afraid to admit it. Sam, her brother, had taught her all she knew about how to get what she wanted in life and he made sure that she was always looked after by anyone she decided to date. Maddie was always getting gifts, nights out, weekends away. Her parents didn't really have a clue what she was into either. She was shady too, something wasn't quite right about her. But this girl had seemed to have lost her shine lately. The weight had dropped from her, she didn't seem to dress the way she used to and she was always snappy.

Harpur snarled over at daughter and she knew she was treading on thin ice. Alright, she was right about Neil still treating her like a baby, but there was no need for her reaction when he was only trying to help her. "Oi, lippy. Your dad is just showing he cares about you that's all. Stop being so cocky with him."

Neil could see Harpur was getting ready to kick off and sat up in bed. "It's okay, love. She doesn't mean anything by it. I know what she means, I am a bit too protective of her and I suppose she's right, I do need to back off." Neil was making excuses for her again. He should have just put his foot down and told her there and then that Dad's taxi was now no longer available for her. That would have shut her up, that would have made her think twice before she started with her attitude towards her father. Maddie left the bedroom in a huff. No wonder she'd moved in with Diane, they did her head in. Harpur looked over at her husband. "She's getting a right attitude on her. She doesn't talk to me like that so why do you allow her to do it with you?"

Neil touched the side of her cheek with his finger.

"Give me a kiss and shut up moaning. I'm sure it's time for our once a month sex session isn't it?" Was he taking the piss here or what? She wasn't sure. Sex was nowhere near once a month, his sex drive was low and she was lucky to get any slap and tickle whatsoever. She examined him further, what had changed between them, why was he feeling horny all of a sudden? Harpur smirked at him and her eyes said it all. Neil moved in for a kiss, he was really into this, tongues the lot. Harpur had her eyes half open and watched him carefully, this was different, he'd never kissed her like this before. His hand lifted her t-shirt up and he was kissing and stroking her body. Harpur started to enjoy it now, she was making the most of it, God knows when he would be like this again.

Neil rolled off her body and lay gagging for his breath. The guy had put a graft in for sure. Harpur lay watching him and studied him longer than she needed to. This was so not him, he was never like this in the bedroom. Perhaps he'd been watching more porn than normal, picking up some tips from the filth he watched. Harpur knew he liked watching films like that but in her eyes it was normal, something most men did to get their kicks when their own sex life was stale and boring.

"Right, I better get gone. The lads are starting a new job today and we have to be there early to make sure it all goes to plan."

Harpur watched him get out of bed and couldn't help but notice a few red blemishes on his bum cheeks. Had she just done that to him or were they already there? She wasn't sure. "I'm at the gym tonight Neil, so will you make your own tea when you come home? I could throw something together by all means but you know you hate warming stuff up."

"Yeah, sorted. I'll grab something from the takeaway on my way home. Shall I get you something?" Harpur froze, what was up with him this morning? He would never buy her anything without asking for some money for it first. He was as tight as a fish's arse and never spent a penny more than he had to. She waited on him asking her for some money, but he said nothing. Neil was ready in seconds and after a quick kiss on her cheek he left the room. "See you later babes. Enjoy your day."

Harpur stretched out fully on the bed and yawned. She had no hangover this morning. It was surprising after what she'd drunk. Reaching over to her mobile, she started to read her updates. It was just the usual stuff, friend requests, people poking her begging her to speak to them. Hold on, her eyes were wide open. She rubbed her knuckles deep into her eyes and sat up in her bed. Here it was, a reply from Dessie. She just sat looking at her screen. What had he replied? what if he didn't want to speak to her ever again? Harpur sucked in a large mouthful of air and opened the message. Here goes, the moment of truth.

"Hi there Harpur. How mad is it that we are speaking again after all these years? I've looked at your photographs and you haven't changed a bit, still gorgeous in my eyes, you always will be. What have you been up to? Are you married? Kids? Do you work? Hope to hear from you soon Love Dessie X"

Harpur was gobsmacked, did he really say she was gorgeous? And, he'd looked at her photographs already. Without any hesitation, she clicked onto his profile and scrolled down to view his photo albums. She was eager to see them; hands trembling she waited for them to load.

Harpur's eyes never left the screen. Was it bad that she was looking at his private moments? He'd already told her he'd looked at hers so what was the harm in her checking his out? She was smiling, her fingers slowly clicking onto the next photo. There was a snap of two children. She examined it closely. Was this his family? Was he married too? Once she'd finished she sat back in her bed and read through the message again, analysing it this time. Her heart was fluttering and at that moment she realised there was no going back. What was the harm in having a few male friends anyway... Her fingers hit the keyboard and she began to reply to his message.

"Hi Dessie, glad to hear you are well. I'm married now with two children living in Manchester and I work as a receptionist for a motor company. Life is good at my end and I'm still good friends with Bridget, do you still remember her (the gobby one), love Harpur X"

She re-read her message before she sent it. Should she say she'd looked at his photographs too? No, no way, she was playing this cool. She continued to write.

"P.S Where are you living now? Are you married etc, job? Anyway glad to know you are still alive and well and life is treating you well. Keep smiling and have a nice day."

There it was, her first proper message to Dessie Ryan. Was it too much? Had she asked too many questions? She wasn't sure. Her finger hovered over the keyboard on her phone. Just press the button and send it, what was she waiting for? Harpur took a deep breath and closed her eyes. There it was, she'd sent it. With a hand held around her neck, she itched at her skin. The bedroom door opened and Joseph startled her. Her grandson was just stood there looking at her. She had guilt written all over her face and she was stuck for words for a split second. "Come on, come and get in bed for five minutes." Harpur patted the bed and he ran up towards her.

"Nana, when is my daddy coming home? Every time I ask my mam she says soon. How long is soon, because it seems a very long time."

Harpur raised a smile. Her grandson was so clever and she always made a point of not lying to him. "Your daddy will be home in eight weeks sweetheart. That's not long is it? And, when he's home you and mummy and daddy will all live together and live happily ever after."

Joseph digested what he'd just heard and he scowled. "But I want to stay here with you and Grandad. Daddy is horrible to mummy and he makes her cry all the time."

Harpur gently stroked the top of his head and gasped her breath. She knew exactly what was going on before her son was sent to jail but no matter how much she tried, she could never get him to change his ways. Joanne was just as bad though, she was a loudmouth and just added fuel to the fire when he kicked off. Was it her fault her son had turned out like this? Was it the life he'd led when she lived with his father? Sam had witnessed a lot of violence when he was younger. Horrific domestic abuse and surely it must have affected him. Harpur looked at the scar across her forearm, a long deep abrasion in her skin. Her heart was beating faster than normal now and the memories of what she'd suffered started to flood back to her. Joseph kissed his nana on the cheek and realised something was wrong. "I love you," he whispered in a soft voice.

Harpur sighed and kissed him on his rosy red cheek. "I love you too. Don't you ever worry about anything. I will always be here for you, no matter what. You know that don't you?"

Joseph had switched off now and he was starting to wriggle about on the bed, restless. Harpur got up out of bed and made her way onto the landing with Joseph tagging along behind her. Joanne's bedroom door was shut and she could see her still lay asleep in bed through the small crack in the bedroom door. She was a right lazy cow and she should have been up out of bed with her son. Harpur stomped down the stairs and knew she would be the one making breakfast again for her grandson. What would happen when they moved out? Who would feed Joseph then? Who would make sure he was getting three meals a day? Harpur was going to make a point of mentioning this the next time her and Joanne were together. It was time for her to grow up, to be a proper mother and do all the things expected of her.

Harpur checked the time on the clock on the kitchen wall. She had an appointment today with her counsellor and she just hoped he could help her get through this tough time in her life. Mark had been seeing Harpur on and off for a few months now. Sometimes she was fine and sailed through life but sometimes, everything got on top of her and she felt like the world was caving in on her. Recent events had nearly pushed her over the edge. Grief was such a hard emotion to overcome. There is no time limit on it, no magic pill that takes the pain away. 'Time's a great to healer' they say. But who can say for sure if anyone really gets over a death of a loved one. Does anyone ever really heal? There were always people all over the news still crying years later about the loved ones they'd lost. Perhaps when a loved one dies they take a piece of you with them, a part of you that can never be replaced.

Joseph sat at the kitchen table eating his cornflakes. Harpur sat watching him, sipping on her coffee. Her head was away with the fairies and just like every other morning when she woke up, her brother was lying heavily on her mind. Harpur walked to the back door and she could hear a phone alert in her pocket. Popping a fag into the corner of her mouth, she pulled it out and glanced at the screen. It was him again, Dessie. Harpur. She was in a panic, she checked nobody was watching her and quickly opened the message.

"Hi there, I'm glad you replied to my message. I thought I was a bit too forward in asking all the questions I did but I'm glad you were not offended by them. Anyway, to cut a long story short I live in Spain now with my two sons. I work as a finance manager and enjoy the life I live. It's a bit boring at times but at least I have the sunshine to keep me happy. I've not been in Manchester for over two years now, the rain and misery keeps me away plus a few bad memories I'd rather not speak about. My sons are called Marcus and Arelius, aged ten and six. They're good kids and have great lively personalities. I'd love to meet up if and when I come to Manchester, if you are up for it. No pressure, just a mate date. The sun is hot today here and I'm already in work. Perhaps we could have a Skype chat, you know where we can see each other on screen? Have a great day and I hope you're well. Love Dessie X"

Phew, this was a lot to take in for Harpur, it was all going way too fast. He wanted to meet her, video chat with her, she wasn't sure. Ramming her phone back into her pocket, she decided to stew on his message for a while before replying to it. She needed Bridget's advice first.

She'd know what to do in a situation like this. Quickly, she stubbed her cigarette out and went back into the house. Joseph was still sat at the table eating his breakfast and he was oblivious to her newfound excitement. Harpur checked the clock again. She was going to be late if she didn't get a move on. Her counsellor was a busy man and if she turned up late for her appointment with him, there was a good chance he'd turn her away. She needed someone to open up to, someone to listen and give her some advice. Now Dessie was back on the scene anything could happen, she was vulnerable and in need of two loving arms to hold her.

Joanne stomped into the kitchen and ragged her fingers through her hair. She yawned and walked over to the kettle. "Do you want a brew Harpur?"

"No, I've already had one. I've got to get ready now anyway. Make sure Joseph is on time for school, don't be late again or you will be getting another letter home about it."

Joanne rolled her eyes. This was her son and she was sick of Harpur telling her what she was doing wrong. Every day she moaned at her regarding the way she was bringing her son up. Who was she to talk anyway after what Sam had told her about his childhood? This woman had no room to talk. People who live in glass houses shouldn't throw stones, so the saying goes. Joanne had told her this too. Oh yes, one night after a few too many they had locked horns and a few home truths were told. If Neil hadn't been there to restrain Harpur, she would have knocked her block right off. It took weeks for that argument to blow over and it was touch and go if Joanne was going to be made homeless. Sam had gone ballistic at his girlfriend when he found out what had happened and warned Joanne that if she ever disrespected his mother again he would not be held responsible for his actions. You see, Sam was a mummy's boy, her word was gospel and he always felt the need to protect her. Even as a small child when his father was pummelling his fists deep into her body, he had tried to help her. It was such a shame he had to witness this and somewhere deep in his memory bank he would never forget the torment his father put his mother through. Harpur left the room and hurried upstairs to get ready.

★

"I thought you weren't going to get here on time Harpur. A few minutes more and I would have had to cancel your appointment." Mark was an older man. around fifty-five years of age. Bald as a coot, he had the most overgrown eyebrows Harpur had ever seen in her life, coarse bristles and long grey hairs grew in all directions. Even his nasal passage was hairy. Wouldn't you think somebody would have told him about his personal hygiene, told him to trim all the hair that made himself look presentable.

Harpur composed herself and gasped her breath. "I'm sorry Mark. I just got caught up at home and lost track of time. Anyway, I'm here now aren't I?"

Mark sat faced her, a notepad placed near him and two glasses of water on the desk. The room was only small and the two chairs were positioned facing each other. Mark made sure he could look his client in the eyes when he spoke to them, see their pain, help them release any emotions they were storing. From the window in the room you could see trees in the distance, lots of greenery and large branches swaying about in the wind. Harpur made herself comfortable in the brown leather chair and twiddled her thumbs nervously. She was always like this at the start of her session and it took a while before she could open up and talk about her problems, her fears, her traumas. Mark coughed to clear his throat and looked over at her. "So, how have you been? It's been a while since we have spoken. Has everything been alright since our last session? I know you have been struggling lately and I thought you would be here sooner to see me." Mark dipped his glasses low and looked her in the eye as he continued. "You know I never judge the people who come here and whatever you tell me stays inside these four walls."

Every time she'd been here to see him, he always started every session with the same old spiel. Harpur knew the crack inside out and just nodded to let him know she understood that everything she spoke about was confidential. Mark led the conversation and got her started. "Last time you were here you said you were ready to talk about your past, the violence and the man who nearly ruined you."

Harpur swallowed hard as her windpipe tightened. She wasn't sure if she was ready or not. Was it too soon? Was she ready to face her demons? But how long could she keep this torment locked away inside her, it was eating her up each day, messing with her head, destroying her. No, she had to get it all out, release the pain, put her past behind her. Her eyes gazed out of the window and she began to speak for the first time about her previous relationship. Although it was so long ago it all seemed like yesterday to her. She was constantly pulling and scratching at her skin as if it was burning her, irritating her. "I feel like a fool now when I look back at what he put me through. I'm angry at myself that I let it happen. I don't ever want to be weak like that again. He could have killed me you know. That's what he always told me and I believe he was capable of it too. He said he would put me six foot under. And if I'd stayed with him I would be in a morgue by now."

Mark's voice was calming. He knew his job well and had many years of therapy under his belt. "You were younger then and probably knew no better. That man took advantage of your good nature and bullied you. He wanted to control you. No woman ever belongs to a man, you know that." His words became soft and endearing as if he understood what she had been through. "If someone loves you they must earn your trust and your love, it's not something given to them for free. They have to earn it, deserve it."

Harpur's eyes squeezed together tightly, she could see her abuser's face right there in front of her. She visualised the misery he put her through. He was there large as life in her mind's eye. She could feel his presence, his warm breath creeping up her skin as if he was stood next to her, listening to her every word. Sucking hard on her gums she continued, her fist curled into tight rounded balls at the side of her thighs. Her tone changed. Rage filtered through every vein in her body and her eyes bulged out from their sockets. "He told me it was all my fault and I deserved everything he did to me. I wasn't a bad person, Mark. I did everything to make him happy. How dare he treat me like that after all I had done for him. If I ever set eyes on him again I would plunge a knife deep into his heart. Honest, I would torture him like he done to me."

Mark reached over and gripped the small glass of water.

He'd never seen this side of Harpur before and he was starting to feel uncomfortable. He passed a glass of water over to her and spoke. "What did he do to you?"

Harpur wriggled about in her seat and her nostrils flared. The emotion was pumping up inside her, rising to the back of her throat, palms sweating, clothes itching her skin. The words were hanging on the end of her tongue and Mark knew he had to be calm and let her take all the time she needed to get this out of her system. "It was late and he'd not been home for days. Nothing new there though, he was always going AWOL. He was like that, he treated our house like a hotel. I was just his skivvy when I think about it. He just used to stroll in and get a bath, get changed and sit down for a few minutes before he was back out again. He hardly said a word to me unless it was verbal abuse."

Mark held his head to the side and twisted his black pen around his fingers. He was intrigued. "Where had he been all the time he was missing, did he tell you?"

Harpur spoke in a sarcastic tone. "He said it was 'none of my fucking business' and if I carried on interrogating him he would 'shut me up for good'." Mark sat back in his chair and crossed his legs. It was her turn to talk now and he waited eagerly for her to continue. "I was asleep in bed and he must have sneaked into the house without me knowing. I'd told him we were over earlier in the day and he just left without saying a word. He took it quite well, or so I thought. Honest, I was overjoyed and thought I'd seen the back of him for good." There were a few seconds silence. She was gathering her thoughts, ready to proceed. "I heard a few sounds coming from outside my bedroom and I just lay listening, thinking it was my mind playing tricks on me. I was always hearing strange noises throughout the night. Anyway, it all went quiet again and I settled back to sleep. The sounds had stopped." Harpur played with her fingers rapidly, she was cracking her knuckles. "He must have moved so quietly into the bedroom because I never heard a thing, nothing, not a sound. I remember waking up and I was wet, liquid dripping from my head into my eyes. That's when I saw him stood over me. All I could see was the whites of his eyes, the stale smell of tobacco. The fumes from the liquid were choking me," her eyes were wide open and her breathing was rapid, she sucked in large mouthfuls of air and she was doing her best to get this out.

"Breathe, take your time. You're in a safe place he can't hurt you anymore, just take your time," Mark reassured her.

Harpur continued. "His hand reached over and he ragged me towards him by my hair. All I could see was a bright yellow flame. One second it was there and the next it was gone. He sank his teeth deep into my face and his voice was chilling. I'll never forget what he said to me..."

Mark's eyes were wide open and he was now realising how much abuse this woman had been through. He urged her to continue. "What was happening, did he let you go? What was he doing?"

"No, I was his prisoner now just as I always was when he was twisted and off his head. He was sick like that, he enjoyed watching me suffer, to beg him for mercy. To let him know he was my master," her feet bounced about on the floor nervously as she continued. "He held the lighter next to my face and he told me he was going to let me burn to death. He said he wanted me to feel pain like he'd felt when I told him I no longer loved him." Harpur's eyes started to flood with tears and she reached over to grab a tissue from the table nearby. She had to continue, to tell somebody how she was treated by her former partner.

Mark was engrossed by this story and for a few seconds he forgot he was her therapist. "So, why did he stop?"

Harpur snivelled and dropped her head low, whatever it was she about to say she was ashamed of. This wasn't easy for her, this took guts, bottle to expose her suffering. Harpur kept her head low and didn't lift her eyes once. "He told me if I sucked his dick he would let me live. I'm sorry to be so crude Mark, but that's what he demanded from me. I couldn't say no could I? I did what I had to do to survive. He raped me after that too, not that that was the first time he forced himself on me either. He said I was his and he could do what the hell he wanted with me." A tear streamed down her cheek, rolling near her lip. This woman just needed a cuddle at this moment, someone to hold her. Her shoulders were shaking. "I just lost all sense of self-worth I suppose. I had nowhere to turn, nowhere to go. Nobody who would listen."

"Did you ever think of telling the police about him. They would have helped you, put you in touch with people who could have helped you get away from him."

Harpur snapped, did this guy think she was brain-dead or something? Had he ever lived in the real world where grassing was frowned upon by the community? She shook her head and let out a sarcastic laugh. "What, and you think the police could have stopped him? He was a law unto himself. They would have taken a statement from me and probably gone and had a word with him. I've seen it so many times before. A few women I have spoken to have all said the same. The police can't protect you, nobody can when you're in a relationship with someone who is tapped in the head."

Mark could see this was all getting too much for her and tried to calm her down. "And, your son. Did he see any of the violence?"

Harpur covered her eyes with her hands. This was her jugular, the stuff that made her blood boil. Her bottom lip trembled and her hand slowly slid to the side of her head and started gripping her hair, ragging at it. "He didn't care who saw what he was doing. Sam came in once and he spat at him and told him to close the door and to go back to bed. He was only six years old at the time – he was a child, innocent to the world. He was scared, shaking he was. His dad dragged him from the doorway and leathered him. I could hear the screaming from the next room and there was nothing I could do about it. I wanted to. God, I wanted to, but I just lay frozen, helpless to my abuser. I knew I needed to do something but if I would have moved an inch he would have left me for dead. I know you might think I'm lying about this Mark but on my life he would have savaged me if I had made a move to go anywhere."

Her words were hard to get out now, there was so much emotion, so much pain. "I know Sam has been affected by all this. He's violent towards his girlfriend too. It's all he knows. He thinks women should be treated like that and who can blame him after what he witnessed? He's got a chip on his shoulder just like his dad."

Mark stopped her dead in her tracks. "But you moved on into a stable relationship and he never witnessed any abuse there did he?"

Harpur sighed and shook her head. "No, never. Neil has never laid a finger on me or any of the kids. And if he ever did I would knock him out. I would never be treated like that again. I hate that I was never strong enough to stand up to that bastard and I let him rule my life."

Mark studied her and crossed his arms tightly across his chest. He wanted to know more about this women's life because as it stood, she didn't strike him as a candidate who would put up with any shit from anyone, she seemed streetwise, able to look after herself. "Did you ever try to fight back when he attacked you?"

Harpur smirked and whatever she was about to say was amusing her. She looked him directly in the eye. "I suppose I became as bad as him in the end. I lost the plot I think and didn't care what he did to me anymore. He shit himself when I fought back," she let out a menacing laugh. "He didn't know what had hit him. He was shocked let me tell you," she shrugged her shoulders and she seemed in a world of her own as she continued. "I just couldn't take it anymore. And if I was to die trying to defend myself, then so be it. I was dead inside anyway and I had nothing else to lose. Death would have been a godsend, rather than spending another second with that prick. I let him see exactly what he'd turned me into to. I scratched his eyes out, bit him, kicked him and launched everything at him that I could get my hands on. I wanted me back. I was sick of just existing. I wanted to live again. And if I was to die trying to get what I wanted then it was a fair price to pay," she licked her lips slowly and her voice was low. "I stabbed him," her eyes danced with madness and her breathing increased. Small balls of sweat formed on her forehead.

Mark coughed to clear his throat, he'd never seen this side of Harpur before and he wasn't sure if she was thinking straight. Was this just grief or was it something more raising its ugly head, he wasn't sure. He urged her to continue, he was taking notes now, making sure he recorded everything for future reference. "I started to see his weaknesses and destroyed the things he loved most. Money was his Achilles' heel. Yeah, he loved cash and the power it gave him. Usually, after he'd tormented me all night long and bruised every inch of my body, he was always sorry and wanted to buy me the world. He bought me everything to keep me by his side. And for a while it worked. I did believe he was sorry and I forgave him. He did the same thing with Sam too, he bought him all the top clobber and the best toys money could buy. I was a fool I know but at the time, I was oblivious to his ways and the way he treated me."

"Did you love him?"

Mark's question knocked her for six. She sat forward in her seat and gripped her knees with her hands tightly. She was taking what seemed like forever to reply, had he overstepped the mark? Was she even ready to go this deep into her previous relationship? After thinking for a few seconds she was ready to answer. "No, he was just there at the right time when I needed someone I think. I was young and mixed up and searching for something more. He was older than me and he made me feel special when I was with him. Love never really came into it for me. I didn't even know what love was. He told me nobody would ever care for me like he did and if I ever left him he would hunt me down and make sure he scarred me for life," her eyes were wide open now and she held a serious look of concern in her eyes. "He said he would shred my face into ribbons, slice me up. So, in answer to your question I never experienced love with him."

Mark could see she was struggling with this topic and thought she needed a breather away from it. Harpur was staring out of the window and she'd dried up with any kind of conversation, completely switched herself off. "And how are things at home? You've been through a lot lately with losing your brother, it must be hard on all your family."

There was no stopping the tears now, the floodgates opened - this woman was heartbroken. She eyes stared out of the window. "I can't believe he's gone, Mark. Every time my phone rings I think it's him ringing me for a chat. I think I see him in the street too. Am I losing the plot or what?"

Mark shook his head slowly and he could see he had to tread on eggshells here. "It's all a form of grieving, Harpur. Everybody must go through the same kind of stuff. Some people never get over the death of a loved one. I suppose they just learn to cope with it that's all."

She snarled over at him and sighed. What did he know about the way she was feeling? Perhaps she should have held her thoughts to herself but the words just leapt out without any control over them. "Nobody is hurting the way I am. I don't care what you say. He wasn't just my brother you know, he was my best friend. We went through a lot together, stuff people like you would never understand. When I was at my lowest he was there to pick me back up and even when I was in an abusive relationship, he was the only person who tried to help me. He was willing to go to jail to help me. He told me so, he would have killed that bastard stone dead if I would have let him."

Mark was getting it all today, usually in his sessions he would just sit back and listen but today he was earning his wages. This woman was gunning for him and no matter what he said, she was giving him a hard time. "Harpur, I'm here to listen that's all. If you want to talk about anything and clear your head, my job is to help you." She pulled a sour expression. This was enough for one day, her heart was heavy and if she didn't start to calm down now, she was sure to end up having a panic attack again. Perhaps Mark could have a word with the doctor and help her find something to take the edge off her anxiety, a few calming pills, something to make her sleep. After all, that was his job wasn't it? He had said he was there to help her. Mark knew his client wasn't going to expose any more of her past or anything that what was going on in her head. He was genuinely concerned about this woman and he just hoped there was something he could do to help her. He was seeing a side of her he never knew existed; a dark, deep side. The kind that sent shivers up his spine.

After her appointment, Harpur went to see the doctor and had a quick chat with him. Mark had made sure she got some short-term medication. Perhaps with a good night's sleep she would start to think straight, sort her head out. The roads were quiet today, there were very few cars about. It was raining too, pissing down. Harpur headed up the main road and looked over at the estate where she had grown up. Harpurhey had been named one of the worst places to live in the north of England. The crime rate there was high and drugs were on every street corner. But she had never feared the place, she was one of them, she knew the score. Her pace quickened and from the corner of her eye she spotted a familiar face. Tony Wallis was stood across the road, leaning against a brick wall waiting near a phone box. The guy must have been waiting to score. This phone box was well known as a pick up point for drugs. It was simple; all you had to do was make a phone call and within minutes a car or a runner would turn up and you would be supplied with anything you wanted. Usually heroin, crack or cocaine; brown or white as they called it on the street.

Harpur dodged the cars on the road to make sure she got to him before he got on his toes. She'd been looking for this man for a few weeks now. He was like that Tony, if he didn't want to be found, there was no way of finding him. Usually he would just go on a mad one and pump drugs into his body all day long. He was fucked really and it was a wonder he'd not been found dead somewhere before now. Tony was tall and thin. His face was long and his cheekbones sank in at both sides of his face. He never looked healthy, just gaunt looking with grey skin, like death warmed up. He'd seen her now and his face dropped. There was no way he could get on his toes either, he had to stay put and face her. Harpur stood opposite him and poked her finger deep into his bony chest. "I've been looking for you for time, Tony, where have you been hiding?"

"You know me love, ducking and diving, wheeling and dealing, just trying to earn a crust and make my life a bit easier that's all."

Harpur checked the area and made sure they were alone. She had to be quick, get straight to the point. "I need a word with you. Things have been playing on my mind and I think you can help me."

Tony dragged at his skin, scratched his beard and picked his nose. He was a bag of nerves. "Yeah, sorted, just say the word, what do you need to know?" he replied trying to sound chilled out.

Harpur moved closer to his side, she was absorbing him, taking note of every move he made before she spoke.

"It's our Brady's death," she pulled a cigarette out of her pocket and slid one into her mouth before she lit it. Tony made the sign of the cross across over his body and dipped his head at the mention of his mate's name. "I think there is something that you're not telling me about what really happened before our Brady took his life. You're forgetting, I knew him inside out and he would never have done himself in without speaking to me first. He left no letters, no nothing. Something went on and I won't rest until I get to the bottom of it. So, Tony, don't insult my intelligence by lying to me. I want to know the truth. I know you know something so you better tell me, cut the bullshit. Brady was my brother and your best mate, you owe his family that much don't you?"

This junkie was on the spot, his body was pumping sweat, his mouth dry, eyelids flicking rapidly. "Nar, Harpur, on my life. I know as much as you. Your kid was depressed, come on you know that more than anyone. It wasn't the first time he'd tried ending it all. I just think he'd had enough, nothing else."

Did this guy think she was green or what? He knew she was smarter than that and he had his work cut out today. "Tony, look me in the eye and tell me you know nothing. Our Brady has gone now and no matter what he was into, I want to know. Nothing can hurt me as much as me losing my brother and all I want is the truth. So, I'll ask you again. Tell me the truth." Tony was rattling for drugs and his head was all over the place. He was in no fit state to sit down and have a chat about Brady. His eyes were rolling to the back of his head and she could see he was roasting his nuts off. But she could tell he knew more than he was saying. "Tony, can we meet up later and have a talk. You've been dodging my mam's house for weeks now and don't you think she feels it? It would be nice for you to pop in and say hello. You can't just ignore her now he's gone. My mam was there for you when you were on your arse and had nowhere to stay. Are you forgetting that?"

Harpur was smart to remind him of all the times her family had helped him out. Feeding him, putting a roof over his head. Yes, he owed them a lot. But to reveal what he knew about his best mate, could he ever do that? Harpur pulled a crisp ten pound note from her pocket. What the hell was she doing, this was so bad. "Here's a tenner to sort yourself out later. That means you can meet me at my mam's at nine o'clock tonight and you won't have to rush off anywhere doesn't it?"

Tony was holding his lower stomach and sweat was pumping from his body. This girl knew how to get him talking for sure and she struck a deal with him. A car pulled up nearby and Tony was flapping. "I've got to go Harpur but I'll call round to your mam's later. I don't know what you're expecting me to tell you but I'll see you there. I've got to go, see you later."

The deal was done now and the ball was rolling. Harpur was feeling positive and knew once she spoke to Tony later in the evening, things inside her head would be clearer. The clock was ticking and sooner or later she would get to the bottom of the real reason her brother had taken his own life. She smelt a rat and by hook or by crook she was ready to reveal the truth.

CHAPTER SEVEN

HARPUR LET HERSELF INTO her mother's house and scanned the room, nobody was about. That was strange, Sheila was always sat in her chair at this time of the day watching television. Harpur sat down in the chair and looked around the living room. Sadness filled her body, her heart ached. It wasn't the same anymore at this house; the place on the sofa where her brother always lay at this time of the day looked so bare. There was no life here anymore, no laughter, no banter, it was just filled with doom and gloom. Harpur sat staring into space, reminiscing about the days gone by. Suddenly she could hear noises from upstairs. Harpur moved to the edge of her seat and listened carefully. After a few seconds she stood up and headed to the hallway. "Mam, what are you doing up there?" she shouted. There were footsteps heard from upstairs across the landing. Harpur crept up the stairs. Her eyes were wide open and she was anxious by the time she reached the top. Brady's bedroom door was open slightly. A gentle breeze was coming from inside the room. She froze, unable to move another step, her heart was racing. This was the place he'd done it, taken his own life, ended it all. She'd only been in his room twice since he'd passed away. It freaked her out too much, gave her nightmares. What on earth was her mother doing in there on her own? She thought they made an agreement that the door was always kept locked. There was no reason for her to be inside the bedroom, none whatsoever. All Brady's stuff had been removed from here weeks ago. Even his clothes had gone, anything that he'd owned had now been removed from this room. Harpur took a deep breath and took small steps to look inside.

Sheila was sat on the edge of the bed talking to herself, there was nobody there, not a living soul. She dipped her head back and stood listening. This was a private affair, a special moment between a mother and her son. Harpur closed her eyes tightly as she listened carefully to every word that what was being said. "Another day has passed now son and you're drugs-free. No more pain, no more lying, it's just how you wanted it to be isn't it? I know you're at peace and the pain and suffering is all over." Harpur watched her mother smelling the jumper she was holding in her hand, it was Brady's, the one he wore all the time. Her expression changed as she inhaled his fragrance. "I've been at peace myself since you've been gone. I don't have to watch you hurting yourself anymore. It was bad wasn't it? You couldn't have gone on the way you were doing. I couldn't either, you were making me ill." Sheila inhaled the body odour from the black jumper again, her eyes closing slowly. "I know you are still here with me. I can feel you near me and I know you hear every word I say to you. Drugs just got the better of you and you had no other way out. We all tried to help you. God knows I tried everything but you were beyond any kind of help. Lost you were, I could see it in your eyes."

Harpur covered her mouth with her hand and she was blubbering, her emotions were rising and she couldn't contain it any longer. She edged closer to the bedroom door and stepped inside. "Mam, are you alright?" Sheila lifted her head up slightly and she smiled gently.

"No love, not really. I'll never be alright but I've got to try and get on with life just like you have. I feel dead inside. I've got nothing left, I'm drained."

Harpur went to her side and cuddled her. Sheila just stared into space, there were no tears. This wasn't a good room to be in, Brady's presence could still be felt here. Something was just not right, a feeling that he was there in the room with them, listening. "Come on mam, I'll make you a cup of tea. Don't be sitting in here on your own. It just makes you depressed." Harpur's eyes focused on a small cupboard facing her and the pain in her expression was there for everyone to see. This was where it all happened, this was where he took his final breath. She examined the cupboard further. It didn't make sense, it just didn't add up. There were so many unanswered questions spinning around in her head and somehow, some way, she had to find out her brother's last moments. She had to make sense of it all, see what he was up against, know exactly what pushed him over the edge. Harpur pulled away from her mother and looked her directly in the eye. "Mam, I know you don't want to speak about what happened but it's doing my head in and I need to know some stuff. If Brady hung himself inside there," she flicked her eyes to the side of her. "How the hell did he do it? He is nearly as tall as the height of it and he could have stood up if he wanted to. There is no way he could have hung himself, no way in this world."

Sheila walked to the window, eyes peering outside, chin resting in her hands as she leant on the window ledge. "Please love, don't make me go through it again. Don't you think I've been through it enough times with the police? I can't get that image of him hanging there out of my mind and I need to try and forget about it. Just don't go there, leave me alone."

Harpur opened the cupboard and stood inside it. There was a cold breeze that passed through her body and every hair on the back of her neck stood on end. Taking a deep breath, she examined the small cupboard. No, her thoughts were right, it didn't add up. Sheila started to walk out of the bedroom and she urged Harpur to come with her. "Come on, I can't stay in here for long. I only popped in to make sure everything was alright." This room was cold and eerie and not a place she wanted to stay for any length of time. Sheila's footsteps could be heard plodding slowly down the stairs, a step at a time. Harpur walked out of the cupboard and paused for a few seconds. Her voice was low as she whispered under her breath. "Brady, tell me what went on please. Do something to guide me to the truth. That's all I ask of you, let me find peace too." Harpur left the bedroom, but before she closed the bedroom door she had one final glance about the room. There was heartache in this room for sure. A presence, Brady was definitely still with them.

Sheila sat in the armchair in the front room and flicked the television on. Harpur came in shortly after her and sat down. Her eyes were red and you could see she'd been crying. Dabbing the tissue in the corner of her eye, she tried to compose herself but she was reliving her brother's death again. The day she got the call would haunt her forever. It was a Tuesday night and she'd not long finished work, it was just a normal working day. Harpur had already called at her mother's house earlier and Brady was there just like he always was at that time of the day. He always waited to see his sister, no matter what he never moved a muscle until she had called to see him. Usually he just lay on the sofa chilling, eating junk food, feeding his sweet tooth. He'd gained so much weight lately and even though he said he was cutting down on his food intake, he never did. If she closed her eyes she could still see him lying there talking to her, laughing and joking. He was like that Brady, he had a great sense of humour and always found the funny side of things. Before his death he had gone two weeks without any drugs. Yes, he was clean for fourteen days before it happened. Everyone was proud of him and with each day that went by, they were all seeing the family member they loved coming back to them, being normal again. He was no longer off his head on smack or tablets. Over the years Harpur had seen her brother in some really bad states. A lot of the time he couldn't even speak or hold a conversation. But every day he promised her that one day he would get clean and free from drugs. Kick the habit, mend his ways. Was it the life he led that made it so hard for him to break the cycle or was it just that he was weak and couldn't face another day without being off his face? Brady had told Harpur that his world was black and white without any drugs in it and as soon as he took the heroin, his world was bright and it had colour in it. I suppose the way he described his addiction was quite clever really. It made her understand. Was it really that bad for him? Was he in that deep that he would never be free from the drugs that ruled his life? It was such a vicious circle he was in. His mates were all junkies and every time he tried getting clean, the temptation was there every time he set foot out of the house. His mate Tony was always there begging him to score, asking him to help him graft to earn the money he needed for a fix, it was so hard, especially when drugs were on every street corner.

Sheila had been so proud of her son when he was free from drugs. Every day she was telling everyone how well he was doing and that he'd not set foot out of the front door for days. She was waiting on him hand and foot, feeding him, providing him with everything he needed to withdraw from the drugs, to stay away from his old circle of friends. Sheila had seen more than she was letting on about. Something in this woman's eye was not right. She knew too much about her son's drugs life. Sheila knew every dealer he scored from. The names of every pill he popped. Harpur had picked up on bits of things she'd let slip but to this day she had never confronted her about it. How on earth did she know so much? It was such a sad time for all the people Brady left behind. Some people might say he took the easy way out in committing suicide but it took strength and courage to do what he'd done. Nobody can ever judge a person until they have walked in their shoes and lived the life that they had. Mental illness is something that a lot of people will never understand, or that they choose to ignore. It was so easy for people to comment on Brady's death but none of them knew what was going on in his head, the quality of life he was living. The demons he was fighting. It must have been horrible to be ruled by a drug that once it had a grip on you, would never let go. People should have kept their snide comments to themselves. Left him to rest in peace without all the stories going round about him. They were lies, mostly; vicious rumours and gossip.

With the funeral over, all that was left was the inquest to get through. The day he had his send-off was something Harpur would never forget. The family had done him proud and each detail was paid attention to. Even the songs he had played at his graveside was something he'd spoken about. Morbid maybe, but he'd already told Harpur which tunes he wanted playing if he ever died. She supposed she always knew in the back of her mind that the time she spent with her brother was golden. He'd tried a few times to end it all and she'd always been by his side when he pulled through. It was a regular occurrence, taking tablets; overdosing. Sometimes he just couldn't handle the stress anymore, but he was lucky like that, he always pulled through, was saved, given another chance to sort himself out. Not this time though, his number was up. Harpur wouldn't leave Brady's side when he was feeling low, she talked to him for hours, got his head straight, made him think positively, told him that there was light at the end of the tunnel. He always listened to her and seemed to take her advice on board. Now, Brady had left a massive void in all their lives; an emptiness, a memory that would stay with them until their dying breath. All that was left of his existence was a small plot of land with his headstone, a few words engraved on it about his life and the people he had left behind.

Harpur didn't know if the time was right but she had to say something. "Mam, I spoke with Tony before and he's going to call round later on to see us. I'm going to ask him a few questions, stuff I think he knows."

These were words that Sheila did not want to hear. She kept her eyes on the television and spoke in a loud clear voice. "There is nothing to know. Brady is gone and we just have to deal with it. Let sleeping dogs lie will you! Don't have him coming around here upsetting me. He's just like our Brady was, a druggie. Do you think I need to see him roasting for drugs, off his head, eyes rolling to the back of his head? No, keep that arsehole as far away from me as you can."

Harpur confronted her. "No mam, he can tell me what he knows. You know as much as me that things just don't add up. Go on, what did Brady tell you about what was going on because I know you know something that you're not letting on about? He told you everything when he was twisted, so tell me, what the hell was he involved in?"

Sheila slammed her flat palm on the arm of the chair and twisted her head to face Harpur. She was raging. "Stop doing my head in! He's gone and nothing will bring him back. Whatever Brady told me doesn't matter anymore, does it? Just let him go and stop raking up the past."

Harpur's bottom lip trembled as she replied. "No mam, he belonged to us all and we're all hurting here, not just you. Every day it's always running through my mind and I need closure on it. You can't just tell me to be quiet all the time. I need to know."

Suddenly, the back door flung open and in marched Diane. This was Sheila's younger sister and since the loss of her nephew, she'd been at the house constantly. If Sheila was being honest, she would rather have sat on her own every day, she liked her own space, she loved her own company. Diane shook her hair and couldn't wait to take her coat off. "I'll tell you what it's bleeding freezing out there. I shouldn't have bothered even washing this mop. Look at the state of it now, it was perfect before I came out." Sheila shot a look over at Harpur and that was enough to let her know that that was the end of their conversation. This was their business and she didn't want anybody else getting involved in things that didn't concern them. "Put the kettle on Harpur, do your favourite auntie a nice cuppa, two sugars and plenty of milk, you know how I like it."

Harpur stood up and walked over to her aunt, kissed her on her cheek and took her coat from her. Diane walked to Sheila's side. "How've you been? I've tried ringing you all morning but you never answered, have you been out or something?"

Sheila sat up and straightened her clothes. She'd heard the phone ringing of course but she just wasn't in the mood to talk to anyone today. Diane sat down and kicked her shoes off. "We can have a walk on the market if you want, love. I need a few bits and it will do you good to get out for a bit of fresh air anyway."

Sheila growled over at her sister. "Stop thinking you can rule me. I've been out this morning for your information. I always go out and get my paper from the shops."

Diane chuckled, "Sheila, stop being so bleeding defensive. I'm just saying that's all. For crying out loud, stop biting my head off when all I'm trying to do is help."

"I don't need any help from you or anyone. I wish you would all piss off and leave me alone."

Harpur came back into the room and she'd heard the conversation from the kitchen, she rolled her eyes over at Diane. "Oh, just leave her to be miserable Diane, you know what she's like when she sees her arse." Harpur knew exactly what she was doing; she winked over at her auntie and carried on talking. "She just wants to sit in here all day moping about. I've asked her lots of times to come out for something to eat or even to come shopping, but she's set in her ways and she won't ever change."

Sheila shrugged her shoulders and sucked hard on her lips. "I'm not stuck in a rut at all. I'm just saying that today I'm not in the mood. Give me half an hour or so and I might change my mind, just let's have a cup of tea and see how I feel after it."

The battle was won and Harpur smirked over at Diane. She sat down next to her and nudged her in the waist with a single finger. "So, come on, how did the date go? Are you seeing him again, did he tick all your boxes?"

"Did he bleeding hell. I swear, all I seem to attract at the moment are unstable guys. Every one of them has something wrong with them. Whatever happened to all the normal blokes around here? All I seem to attract are weirdos and Clampetts." Harpur started to giggle. Diane made her laugh so much and she was so different than her sister Sheila, she was fun, outgoing and never afraid to try something new. "Ay, Sheila you should try a bit of dating too. I mean, when was the last time you had a date or even a kiss?"

Sheila shook her head and folded her arms tightly in front of her. "I've not got time for all that nonsense. Anyway, men are ten a penny and if I wanted one I would go out and find one. It's not rocket science is it? So wind your neck back in. I'm happy being single."

Diane let out a laboured breath. There was some sibling rivalry going on here and her older sister was getting the better of her. "Well you won't find a fella sat there will you. At least I'm out there looking for something new, not like you." Harpur's phone alert stopped the conversation from continuing and both Sheila and Diane were looking at her. "Is that your phone?" Diane asked curiously. Harpur pulled her handset out of her pocket and she was aware that all eyes were on her. "Who is it?" Diane asked.

Harpur's cheeks were bright red and for the first time ever she lied to her auntie. "Oh, it's just Neil asking what's for tea."

Diane looked shocked, this was a first. Neil very rarely texted his wife for anything, it was strange. "How is Neil anyway, I've not seen him in ages is he still looking after you?"

Harpur let out a sarcastic laugh and rolled her eyes. "Since when has that man ever looked after me. I'm the one who looks after him more like."

Sheila jumped into the conversation. "Ay, Neil's a good man and I don't know what's up with you lately but you need to remember all he has done for you."

"Mam, why do you always have to fight his corner? You don't know what I have to put up with in my life. You always think he's perfect when in fact he's far from it. He's a tight-arse for a start."

Sheila pulled a sour expression. "He's far from being tight. That man is devoted to you and you know as well as me that you're his world and he'd do anything for you."

Harpur was just about to say something but stopped at the last moment. What was the point anyway, Sheila would never say a bad word about Neil, not now not ever, he was perfect in her eyes.

Diane watched her niece carefully and as soon as Sheila nipped to the toilet, she confronted her. "Ay, you seem a bit pissed off, is everything all right at home with Neil and that?"

Harpur was stuck for words, was it that obvious that her marriage was breaking down? She flicked her hair over her shoulder and started to chew on her fingernails. "It's the same shit, different day Diane. I just don't know anymore. We used to be fine but lately everything he does just rubs me up the wrong way, he just irritates me."

Diane was a wise old owl and it was fair to say she'd had her share of problems in her life, especially where men were concerned. "You might need to relight the romance that's all. Go away together for the weekend, get some raunchy underwear. Have a date night."

"You must be joking," Harpur squirmed, "he won't move from the sofa once he comes home from work. I can honestly say I'm so bored with him. Nothing ever changes and if this is how my life is going to be, I'd rather leave him and get a divorce."

Diane was gobsmacked. Until that moment she hadn't realised how bad things were. Every marriage goes a bit stale from time to time and she just thought this relationship was the same. It just needed spicing up. "That's a bit strong love. Is it that bad?"

"Yes, I feel suffocated by him. Since our Brady has gone it's made me look at my life in a different way. It's put everything into perspective I think. I want to feel alive again, go on adventures, go and see stuff. Live life instead of just existing."

"So, tell him how you feel and see what he says?"

Sheila walked back into the room holding the bottom of her back. "I'll have to go to the doctors with this pain. I can't move a muscle with it, honest, all night long I've been awake with it."

Harpur started to read her message as Diane turned to talk to her sister.

"Why don't we Skype, it would be good to see you in the flesh after all this time? What do you think? Love Dessie x"

Harpur's cheeks were on fire and she was fidgeting. Was she even ready to take this to the next level? She wasn't sure. "Right, I better go home and sort Neil's tea out. Mam, if you need me give me a ring. I'll see you both soon anyway, I'm coming back to meet Tony here."

Sheila snarled over at her; she knew by her reaction she wasn't happy. The front door slammed shut and Harpur was gone. What the hell was she playing at? Her marriage was on the line here and she should have been concentrating on her family, not a guy she know years ago. He was in her past for a reason, why could she not see she was heading for trouble? Harpur read the message again and rammed her mobile phone back into her pocket thinking of her next move.

CHAPTER EIGHT

HARPUR SHOVED A SILVER KEY inside the lock and twisted it to open the door. Same shit different day. Neil's car was outside and she was surprised he was home so early from work. Maybe he'd planned a nice romantic evening out for them both, taking her somewhere special. She scanned the hallway and could hear loud music coming from upstairs, the television blaring in the front room. There was no sign of anyone. "Hello?" she shouted as she started to pick the mail up from the floor below the letterbox. Above the din she could make out footsteps upstairs and doors shutting.

Joseph came into the hallway and he ran towards her with open arms. "Nana," he yelled. She scooped him up into her arms.

"Bloody hell, why is the TV on that loud?" Joseph was eager to get back down on the floor and started to wriggle.

"Come on Nana, come and watch this film I'm watching it's called Avatar, the people are blue in it. Quick, come and see them."

Harpur held her grandson's hand and went into the living room. Her eyes were wide open and you could see by her face that she wasn't happy. "Where has all this mess come from?" her eyes were all over as she bent down towards the floor picking things up. "Look, who's squashed crisps into the carpet?"

There was no answer from Joseph and she started to pick the crumbs up as he sat watching the television. This kid was as good as gold and he never asked for much, he just sat there. Harpur reached for the remote control for the TV and turned the volume down. "Where's your mam?" Joseph was engrossed in the film and he never replied, he just pointed his finger up to the ceiling. Harpur kissed him on the side of the cheek and left the room in a huff. Joanne was going to get a piece of her mind, what a scruffy cow she was. She was sick to death of her, every day it was the same, clearing her shit up and waiting on her hand and foot. Harpur marched up the stairs with a face like thunder. When she reached the top she was greeted by Neil. He was wearing only a towel around his waist and she could hear the bath running inside the bathroom. "I was just coming down to see you. Don't do me any tea I'm off out tonight. Man U are playing and a few of the lads are going down to the boozer to watch it. You don't mind do you?"

Harpur looked a bit shocked but she answered him straight away. "Yeah, that's fine. Where's Joanne? Bleeding hell, why didn't you tell her to turn that music down, don't tell me you can't hear it. I bet the neighbours are going mad listening to that racket all day long."

Joanne must have heard her and raised her head from the bedroom. "Sorry, I was just getting ready and forgot to turn it down. I'll do it now."

Harpur shot a look over at her. It was nearly teatime and she still wasn't ready. There she was stood in her housecoat, all her make-up on and not a care in the world. "How long has Joseph been down there on his own? Have you seen the state of it down there, he's wrecked the house? You better get down there and hoover up. I mean, I go to work all day and don't need to be cleaning the minute I walk in the door do I?"

Joanne rolled her eyes and went back into the bedroom. Sam's mother could moan for sure. What the hell was wrong with the woman? It was only a bit of bleeding cleaning. Harpur stomped down the stairs and went into the kitchen. Her face was bright red. Cups and pans were stacked high in the kitchen sink, the worktops were covered in food, there was spilt milk on the kitchen floor. She let out a laboured breath and plonked down on a chair at the kitchen table. Why did she even bother anymore? Nobody listened to her anyway, she was pissing in the wind. Staring at the wall, she shook her head slowly. Was this how her life would always be? Work, cooking, cleaning... Surely she was meant for more in life. This couldn't be it?

Harpur checked nobody was about and pulled her mobile from her pocket. She unlocked the screen with her password and read over Dessie's message again. He did make her smile, that was certain. Something was happening here, a bond was forming, a friend, a soul mate. Her fingers started to type slowly, she was thinking about every word she sent.

"Hi Dessie, I don't think it's a good idea us Skyping at the moment. Just let's be friends for now. You have a family remember and I'm married. Anyway, I'm a lot older than when I last saw you and I don't want to spoil the image you have in your head of me. How's your day been? Mine has been crap if I'm being honest. At least you have sunshine to keep you smiling, come and rescue me and take me to the sun, God I need it at the moment. Love Harpur X"

She sent the message straight away without reading it through. She didn't care anymore and when the time was right she would have a video chat with her old flame, just not yet. She had nothing to lose, nothing at all. Harpur dialled a number and held the phone to her ear. "Hiya love, do you fancy nipping round to my mam's house with me later on? Tony Wallis is coming round and I want a chat with him. I'd like you to be there if you can make it, Bridget. Just for a bit of support." Harpur nodded as she listened to her reply. "Alright then, I'll pick you up about half past eight. Please be ready, don't have me waiting about for you. If I miss him, I'll be gutted." Harpur was giggling. Bridget must have cracked a joke or something. This woman was always so happy, without a care in the world. She was a great friend to have onside.

Neil stood at the kitchen door and rubbed his hands together. "What's for tea lovely?"

Noel twisted her head around and hissed at him. "I've just this minute walked in. I've not had time to have a bath like you have. Why didn't you start the tea if you was that hungry?"

Neil walked over to her and bent down slightly to kiss her but she moved away from him. He made her skin crawl, his touch made her cringe inside. "Piss off Neil. It's always the same old story with you. In fact, while we are on the subject, when did you last take me out or want to do something with me?" She didn't gave him time to reply, she was all over him like a rash. "No, but the lads phone you and you're up and ready in seconds and full of life. If I ask to do something you're always too bleeding tired. It's a task to even get a conversation out of you lately. I don't know why I bother. Fuck it anyway, I'm not arsed anymore. Do whatever you're doing. Just think on though, one night you'll walk through this door and I won't be here. Remember that."

Harpur's knew she'd rattled his cage. She'd seen her

arse. Neil held his head back and chuckled. "Bleeding hell, where did that come from? You never want to go anywhere with me anyway. Well, unless it's shopping and you know me love, I hate shopping. What man likes being dragged around the shopping centre, go on tell me that. Only faggots like shopping."

"You hate a lot of things I like don't you. Tell me again, why are we even together anymore?"

This was a bit strong and just because he was going out for a few pints there seemed no need for this. Neil was gobsmacked. He knew she'd been feeling a bit low lately but he just took it that she was grieving and a bit touchy. Yeah, he should have showed her more love, helped out in the house a bit more, but he just forgot. He was a man. "Babes, come on, give us a cuddle. I'm sorry if I've upset you. I'll stay in tonight with you if you want?"

Harpur was never one for pity and she screwed her face up as she spoke to him. "No, you go out and enjoy yourself. Just remember this when you come home one night and I'm not here. It will be all your own doing. You've been warned. Coulda, woulda, shoulda is the story of your life, Neil." Joanne walked into the kitchen and she was dressed now, she wore a short black mini skirt, and her hair was all done up and her make-up was perfect. "Harpur is there any chance you can watch Joseph later on tonight. It's my mate's birthday and they're all going out for a few drinks?"

By the look on Harpur's face she was ready to explode. It was true, everybody just used her, took liberties, looked after themselves without a care in the world for her feelings. She was sick to death of it all, she'd had enough. "I'm going out myself. I don't know what time I'll be back either. Sorry about that but I do have a life as well. Ask your mam to have him." Joanne was blushing, stuck for words. Harpur always babysat for her, she never said no. "I thought we were on a visit tomorrow with Sam anyway. Do you really want to be going to see him with a hangover, stinking of stale beer?"

Neil made a quick exit before she flipped on him again. He'd seen the other side of his wife when she was angry and there was no way he was crossing her when she was like this, no way in this world. Joanne sat down at the table and did her usual speech when things were not going her way. "It's alright. Thanks anyway, I know you do a lot for me and I shouldn't take advantage of you. It's just sometimes I get so fed up with Sam being banged up in that place and I just get lonely." Oh, this girl knew how to work a sob story, she was a professional at it. A leading lady if ever you saw one. "I'll make us something for tea if you want, you sit down and put your feet up."

Harpur was already regretting the way she'd spoken to them both. But they wound her up, took the piss out of her, what did they expect? Joanne started to look in the freezer, eyes flicking one way then the other. She was a crap cook and she knew any minute now Harpur would spring into action. She didn't have to wait long either. "Just leave making tea. I'll order us something. I've not got long so we need to have something quick." Joanne smirked and sat at the kitchen table. What a cunning cow she was. Thank God for that, there was no way she fancied getting all grubby after the time and effort she'd put in to get ready. Harpur opened the kitchen drawer and passed Joanne a takeaway menu. "You order something and shout me when it's here. I'm just going to get a bath before I go out."

Joanne looked wounded, there was not a single mention

of her staying in to watch Joseph. She sat with her arms folded and had a face like a smacked arse. All that time and effort she'd put in for a night on the tiles was wasted. No dancing, no copping off, nothing, just a boring night sat in front of the television. Her phone got a text alert and she checked nobody was looking before she answered it. Once she replied she sat back and smirked, humming a song.

Harpur plodded upstairs and headed into the bathroom. The place was a pig sty, there were wet towels everywhere. Lifting her head slightly, she clocked the toothpaste squirted all over the white sink. The bath was still full of dirty water and the cold tap was dripping. Pulling the plug out, she sat on the toilet seat and waited for the bath to empty. She inhaled and looked at the side of her, there was aftershave left with the lid still off. This was Neil's favourite one too, his Armani one. She looked puzzled and held her head to the side. Her husband only really wore this when it was a special occasion; weddings, christenings. He would never waste it, he was too much of a penny pincher. When Sam was at home he would go ballistic if he ever found out he'd been using it. The heated arguments they'd had in the past about him using Neil's stuff was endless. You see, Neil didn't really know how to share. In some things he was selfish, a brat in fact. Sam knew how much it wound his stepfather up and Harper was sure he only used it to cause some friction in the household. Harpur reached over and screwed the gold top back on the bottle. If Joseph would have got his hands on this he would have squirted it all over the place. It would have been Neil's own fault too. Fancy leaving expensive aftershave lying about where anyone could their hands on it anyway.

Harpur looked down at the floor again and in the

corner she could see Joanne's dirty underwear, just left there for everyone to see. Did this girl have no shame? There were men in the house too. Harpur stood up and walked towards them with a look of disgust in her eye. As she picked them up with the tips of her fingers she cringed. "Dirty cow," she mumbled under her breath. Harpur swilled the bath out now and put the silver plug in the bottom of the bath. All she needed was a nice hot bath to ease her stress and worries. Sticking her finger slightly under the hot tap her cheeks were bright red, she clenched her teeth together tightly. Bleeding hell, there was no hot water. "I'm sick to death of this house. Does anyone ever think that I might like a hot bath every now and then?" Oh, she was on one now. She hurried to the bathroom door and yanked it open. If Joanne would have been in her bedroom she would have given her a mouthful. Here she was grafting all day long and Joanne just jumps in the bath with no consideration for her or anyone else in the house either. She should have got washed early in the day, not waited until she was ready to come home from work. Things were going to change in this house for sure. Starting from tomorrow she was telling them all that she was no longer a maid for them. Let's see what happens then when she's stopped picking stuff up after them all the time. They'd see then exactly how much she actually did in the house. Yes, fuck them all, she was putting her foot down.

Harpur sat in the car waiting for Bridget to come out of her house, she was late again. She sat playing with her phone when a message from Dessie came through, she smiled softly and sat twisting her hair around her finger as she looked at it. He just seemed to cheer her up, know the times when she was feeling down. She opened the message and started to read.

"Hi there, thanks for your message. I can't ever imagine you being hanging or not pretty anymore. Stop being boring and let's Skype. What's wrong ay, scared you might still fancy me? Love Dessie."

Harpur fanned her fingers in front of her face, she was having a hot flush. This guy was so upfront, he just said what he thought and the cheek of him even suggesting that she fancied him, what on earth was he thinking? Harpur had a mischievous look on her face as she started to type a reply. There was no way he was getting the upper hand with her, she was retaliating.

"Hi there, Mr Full of Yourself, why on earth would I still fancy you? Get over yourself, you're yesterday's news. I think it's maybe you who still has a crush on me don't you think? Ok, let's Skype soon. Get a wash and make a bit of an effort too if you're trying to impress me. We'll soon see who fancies who? Love Harpur X"

She added some laughing emoji faces and pressed the send button. That would shut him up, let's see what he had to say about that. Inside she was excited, something was happening. Although this was just a few text messages it was making her feel alive again; smiling, refreshed. They were messaging each other all day long now, non-stop. The car door opened quickly and a strong gust of wind flew in behind Bridget. "Sorry I'm late. You know what I'm like. I just always end up getting distracted. So, fill me in, what's been going on?"

Harpur flicked the ignition over and started to pull onto the main road. "Nothing much really. Well, Neil's out tonight for football so I'm in no rush to get home. I swear to you, I walked in from work and the house was such a shit-tip. Neil was running about like a blue-arsed fly getting ready and Lady Muck was caked in make-up getting ready for a big night out on the town. Honest, on my life, Joseph was downstairs on his own watching television while she totted herself up. I'm sure she forgets she's got a kid. Bone idle isn't the word for her."

Bridget pulled the car mirror down and started to apply a baby pink coloured lip gloss, her mouth open slightly. "More fool you then. There is no way in this world that I would run about after them like you do all the time. Tell her to piss off back to her own mother's anyway. I can't see why she's even staying at your house to start with. She's a woman, not a bleeding kid. Let her stand on her own two feet."

Harpur was driving now, concentrating. "Her own mother threw her out when Joseph was a small baby. They don't get on well, they never used to anyway. I just feel while Sam is in prison that I should help her out. It's hard work on your own with a small child. I should know, I've been there."

"But she's not your problem. Okay, if she helped out a bit in the house, put a wash on or hoovered up and made your life a bit easier, that would be fine but from what you tell me, she doesn't do a tap, she's a lazy bitch if you ask me. Either you step up and tell her straight or stop moaning about it." Harpur shook her head, why did she even think she would get a bit of sympathy from her friend anyway? Bridget was hard like that. It was her way or the highway. As they sat in the car waiting for the traffic lights to change Harpur changed the subject, she was sick to death of doom and gloom. "You never guess what, me and Dessie have been sending messages to each other for days now. The cheeky get said I still fancy him. He wants to Skype me, you know, video chat."

Bridget was listening eagerly, urging her to continue. "No way, what did you say?"

Harpur tapped her fingers on the steering wheel. "At first I thought no way, but I'm going to chat with him and have a bit of banter. It's what my life needs at the moment. He cheers me up. I know I'm married but, what the hell. What harm can it do anyway."

Bridget knew this would have happened sooner or later and she was smiling. "Well, get yourself in the hairdressers and sort your hair out, perhaps a spray tan too and book to get your nails done. If you're going to see Dessie Ryan you better make sure you are top notch, show him what he missed out on. Has he said anything about his wife to you?"

"No, there are no photographs of her either. I think he's going through a rough patch like me." As the traffic started to move again, Harpur started to giggle to herself. She turned the radio up and started singing. Bridget watched her from the corner of her eye. Things were moving on nicely, just like she'd hoped they would. Dessie Ryan was just the medicine her friend needed at a time like this.

The car pulled up outside her mother's house. Just the look of the place had misery written all over it; dark, dreary and morbid. Harpur let out a laboured breath and looked over at Bridget. "You know she's going to kick off don't you. She's already told me she doesn't want Tony anywhere near the house but I'm not listening. I need to see him, to speak to him and see what he knows."

Bridget scratched the top of her head and hesitated before she spoke. "Perhaps your mam is right. Tony can't bring Brady back can he and seeing him, well, it just brings it all back to her doesn't it?"

"For crying out loud Bridget, please stick with me on this one. I don't need you saying that in front of my mam. I thought you had my back?"

"I do, but I'm just saying that's all. You know what she's like. And I don't want to be sat there when she kicks off with you." Harpur opened the car door. A text alert sounded but she ignored it and locked the car up once Bridget was out of the other side. The girls walked down the garden path together. Bridget slowed down a bit and let Harpur take the lead. She was just there for support, she wanted no part of this family drama.

Harpur walked into the living room and Sheila was watching Coronation Street. She held a single finger up at them both and never took her eyes from the television. "Not a word, be quiet until this has gone off. We're going to find out who killed her now." Harpur rolled her eyes and sat down on a chair. They both knew not to mutter a single word until the show was over. She was like that Sheila, she loved her soaps, she really thought they were real people with real lives. Everyone told her it was make-believe but she chose to ignore them. This was reality in her eyes, a real street with people she was familiar with. Not a word was whispered until the episode was over. Sheila sat back in her seat and shook her head. "We've waited weeks now to find out who did it and now I've got to wait until Friday until they reveal who knocked her off. I suppose it keeps the viewing up but to tell you the truth it does my head in. They just kick the arse out of every storyline when they should just reveal who it was and not have you holding on for weeks."

At last, they could talk. Sheila popped a fag into her mouth and lit it. She sucked hard and both sides of her cheeks sank in. It was fair to say she was a heavy smoker and since Brady had passed away she had been chain smoking. Harpur followed suit and sparked one up too. Sheila squinted her eyes together and checked the wall clock. "What are you doing here at this time anyway?"

Bridget shuffled about in her chair and kept her head down. Here it was, the start of World War Three. "I told you earlier that Tony was calling here to see you. Plus, I wanted a quick word with him too."

Sheila gritted her teeth and twisted her head quickly towards her daughter. "What did I tell you about having him around here? He's a scumbag, nothing less. He said he was Brady's mate but has he been near here since he's been gone?" Her eyes were wide open waiting on an answer. "Has he bleeding hell. So do me a favour, if he knocks on this door tell him to piss off before I do."

"Mam, don't be like that with him. When Brady was here you always let him in, it must be hard for him too."

Bridget sat fidgeting, this was going to blow soon she was sure of it. "Are you having a laugh or what? I let him in here so Brady wouldn't go out with him. It was him feeding him the drugs, helping him score. He's a dirty no-good lying bastard. And now my son's gone I don't have to be nice to him anymore. He's a smackhead who cares about no one but himself. That's the thing with people like him, they're selfish, they've got no morals. He knew Brady was trying to get clean yet he made him go back to his old life all the time. It was him, yes him, who's to blame for our

Brady not being here now."

Harpur wasn't taking it anymore, she snapped. "Are you for real or what? Nobody forced Brady to take drugs. He was his own person. He never gave a shit about anyone when he was off his head on drugs and you know it. You just blamed everyone else for the way he was. Face it mother, Brady was responsible for his own actions, nobody else."

Sheila smashed her clenched fist on the arm of the chair, dust flew into the air. "Don't you ever say I didn't know what my son was! I knew every little seedy secret he had. More than you will ever know. He was an addict, look the word up and see what it means. I'll tell you shall I, and save you the time." Harpur sat back in her chair and folded her arms tightly across her chest. "It means he could not survive without the drugs. He had an addiction. That means he had to have heroin every day to make him function. So don't you come around here on your high horse preaching to me about what happened to my son."

Harpur wasn't backing down, no way. "Tony knows what went on and I'm going to get to the bottom of it, like it or not."

Sheila hissed over at her, she was being sarcastic now. "And who are you all of a sudden? The police investigated it all and found nothing. They left no stone unturned so keep your bleeding nose out and concentrate on your own life. Stop trying to hurt everybody when we should be putting this behind us."

Harpur snarled over at her mother. She could be so evil with her mouth, ruthless she was when she started. Well, so much for having a chat with Sheila, it had all backfired on her. "Bridget, are we ready to go. I'll wait in the car for

Tony. What's the point of bringing him in here when all she wants to do is verbally abuse him."

Sheila nodded her head. "At least you got that right. So when you see him, tell him from me to never darken my door again or he will feel my foot right up his arse. Tell him to keep away from me."

Bridget stood but in truth she didn't know where to look. She kept her voice low as Harpur marched past her in a strop. "Take care Sheila, see you soon." There was no reply from Harpur's mother, not a word, she just plonked down in her seat and changed the television channel. The front door slammed shut and Sheila looked up at the large photograph of her son hanging on the wall in front of her. "See what you have caused. It's a mess, a bloody big pile of shit. I hope you're happy now."

Harpur dropped her head onto the steering wheel. "Why did I ever expect anything else from her? I swear, she bugs the life out of me sometimes. She thinks she knows it all when she knows fuck all."

"You knew what she would say. Can't say I didn't warn you."

"Oh, you can piss off as well if you're sticking up for her. Did you hear the way she talks to me? Come on, that would wind anybody up. She's hysterical every time I mention our kid. It's like I'm not supposed to have any feelings where he is concerned."

"It's just all still raw at the moment that's all. You're both still hurting."

Harpur was raging inside and Bridget wasn't helping one little bit, she was adding fuel to the fire. "Oh forget it, what's the point anyway." Harpur quickly checked her wristwatch. "Tony should be here anytime now. I'll just get him in the car and tell him my mam's not well. I'm not lying anyway, she's in bad pain. She tries to hide it but did you see the way she was sat; I can see she's suffering."

"Has she been to the doctors?"

"Yes but she only tells half the bleeding story anyway. She doesn't want to worry anyone." There was a silence in the car and Harpur was surveying the area. Bridget hated that they'd had words and wanted to get things back to normal. "Let's go and see Neil down the boozer after you've seen Tony. We can have a couple of drinks and chill out."

Harpur pulled a sour expression. "No, I'll give that a miss. I see enough of his moaning face at home, he's the last person I want to see right now, he's in the bad books."

Bridget pulled the mirror down again and started to examine her complexion, dragging at her skin. "I'm not getting any younger am I. I swear to you I'm getting more wrinkles every day that passes. I need some TLC. Why don't we get a bit of Botox, just a freshen up, not like some of the women you see who have that frozen look?"

Harpur was cooling down now and she started to smile as she looked over at her stressed friend. "I feel the same love, I need more than Botox. I need a facelift, a nip and tuck, a boob job, the list is endless."

"So, let's do it then. There is a place in Whitefield where I've seen it advertised. The girl is mint and it doesn't cost a bomb."

Harpur digested what she just said and sat thinking for a few seconds. Yes, why not, it was about time she did something for herself. "Ok, book us in. And see if she does anything for this fat around my stomach too. I think I've got middle-age spread." The girls sat laughing and their little dispute was over now.

They had been sat in the car for over an hour now and there was no sign of Tony Wallis. Harpur checked her watch again and let out a laboured breath. "I'll skin that rat alive! Who does he think he is letting me down like this? I'll tell you something for nothing, he must know that I know he knows something. Otherwise why is the dirty ferret dodging me. I'll make it my business now to find him. He's not going to be far is he. I'll just park up on Tavistock Square and wait for him. That's where they all score from isn't it?"

"Are you sure you're not getting in too deep Harpur? The world Tony lives in is dangerous. Come on, you've heard the stories. More to the point, you've seen Tony's scars." Harpur had no fear, all she wanted was the truth and if she got injured finding it, so be it, she was ready to risk it all. "Come on, I'll come back to your house for a bit. We can pick a bottle of wine up on the way home. I can't be getting steaming though I've got a visit with Sam tomorrow and I don't want to be reeking of booze." Bridget snarled and looked out of the window. The last thing she wanted to do was to sit in her house again. She wanted to socialise, meet people, take a break from her normal everyday life. The car pulled out from the street and the radio was on low. Bridget was in a mood and it was obvious she wasn't happy. Harpur shot a look over at her and gasped her breath. "Okay then mard arse, we'll go to the pub. But don't expect me to be a barrel of laughs. Especially, if that arsehole of a husband is in." There it was, Bridget was smiling again. She was easily pleased.

The boozer was buzzing. The football match was coming to a climax on the big screen and all the blokes were sat watching it. Some of them were stood up and it was a nail-biting situation. Bridget stood at the bar and smiled at the man near her, dishy he was, eye candy. "What score is it, are we winning or what?" The man smiled at her and loved that she was interested in football. Usually the females in the pub sat as far away from the big screen as possible. "It's one each darling. We've had a few shots at goal but up to now nothing. There's ten minutes left so anything could happen. Rooney's playing like a fairy though, they should take him off and let one of the others have a crack at it. The fat scouser needs to leave the pies alone."

Bridget fluttered her eyelashes, she had his full attention. "The team is struggling since Sir Alex left. He should have stayed a bit longer I think." Oh this girl knew her stuff, or so he thought. Little did he know that she couldn't have given a toss about the score, she was more interested in him, his body, his come-to-bed eyes. Harpur looked round at the men watching the football. Where was Neil? She couldn't see him. Stretching her neck further she spotted him sat in the corner looking at his phone. This was weird, he never ever missed a second of the game. Raising his head he spotted her. Harpur walked over to where he was, he was shocked to see her. "Alright babes, what are you doing here, are you getting the beer in then or what?"

"I don't need a reason do I? I just popped in with Bridget, wherever she is." She turned her head, trying to locate her. She could see her friend at the bar chatting away to her newfound friend.

"She's like a dog on heat," Neil mumbled under his

breath.

Harpur heard him and poked a single finger in his waist. "Turn it in gobshite, that's my friend, remember that." Why had she even come here? She was depressed now, fed up. Neil looked over at the TV as his football team made an attack on the goal. "Go on you red fuckers, go on, shoot. Orr, for fuck's sake, pass it you muppet."

Harpur couldn't take it a second longer. She walked back over to Bridget and stood at the side of her. "Are you alright here, I'm going to shoot off. Neil's doing my head in already." Bridget nodded and whispered in her ear. "He's mint isn't he? I'm sorted you get off. I'll ring you tomorrow and fill you in." The girls pecked each other on the cheek. "See you love, sorry I'm no fun tonight." Bridget had already turned her head and never heard what she's said. One last glance over her shoulder and she was gone.

Harpur drove around Harpurhey for at least ten minutes looking for Tony Wallis. There was no sign of him. Where was he hiding? His days were numbered and when she got her hands on him she would wring his neck. Tomorrow was another day though and she was going to make it her business to corner him. Oh yes, she wanted answers and she was going nowhere until he told her what he knew about how her brother met his death.

CHAPTER NINE

THE MURRAY HOUSEHOLD was in a state, it looked like a bomb had hit the place. Harpur was running around like a headless chicken, rushing, moaning. "Joanne, where are Joseph's shoes? We're going to be late for the visit if you don't get a move on. Neil, are you ready?" Harpur dipped her head under the coffee table and reached for her grandson's trainers. Joanne walked into the room and was giving herself the once-over in the mirror. Harpur caught a glimpse of her from where she was. "Never mind totting yourself up, get him sorted out. Bleeding hell, is this family ever early for anything?"

Neil walked into the room and winked over at Joanne. "You're looking nice."

Harpur twisted her head back over her shoulder and growled over at her husband. "She will do, all bleeding morning she's been getting ready. Who do you think cleans this house, the fairies? I wish I had the time to dress up too?"

Ouch, someone was jealous. It was fair to say she'd seen her arse that her husband was giving out compliments. When was the last time he said anything nice to her, she couldn't remember? From the corner of her eye she studied Joanne. She did look pretty; nice legs, big tits, what more could a man ask for she supposed. Harpur hadn't even had time to brush her hair properly, she looked haggard. Well, that was all going to change as from today. She was sick to the back teeth of feeling like shite. It was time to get herself back in the game. Yes, she would have a revamp of her wardrobe, a new hairstyle, and start eating healthily again. Things in her life had slipped over these last few months and it was fair to say she's let herself go a bit. Bridget was right, Botox was the way forward. Yeah, a bit of facial tightening was just what she needed. Neil came over to where she was and sighed. "I've got to put petrol in the car too. I'll tell you what, it costs a fortune each week to go and see Sam."

She shook her head he was such a tight bastard. "Will you stop moaning about money. If you're that arsed about putting petrol in the car, then I'll give you the money myself."

Neil never said a word. Honest to God, this man kept his mouth shut. No shame whatsoever. There was no, 'Oh, I was only joking put your money away.' He was really willing for her to pay for the fuel to go and see Sam. No wonder she was drifting away from him. Harpur was no gold digger but to have a man treating her to nice things every now and then wouldn't have gone amiss. Her husband didn't make her feel special anymore. Joanne stood up and swung her handbag over her shoulder. "Joseph, come on put your coat on now. We are going to see your daddy. You can draw him a picture like you did last time."

"Mummy, can I have some hot chocolate again and some crisps?" Joanne ignored him and dropped her head low. Yep, Harpur would be stuck with the food bill too. It was always the same when they went to visit her son because Neil never stuck his hand in his pocket for anything. One last look around the house and the family left. It took over an hour to drive to the prison and that was if the traffic was good. It was a ball ache really and the sooner he was home, the better it would be. Neil stood at the car waiting to let Joanne and Joseph in the car. It was only a two-door vehicle and you could see he was losing his rag waiting for them both to get inside. The journey began and after a stop at the petrol station they headed straight for the motorway. Joseph looked out of the window taking in everything he saw, sheep and cows. Harpur sat in the front of the car and her phone vibrated. It was on silent mode and that was the way she was keeping it. There was no way she wanted any nosy parkers monitoring her phone. Dipping her head low, she checked her message. Neil was singing and seemed oblivious to anything she was doing.

"Good morning gorgeous, maybe you are right. I do still fancy you. So, lets Skype and see if you still fancy me. I know you're married but we are only chatting aren't we, or are you planning to run away with me? Love Dessie X"

Oh this man had her heart racing for sure, her cheeks were bright red and she was burning up. Quickly, she opened the window and let some fresh air inside. She smirked to herself, this was exciting, dangerous even, but she didn't care anymore. She started to type a reply back.

"Me, running away with you? Get a grip! Once bitten, twice shy. You had your chance with me and blew it. Go and find someone who will listen to your bullshit. I'm immune to it. Love Harpur X"

She added lots of laughing faces. Harpur stuck her phone back in her pocket. It was never far from her side these days, she was constantly on it. Twenty-four hours a day they were texting each other, it was non-stop. Joanne leaned forward in her chair and rested her hand on the back of Harpur's seat. "Erm, I've decided I'm not telling Sam I've been going out to the pub. You know what he's like, he just goes skitz and makes my life a misery. It's just easier if I don't tell him. If that's alright with you two?"

Neil looked at her through his rear view mirror. "Oh, we don't like liars in our house do we Harpur?" he was being smart with himself and trying to make a joke out of it. Harpur looked over at him and wondered if he was having a pop at her. Did he know she was texting somebody? No, he never checked her phone, he didn't care what she did, surely she was being paranoid. She licked her bottom lip and turned her head away, looking out of the window as she replied. "It's up to you love, but don't ask me to lie to my son. I mean, if you've been out, just tell him the truth. I don't want any part of it."

Neil gasped his breath. "Bleeding hell, help the girl out. She's not asking for much is she? You've heard him when he has a go at her. Why would you put her through that?"

Harpur was sick to death of him sticking his nose in where it wasn't wanted and for that matter, since when did he start caring about Joanne getting into shit? Usually he was slagging her off himself. "I said I'm not lying. If he doesn't ask, then I won't tell him."

"Oh, I forgot about mummy's boy. He's her golden balls Joanne. A bond that can never be broken. You know, mother and son." What a prick her husband was today. If he had something to say then he should just come out and say it instead of going round the houses. It was obvious that something had got his back up. It couldn't have been the price of petrol because his wife had just paid for it, not him. They travelled on in silence, you could have cut the atmosphere with a knife.

The car pulled at Lancaster Farms Prison grounds. It was a fairly new jail and a lot nicer than some she'd been to visit in the past. And this woman had been to some shitholes. Brady had always been in and out of the nick in his younger days and she'd travelled up and down the country to see him. Strangeways was the jail her brother tended to end up in. In his own words, he loved a bit of time behind bars. He always told her it helped him to get clean and sort his head out. His last stretch was a three-year sentence. It broke his back if he was being honest and he said that would be the last time he would ever go back to jail. He was getting too old for it, he said. And funnily enough, Brady stayed true to his word. He never went back, he kept a low profile and never put his neck on the line anymore. In his younger days he would take the blame for all his mates and never grass them up. He was a fool, he'd wasted so many years stuck in the big house doing time for other people while they walked the streets without a care in the world. His criminal record was lengthy. Everything was on it; burglary, GBH, kidnapping, supplying class A drugs, the list was endless.

Harpur got out of the car and stretched her legs. She reached in her coat pocket and pulled out a cigarette. She needed nicotine and fast, her nerves were shattered today. This place always made her feel anxious and she hated that her son was locked away behind the big brick walls. Lots of other visitors were pulling up in the car park now and it was a rush to get in before them. Booking in the jail was a task in itself. You had to show your proof of address, passport, get searched, get your hand stamped, empty your pockets and that was just the start of it. "Neil, go and start booking us in. I'll finish my cig and I'll follow you in. Joanne, get a grip of Joseph before he gets knocked down. Hold his hand or something. For crying out loud! Look!

Get him before he goes missing."

Joanne rolled her eyes and her heels clicked along the gravel path leading towards the visiting centre. Neil lagged slowly behind her. Harpur took a few more blasts of her fag before she flicked the butt into the area behind her. Her hands were shaking and she was starting to feel hot and sweaty. Taking deep breaths, she started to walk towards the centre. The prison was busy today. Young girls holding babies, mothers sat staring at four walls, wondering how it was possible that the fruit of their womb had ended up in such a horrific place. Then there were the thugs, the toy gangsters, loud and full of attitude. Yes, there were lots of different people here today from different walks of life.

The family booked into the prison and they knew they had a good twenty-minute or so wait before they would be let over to the main prison. That's when they would be searched, frisked, made to feel like they were criminals too. The screws treated everyone the same really, no matter how you looked. They were aware that getting drugs into the prison was something that people would do anything to blag the system for, even placing drugs into their arses, vaginas. Yes, you would be amazed at the lengths people had gone to conceal drugs.

Harpur lifted Joseph up onto her lap and bounced him about. "Are you looking forward to seeing your daddy? He will be so happy to see his big boy. Look how big you've grown over these last few months." It was true, Joseph had sprung up in size. His clothes were all too small for him now and Harpur had been out and replaced most of his old stuff. She loved her grandson and she was doing her best for him. In her eyes, she let her own son down and wanted to make amends by doing it right this time with his son.

A screw appeared and cleared his throat to grab their attention and started to read out the names for the visit. Once she heard her son's name she stood up. "Make sure all your stuff is in the locker, we don't want to have to come back over here do we?" The sentence was aimed at Neil. He was a right dimwit. He never checked his pockets and always found something inside them as soon as they got over to the main prison. The noise was deafening, visitors chatting to each other, screws hovering around them all, watching their every move, looking out for anyone who looked suspicious. Harpur stepped forward and placed her money into a small plastic dish. She walked through the security check and was met by a female officer to be frisked. Harpur was panicking, her heart was racing. Even though she knew she was clean, she always had a vision that they were going to find something on her. Daft, but she always went through the same emotion. Joseph loved getting searched, he giggled and pulled his pockets out showing he was hiding nothing either.

At last, all the visitors were searched and ready to go into the main prison where their loved ones would be waiting for them. Harpur passed a twenty pound note over to her husband. There was no way the tight get would fork out any money when he didn't need to. "Will you get the drinks and get our Sam some crisps and chocolate, you know which ones he likes?" Neil took the money and shoved it inside his pocket. He never replied. Joanne straightened her hair and pushed her breasts out in front of her.

The family walked through the doors and Joseph spotted his father first, then started to run towards the table he was sitting at. "Daddy, daddy!" he screamed. Harpur choked up and her eyes started to cloud over. What was wrong with her lately, she cried at the least thing. It was all since her brother's death really.

The day of the funeral would haunt her forever and it was probably the reason her emotions were all over the place at the moment. It didn't seem real, it was just like a bad dream that never went away. She could see it, every time she closed her eyes it was there. The minute the hearse pulled around the corner and she spotted Brady's coffin in the back of it, her world fell apart. Was he really inside there? Was this the end of his existence? It was such a heart-wrenching day. Harpur couldn't deal with death. It scared her, the unknown. And in the past she'd run a thousand miles from any bereavement if she could. But there was no running from this, there was no escape. She had to face it head-on. Brady had been in the chapel of rest for over three days and even though she'd been there with her mother, she could never set foot inside the room where he was laid. How could she sit there with him, looking at the brother she loved so much? He couldn't talk to her, he couldn't laugh anymore or give her any advice. All she could have done was whisper her last goodbye to him. It was as though in her eyes, if she never said goodbye, then it wasn't real. Sheila, however, had sat for hours with her son, talking to him, touching his cold skin, playing with his hair, straightening his clothes, talking about the day just gone. No, she could never do that, never in a million years. The hearse was full of wreaths and flowers and a photo of her brother stood on the top of the coffin. She never took her eyes from that image all the way to the church. The day was bright and sunny and the pied piper played all the way to the chapel of rest. Harpur and a lot of his family members walked behind the car all the way there. It was a sign of respect, to show they were strong, to do him proud. The neighbourhood was out that morning and each of them made the sign of the cross as the funeral passed them. Harpur even stood up in the church and told the people who loved him all about the life Brady had led. She never told them the dark side of it though, no, she kept his memory clean. Nobody had to know about the bad choices he'd made, the tears he'd caused. The priest knew though, he was given every last detail of the deceased's past. On his visit to the family home, Sheila had told him all about Brady's addiction to heroin and how it had changed the son she loved so much. She blamed everybody but her son. Every friend he'd ever had got the blame for the choices he'd made. It was never him, she turned a blind eye to it all. Brady's mother confessed all to the priest, everything she knew about the life her son led. How can anyone ever get over the loss of a loved one anyway? Did the pain, the aching in their hearts, ever leave them? When the coffin was lowered to the ground, Harpur stood above it with her family close by. Red roses were given to them all to place on his coffin. It was such a sad day, and one she would never forget. It was all over now, there was nothing left but his memory. No second chance, no coming back.

Harpur let Joanne hug and kiss Sam first. She was all over him like a rash and it was a bit embarrassing to watch. Sam smiled at his mother and wrapped his arms around her. She was the only woman he could totally trust, the one who stood by him no matter what. "Hiya mam, how have you been?" Harpur smiled gently and hid the fact that her life was in tatters. There was no way she would burden him what was going on. Sam took the news of his uncle's death badly too. The two of them had a strong bond and he was always trying to help get Brady clean when he was on the out. He'd take him out with him, buy him clothes, anything to keep him away from the drugs. But Sam was a hypocrite, he was involved in the drugs world too. That's why he'd landed himself in the slammer. Harpur hated drugs, they were the root of all evil, stole children from families, changed people into zombies. Sam was not allowed to attend the funeral of his uncle. The prison service said it needed to be a direct member of his family before they could even consider letting a prisoner attend and Sam didn't fit the criteria. How sad was that. Somebody needed to look at the prison rules again and have a bit of sympathy for inmates who lost someone they loved. Where were their hearts?

Harpur sat at the table and watched as Joseph hung around his father's neck, kissing and squeezing him. Neil was on his way towards them now carrying a red tray full of food and drinks. Sam watched his mother with a close eye and he could see by the way she looked at him that something wasn't right. He knew her inside out and he could tell when she wasn't happy. Neil reached his hand over and shook Sam's hand. "How are you lad, you still smiling?"

"You know me, it will take more than this jail to break me," he held his head back laughing. The screw nearby paused and shot a look over at him. Sam was well-known to the officers and he'd given them a hard time from the moment he'd landed there. He hated authority figures and struggled following rules, he wouldn't answer to anybody. Sam opened his chocolate bar and started to munch on it. He smiled over at Joanne and touched her fingertips. "So what have you been up to, have you been out?" There was a silence and Harpur dropped her eyes down, she wanted no part of this.

Joanne swallowed hard and kept her voice low. "No, babes. I've been around to Gemma's for a few drinks but I've not been out partying. I can't be arsed with it anymore."

Neil watched the conversation closely and jumped in to change the subject. "You look hench, have you been training?"

Sam flexed his biceps and twisted his arm about. "Of course, these muscles don't just grow you know," he reached over and touched Neil's forearm. "You look like you've been doing a bit too. Have you been to the gym?"

"I've been eating healthy I suppose and when I get a chance I have a go of them weights you left at our house, just a few curls and bench-presses I do, that's all." Harpur quickly looked at him. This was news to her, she'd never seen him once doing any kind of weight training, she was sure he was lying.

Sam made sure the screw had left his side and leaned over the table slightly. "Mam, some guy in here said he knew our Brady. I was talking to him the other night and he said he had been in some serious shit."

She was listening now and urged him to continue. "Serious as in what?"

"I don't know but I'll get back onto him when we have social later tonight. He said Brady was seeing a girl called Melanie Byfield who lived in Blackley. Mam, from what this guy was telling me, this girl is bad news. She had her three kids taken from her and put in care and she was up to all sorts, you know, prostitute, selling herself. Word on the street is that she was trying to sell her kids before they were taken away from her too. She's a wrong-un for sure."

Harpur made a mental note of the name. This girl would be getting a visit from her the moment she had a free minute. "I've been trying to get hold of Tony Wallis, he knows something I'm sure of it, but when I arranged to meet him he went on the missing list."

Sam was onside and he knew there was more to his uncle's death than they were letting on. Neil coughed and raised his eyebrows. "You two need to turn it in. Brady has gone now and no matter what you find out, he won't be coming back." Was this man for real? How could he be so callous with his words? Didn't he realise what he'd just said? He was a heartless bastard for sure. If the truth was known, he wasn't keen on Brady and hated Maddie going out with him. He was a deadbeat, a scumbag. He'd caused so much heartache to his wife too and he was sick to death of her running about after him when he was off his head or on the missing list. He just never understood the world his brother-in-law lived in, he never understood addiction. Sam and Harpur locked eyes and they knew he was treading on thin ice. But who was going to put him straight, would it be her or was it going to be her son?

Harpur growled at Neil, she didn't care where she was or who heard what she had to say. This was her flesh and blood he was talking about, how dare he speak about him like that! Sam sat back in his seat and stretched his arms above his head. He could tell by his mother's body language that she was ready to let rip. "Listen you. We all know Brady won't be coming back. But, like I've explained to you over a thousand times now, something is not right. Don't you ever listen to a bleeding word I say anymore?"

Neil brushed some invisible dust from the top of his

shoulder and replied. "There is no need to have a pop at me. I'm just saying that's all. Let him rest in peace and stop raking up the past." She could have smashed her fist right into his face at this moment, she was fuming and knew if she sat there with him for a second longer she wouldn't be held responsible for her actions. He was a clown, a heartless prick, in her eyes. Harpur stood up. "I'm just nipping to the toilet. I won't be long." Neil held his hands up in the air. He knew what he'd done but here he was protesting that he was innocent one in all this.

Sam watched his mother disappear and confronted Neil. "That was a bit below the belt. You know what Brady meant to her, try showing her a bit of understanding ay?"

Neil locked eyes with Sam and studied him. Was this a threat? Was he laying the law down to him? He wasn't sure. This was his wife he was talking about and there was no way he was having this dickhead telling him what he should be doing. These two had a history of not agreeing and in the past Sam had been ready to floor Neil to prove a point. He wasn't his dad, he was just the man his mother married. Sam was the top dog, not him. Neil blew a laboured breath. "Bleeding hell, I was only telling the truth. Why is everyone so touchy today?"

Joanne smiled. "She's been snappy with me too. Honest Sam, it's been a nightmare living with her lately. Everything I do isn't right. I can't wait for us to get our own place." What a cheeky bitch this girl was. There was no stating how much his mother had done for her, the clothes she'd bought her, the money she kept bunging her, no, she kept all that to herself.

Sam was starting to stress. The tops of his ears were turning bright red and he was fidgeting about, unable to sit still. "Listen you two, she's been through a lot. And you Joanne, start pulling your weight. I bet you're just letting my mam fetch and carry you aren't you?"

Joanne was gobsmacked, how dare he accuse her of being lazy! She'd never take the piss out of anyone, would she? "I do my share Sam, ask Neil, go on Neil, tell him that I don't just sit on my arse all day doing nothing."

Neil was onside, he nodded his head and gave her the support she desperately needed. He checked Harpur was nowhere in sight and spoke. "We all help out. Your mam's just on one at the moment. She'll be fine when this inquest is over. It must be playing on her mind all the time. I guess I should be a bit more understanding."

Sam spotted his mother walking back into the room. Joseph had followed her and she was holding his hand on the way back. She looked a bit calmer now, her temper had calmed down. Harpur sat down and started to speak. "Bleeding hell, I've had to go through another search again. It's a joke in here. I'm sure if they didn't find something on me the first time there isn't a chance they're going to find something the second time. It's just all over the top. What do they think I've got in my knickers, a bloody microwave?"

Sam started laughing. This was the woman he was used to; funny, witty - his mum took everything in her stride. Sam loved to stir up a bit of trouble and he knew Joanne wasn't telling him the truth regarding her pulling her weight in the house. He just had to double check he was right. "So mother, Joanne and Neil have been telling me how much they help you out in the house. I bet you're glad of the extra support aren't you?"

Joanne was bright red and Neil was shocked. The little

bastard had dropped him right in it. It was totally out of order, what the hell was he doing? "Are you having a laugh son. None of them do a tap."

Joseph wanted to speak and he made sure he got his moment. "Daddy, mummy lies in bed all the time and tells me to go and wake my Nana for my breakfast. And she always tells me that nana is the cleaner in the house, not her."

Harpur twisted her head to look at Joanne, who was now chewing rapidly on her fingernails. She'd strangle Joseph when she got him home, the little bugger. All eyes were on her and Sam was waiting on an answer. She smiled and tried to make light of the matter. "Stop lying Joseph, honest, he keeps making up lies all the time now. Sam you need to have a word with him about it. It's doing my head in, he makes me out to be a right liar."

Joseph shook his head and he was adamant that his mother was telling fibs. "No, daddy, I don't tell lies. Nana told me it's bad to not tell the truth. Look at my tongue it's not black is it?" Harpur examined her grandson's tongue and shook her head. This was something she'd made up with him to deter any lies, she told him that if he wasn't telling the truth, his tongue would turn black. Joseph believed this and if he was ever hiding the truth, he always covered his mouth so nobody could see his black tongue. Harpur chuckled and spoke directly to her son. "Don't worry though, things are changing in our house. Lots of things are changing." She flicked her eyes over at Neil and he knew this comment was aimed at him. There was no way she was getting into this here. This would keep until she was in the comfort of his own home, then she would tell him a few home truths.

After that, the visit went well and it was nearly time for Neil and Harpur to leave the two love birds to have some quality time together. Usually they would pledge their undying love for each other at this time, say how much they wanted sex, count the days until they would be together. Harpur wasn't sure if Joanne was the girl for her son; his true love; his soul mate. They were a feisty couple and the fights they'd had in the past were sometimes violent. It was fair to say they were as bad as one another. The abuse they shouted at each other was horrendous, she'd call him names and he'd call her every slag and slut's name under the sun. But, funny as it may seem, they always ended up back together. Harpur hated getting involved in her son's relationship. She kept well out of it. That was their business and nothing she wanted a part of. In fairness, she couldn't see it lasting anyway and hoped one day he would find someone who showed him a different way of life; somebody who worked, a girl who wanted a career, a nice home, holidays, dreams and goals.

Harpur walked to the other side of the table and hugged her boy. The screws were alert and stood nearby making sure no illegal items were passed over. "Not long now son. Just another few weeks to go and you'll be home for good. Just promise me that this is the end of it, no more prison please."

Sam dropped his mouth low to his mother's ear. "No more mam. I promise you. I can't keep coming back to jail, I've had enough." Was he telling the truth or not? Harpur believed him and the look in his eyes told her that in fact he was missing home, longing for his family to be nearby. Neil nodded his head at Sam, there were no hugs or a handshake. This idiot had dropped him in it and he was still having trouble trying to forget this. What a wanker he was, he knew what he'd done, and he knew that he knew that too. Harpur and Neil left the table together.

Joseph ran back to the table and kissed his father one last time. "I love you daddy," he shouted behind him. A few of the female visitors held a look of sadness in their eyes as the small child passed them. They all knew how hard it was for anyone leaving a loved one behind in this place but this child was missing precious time with his father; games of football, watching films together, helping him when he was fixing something – valuable bonding time. Harpur left the room first, she couldn't wait to get out of this place. Her heart was racing now and all she wanted to do was grab a cigarette. It had been an hour and a half visit today and in fairness, it was far longer than she needed with her son but leaving him behind killed her inside. The Christmas visit had been the worst. Her heart broke the moment she got out of the door. She couldn't look back, she just knew her son would be filling up, unable to cope with not being with his family at this festive time. And Christmas was for families. They all got together and put their differences behind them, mended bridges, forgave each other for words spoken out of turn. Yes, her household was a nice place to be at that time of year.

All the doors were being unlocked now, they were nearly free. Just once last security door and the open air would be there facing them; fresh air, birds singing, the free will to do as she pleased. Not a word was spoken between Harpur and her husband. They were both speaking to Joseph but neither of them said a single world to each other. Once they collected their personal belongings from the lockers in the visitors centre, they headed for the car.

"Grandad, will you play football with me?" Neil grabbed the opportunity to kick a ball about, anything would be better than sitting with his miserable wife at the moment. She had a face on her like a smacked arse. He opened the car boot and grabbed the white ball there. Kicking it up in the air, he showed off his skills to his grandson. "Grandad, kick it over to me, let me show you my skills." Joseph loved football and he lived and breathed Manchester United. He was always telling them that one day he would play at the Theatre of Dreams and score lots of goals. There was a good chance of that coming true, this child had talent, skills and ambition. Harpur always told him she would be so proud when she was watching him at Old Trafford and he blushed when she cheered his name, pretending he was a professional United first team player.

Neil and Joseph went over to a small area next to the car park so she could see them in full view. Her first job was to light a fag then check her phone. Had he messaged her? What was he going to reply to her last message? The suspense was too much. One last glance over at her husband and she was safe to continue. Her eyes were wide open and her heart was beating ten to the dozen. He'd replied! Quickly, she scrolled through the other messages and got to his.

"Thanks for your reply. You do make me smile, why is it that even after all these years you still make my heart flutter? I'm going to be straight with you here, so don't be shocked but I think I owe you an apology. There you go I've said it. I messed up and probably lost the most important thing in my life. I did still think about you but you'd moved on, so how could I ever get you back after that? It was my fault anyway. I've always had a knack of

messing up all the good things up in my life, you being one of them. Please let's video chat. I can explain a few things when we are face to face. Don't think I've gone all soft either. I'm still me. I don't know if that's a good thing or a bad thing really? Things here at home are all over the place. I suppose I've just been existing, cracking on with a relationship that has had its day if you know what I mean. I don't mean to load all my shit on you but already I feel a connection with you. Speak soon Love Dessie X"

Harpur's mouth was wide open. This is not what she was expecting. It was like these two people were destined to meet. It seemed like fate. And he finally admitted that the relationship breakdown was his fault. He'd never admitted that. He always denied that he'd slept with that slapper Wendy. Harpur hated her with a passion, loathed her and always said if she ever saw her in the street, even after all these years, she'd stick one on her, scratch her eyeballs out. Was Dessie going soft or had he really changed? There was no way she could reply yet, she had to think about this. Was this all getting too deep? Was she getting emotionally involved with a guy she hadn't seen for years? Falling in love with someone online? They were speaking every day. Not a day had gone by without these two lovebirds chatting to each other. She didn't know anymore, her head was all over the place.

★

The family had been home for over an hour now. Harpur checked the clock on the wall and looked frantic. "I need to get to the hairdressers. Bleeding hell, I should have been there to meet Bridget over five minutes ago." She grabbed her handbag and her car keys from the coffee table and headed for the front door. Neil was watching the football on TV again and he was so engrossed in the game he would never have missed her anyway. She usually kissed her husband goodbye, as well as when she came home, she would always kiss him no matter what. She looked at him for a few seconds and left the room. There was no kiss today, no words exchanged, she just headed to her appointment. This wasn't good.

"And you have the cheek to call me for being late. Belle has been waiting to get you started. You need to pick a new hair colour. Come on, get your coat off and sit in the chair. She's not got all day." Bridget was excited, she loved that Harpur was making changes in her life. So what, it was just changing her hair colour but it least it was a start. Belle come over to her and handed her a colour chart to look at. Bridget was involved in this too, it was a group discussion and she wanted Harpur to get something bright, not something boring and dreary. After a few minutes Belle looked happy with the colour that was chosen and it was nice that her client was willing to leave her new hair in her hands. She loved being creative and she didn't really ever get the chance to do as she wished with someone's hair. They all had their own image, style or they wanted to look like somebody else who was famous. Belle quickly left to mix the colour before her client changed her mind.

Harpur beckoned Bridget over to her. Once she was sat in the chair next to her she passed her mobile phone over to her. "Click on Dessie's messages and see what you make of his last one. It's sent my head all over the place. Do you think he's for real or what, or is he playing games?" Bridget snatched the phone from her hand and couldn't wait to read the message. Harpur looked into the mirror as Bridget sat in complete silence, speechless. Belle was back now and she started to section her hair and apply the colour. Bridget lifted her head up and gasped her breath. This woman was actually stuck for words. Yes, for the first time in her life she was gobsmacked. Harpur raised her eyebrows in the mirror at her. "What do you think of that then?"

Bridget waited until Belle walked away to take a call from a customer before she replied. "Oh my God, this is getting out of hand. I didn't know you two were texting each other as much as you have been. You never said."

Harpur smirked and sucked hard on her gums. "It's just happened, I don't know how, but it's just gone to a different level all of a sudden. Honest, I find myself waiting on his replies, thinking about him all day. What the hell am I getting involved with here, Bridget? Do you think I should just stop and tell him I'm happily married?"

Bridget smashed her fist into the chair she was sat on and snarled over at her. "What and go back to being miserable? You know what I think about Neil, so let's not even go there. Dessie is making you smile again. Look at you, you're alive again. I've not seen you like this for years."

Harpur rubbed her flat palm up and down the side of her cheeks, she was stressed out. This was a big decision and once she'd made it, there was no going back. Could she risk losing Neil over texting some other guy? Would she be upset if her marriage was over? Harpur took a deep breath and turned to face Bridget. "You're right, I'm going to video chat with Dessie and we can take it from there. What do you make of his messages anyway? Is he bullshitting or what? You remember what he was like, he's a joker and I don't want to be sucked in by him."

"Have you ever thought that he might be genuine. He

was a kid when you two last met. For crying out loud, just go with the flow and see what happens."

Belle was back and she finished putting the colour on. It was a big change for Harpur and she just hoped she suited the new copper shade she'd picked for her hair. Bridget left her side. She was having her hair washed and blown. Once their hair was done they had to fly up to Whitefield to attend their Botox appointment. It was going to be late when she got home tonight and for the first time ever, she'd not prepared anything for tea. They could fend for themselves, see how they survived when she wasn't there. Let them see exactly how much she looked after the family. Harpur looked down at her phone and started to reply to the last message Dessie had sent her.

"Hi there, your message has knocked me for six if I'm being honest. Wow, at last you admit it was your fault we split. Thanks for that, it's given me peace of mind after all these years. Ok, let's Skype tomorrow at seven o'clock my time. I will be at Bridget's house so we can have a good chat. I'm a bit nervous about all this if I'm being honest. I've never done anything like this before in my life. Honest, never. You just bring out the worst in me Dessie Ryan, you always have. Anyway, if you're free let's talk tomorrow. I'm looking forward to it. Love Harpur X"

The message was sent now and there was no going back. Harpur smiled at herself in the mirror. At last, something exciting was happening in her life. She just hoped it wouldn't come back to bite her on the arse.

Harpur shook her hair about in the mirror. It was fair to say that this woman looked amazing. The new style and the colour change had taken years off her. Even her skin looked fresh and full of life. Bridget came to her side and touched the new coloured hair. "You look stunning, babes.

Honest, on my life, I've not seen you looking this good for years. Come on then, pay your bill and let's fly up to see the fountain of youth, woman." Harpur sniggered and looked at herself one last time. She did look younger and fresher, she was glowing.

★

Bridget lay on the bed and waited for Angela to come back in. Harpur was stood at the side of her and it was fair to say she was shitting herself. Lots of her friends had dabbled in Botox and she'd never really considered it until now, she just thought she would grow old gracefully. Angela was lovely looking and everything about her was perfect. Even her teeth were bright white and straight – perfection. "Is this the first time for Botox for you both?" Bridget nodded, she was quiet for a change and it was Harpur doing all the talking.

"Yes, can you explain to me what it's going to do. I'm not going to look frozen am I?"

Angela chuckled. Every woman who came to her for treatment always had doubts about these products, none of them wanted to look like some of the Hollywood stars they'd seen on TV. They just wanted a natural lift, nothing more. "I'm going to give you both a light treatment to start. I'm going to lift this area here," she pulled some loose skin above Bridget's eyes. "And then I'm going to remove these lines here, crow's feet everybody calls them."

Bridget was getting excited now and her fears were disappearing. "So I'm going to look younger, fresher?"

"Yes, Botox is designed for that reason. I will give you both a printout of what the treatment actually does." The lady started to inject her friend now and there was not a sound. Harpur was peering over her shoulder and making sure there was no pain involved in this procedure. Bridget didn't move a muscle.

"There you go," Angela said soothingly, "all done. It will take between five to ten days for it to kick in but after that you will see the difference."

Bridget jumped up and couldn't wait to look into the mirror. She was examining every bit of skin that had been injected. Harpur lay down now and she was going through the same procedure.

"What other treatments do you do, Angela?" Bridget asked.

"We do lots; fillers, lips, teeth whitening. I'll give you a price list before you leave."

Bridget was at Harpur's side now. Both of them seemed to have rolled back the years. Angela helped Harpur to sit up. It was all over. Bridget's facial expression changed and she ran to the mirror. "I can feel my face going tighter, does that mean it's working already?" Angela smiled and reassured her it was all quite normal. That was it now. The two ladies were addicted to the youthful look. The years would never get the better of them both. Not now they'd found the secret of turning back the hands of time anyway.

It was late now and Harpur had just got home. She took her coat off and walked into the front room. Neil was laid on the sofa watching television and Joanne was sat in the chair playing on her mobile phone. "Wow, your hair is mint," Joanne yelled.

Neil twisted his head slowly and clocked his wife at the side of him. "Let's have a proper look at it then," he said. Harpur ruffled her fingers through her hair and stood where he could get a good look at her. He examined her and held a sour expression. "It's okay I suppose. I liked your old colour better if I'm being honest."

Harpur couldn't hold her tongue and if the truth was known, she was sick to death of her husband being so negative. Never once did he ever say something was good, he just didn't like change. Oh she was ready for him now, the gloves were off. "And I liked you when you had all your hair but you don't hear me complaining about that do you?" Oh, that was a low blow and something she knew would get his back up. Neil had an egg in a nest on the top of his head and she knew how much he hated it. It was about time she gave him a bit back, insulted him like he'd done with her. Give him a taste of his own medicine.

Neil sprung up from the sofa and growled at her. "I just said I liked your hair the way it was, what's with the snide remarks? There is no need to be so insulting!"

Harpur kept her face straight and answered him. "And all I said was that I liked your hair when you didn't have the bald spot," she sneered at him, letting him know that she could be sarcastic too. Joanne left the room, she knew it was going to kick off any second now and didn't want to be anywhere near the line of fire when it did. She closed the door softly behind her and listened from the hallway.

Neil lay back down on the sofa and folded the pillow under his head. "Nasty that. I've never said anything personal to you, ever. It's a good job I can take it isn't it?"

Harpur was in the zone now and she would have scratched his eyes out if he came anywhere near her. Weeks of frustration were coming to the surface here, she'd reached boiling point. "I'm nasty? Are you having a laugh or what? Come on, let's put our cards on the table here. You're miserable and a tight arse. Why I ever married you I'll never know. I'm sick of it, sick of you and coming home each night to the same shit."

Neil was shocked and rolled on his side. "Stop being nasty then! I am who I am! I love you don't I? That should be enough. Why do you always find faults with this marriage? It's real life this, not a bleeding fairytale."

Harpur knew if she stayed in the same room as Neil a second longer, she might have said something she would regret later. She picked up her handbag and left the room. The door slammed behind her and Neil just sat thinking for a few seconds before he turned the football match back on.

"Women," he mumbled under his breath.

Harpur walked along the landing. As she passed Joanne's bedroom she could see her through the small gap in the door. She was lying on the bed texting, smiling, taking selfies. She gasped her breath and went into her own bedroom. This woman was fuming, she kicked her shoes off and couldn't wait to take off her clothes. Once her pyjamas were on she plonked onto the bed and made herself comfortable. There was no way Neil was getting in this bed tonight, he could sleep on the sofa, stay well away from her until she had calmed down. Harpur reached over to her handbag and pulled out her mobile. She started to read all the messages between herself and Dessie. Twiddling a piece of her hair at the side of her cheek, she began to smile. This man was playing havoc with her heart already, who the hell was he and what did he want from her?

A little later, Harpur was nodding off, tossing and turning in her bed. Dessie was on her mind and she couldn't stop thinking about him. Footsteps were coming up the stairs. Harpur rolled onto her side and tucked the quilt tightly around her body. It was Neil, more than likely getting into bed next to her. The footsteps stopped. She held her ear to the door and listened carefully, nothing, not a murmur. Maybe he'd changed his mind and gone back downstairs. She spread her body across the bed and tried to get to sleep. A few minutes later the bedroom door opened and in walked Neil. Harpur looked puzzled, he'd not been in the bathroom, had he been back downstairs, she wasn't sure. He pulled the duvet back slowly and sneaked into the bed at the side of her. His cold body pressed against hers. She cringed as she felt his hands all over her. He'd annoyed her for sure. "Goodnight babes," he whispered into her ear. A small kiss on her back and Neil began to go to sleep. Harpur lay staring out of the window. The moon was full tonight and she wondered if Dessie was looking at the moon too. Her heart was racing, tomorrow was D-day. She was going to see him face to face, to really talk to him after all these years.

CHAPTER TEN

HARPUR SAT BEHIND RECEPTION in work and was clock-watching every few minutes. Her head had been up her arse all day long. She'd got orders wrong, sent the wrong parts to people, she was a dithering wreck. The reception door opened and Harpur was gobsmacked as a man came smiling towards her. He was eye candy; six-foot tall, dark hair, blue eyes and the brightest smile she'd seen on a man in a long time, sexy he was. "Hello my dear, I'm here to pick up a part I ordered earlier on today. My name's Donny. Mark will know what it is if you just give him a shout."

Harpur swallowed hard and flicked her hair back over her shoulder. She was flirting, trying to catch his eye. Pressing the buttons on the phone, she couldn't take her eyes off him, she was dribbling. "Hello Mark, I've got Donny waiting in the reception for a part he ordered." Harpur held her ear to the phone and dipped her head slightly over her desk to get a better look at this beauty. Caught in the act, he'd seen her checking him out. Her cheeks started to turn bright red.

Donny broke the ice and started to talk to her. "The weather is crap isn't it? I need sunshine in my life for sure. I'm sick to death of rain. What's your name anyway, I've not seen you in here before?"

Harpur had been off work a lot lately and perhaps they'd missed each other when he'd called in. "I've worked here for years. I've been on holiday so that could be the reason why."

Donny was up for a conversation. He walked back to where she was sat and rested his head in his hands as he spoke to her. "If I'd have seen you I would have been back here a bit more often. What's your name then?" What was going on here? This was a purple patch for Harpur. Ever since she'd started to talking to Dessie men were all over her. Of course, there'd been a few admirers in the past, but they were like buses now. She didn't have to think about it before she answered him. Her confidence was booming and she was ready for a chat. "My name's Harpur."

"That's a lovely name isn't it? I've not heard that one before. A gorgeous name for a gorgeous lady." This guy knew exactly what he was doing, he was going for gold. "I don't suppose I can have your number. Perhaps we could go out for a drink sometime?"

Harpur was frozen, debating what she should say. She licked her bottom lip slowly and replied with a smirk on her face. "I'm a married woman, sorry."

Donny giggled and held his head to the side. "Bring the hubby with us if you want," he smirked. Harpur chuckled, she liked his sense of humour and she continued to find out a little bit more about him. "Where do you work, are you local?" Donny leaned over her desk further and was actually looking at her legs, absorbing everything about her. "I work for my old man. I don't live far from here really, basically I live near the town centre."

Mark came into reception then, holding a brown box. "Hiya mate, I hope it's the one you ordered. I've checked the name on the box so you shouldn't have any problems." Mark passed over the car part and spoke to his receptionist. "Donny has already paid, so if you can print him out an invoice that would be helpful. Is there anything else I can get for you pal?"

Donny pushed his toned chest out in front of him and he was looking straight at Harpur when he spoke. "Yeah, can you give me this lady's phone number please? She's playing hard to get at the moment."

Mark sniggered and came to Harpur's side. He placed his hand on the top of her shoulder. "You will have to get in the queue Donny. This one is married. If I had a pound for every man that came in here asking about this woman I would be rich."

Harpur was chuffed now, buzzing, her confidence peaking. Mark was actually telling the truth. She was well liked by the men who came here. Donny took a few paces back from the counter and winked at her. "I won't give up that easily. Me and you will be going out soon. You just wait and see."

Harpur sighed and shook her head, she didn't reply. Donny left the store and Mark waited until the door had closed before he spoke. "I'll tell you what love, he's a good catch. Look at him too, he's got it all going on. All the ladies are trying to bag him."

"Well, I'm not. So there. I told him I'm married so he should back off now and leave me alone."

"Well, don't hold your breath. Word on the street is what Donny wants, Donny gets." Mark started to whistle and walked back into the warehouse. Harpur was flustered now, she was hot and sweaty. Checking her new hairstyle in the computer screen, she smiled. It was amazing what a new hair colour could do for a woman. It was back to business now and she flushed Donny right out of her mind. She was flattered of course but no, she was married. There was a text alert on her phone and her eyes shot to the screen. The message was from Dessie.

"I can't wait to see you later. I've not slept a wink all night. I've had a haircut too so I can look top-notch for you. Speak soon, Love Dessie X."

Her heart was pounding inside her ribcage and anxiety was setting in. What the hell was she playing at here? It all seemed a good idea when she had agreed to it but now she was starting to flap, having second thoughts. Making a quick phone call, she tried to get some advice. "Hi Bridget, what's going on with me? I've shit myself now and I don't know if I can go through with it."

The voice at the other end of the phone was shouting, she held her ear back from the phone. "Okay, I was just saying that's all. Take a chill pill will you. I'll be at your house soon. Make sure you have a few bottles of wine in. I need a bit of Dutch courage."

The call ended and Harpur began to log off from her computer. Once it was shut down she collected her belongings together and walked into the warehouse. "Mark can you lock up now, I'm going. I'll see you tomorrow."

Mark's voice shouted from the back of the room. "See you tomorrow love. Make sure Donny isn't waiting for you too."

Harpur loved the banter in the workplace and she always had a joke with the men who worked there. Filthy they were. They didn't care what they told her about the girls they'd been seeing. Harpur walked into the car park and twisted her head around, checking the area. Surely Mark was joking about Donny waiting for her, surely.

Harpur flicked the engine over and turned the radio on. The tunes were decent tonight. They were songs she could sing along to. This was such a big change for her. Her mood was good and all her problems seemed to have been buried deep today. She was due to see her counsellor at the end of the week and for now her panic attacks were at bay. The traffic was at a standstill and moving slowly. Why was it every time she was in a rush to get home, the local council decided to dig a hole in the middle of the road and cause problems with the traffic? This was rush hour for crying out loud. Harpur looked at the other drivers near her and she could see they were as pleased as she was about the delays. A man rushed past a car, dodging the traffic, weaving in and out. She pushed her head forward to get a better look at him. It was him, bleeding Tony Wallis. Harpur was all ready for jumping out of the car and running after him but the traffic started to move. She opened the car window frantically and screamed outside after him. "Oi, Tony, you better get your arse to see me. Don't make me come and find you. Are you listening to me dickhead?" Tony looked like he'd seen a ghost. He knew it was Brady's sister and chose to ignore her. Whatever he was concealing inside his coat seemed more important than stopping to chat with her. He never said a word, just kept on running. Harpur smashed her clenched fist against the steering wheel. If she would have thought she could catch him she would have run down the street. But Tony was fast, he had to be in his line of work and she knew she would never get within yards of him. Brady had told her so many stories about his pal getting on his toes after a graft and it was well known that Tony Wallis would dust anyone to save his bacon. Her eyes were all over as she started to drive. "You rat Tony! Just you wait until I get my hands on you. I'll skin you alive!"

★

Harpur sat looking in the mirror at the end of her bed. She'd made an effort tonight and she knew once Neil clocked her he would start to ask questions. She needed to be ready to deal with anything he threw at her, have answers ready. Her clothes were smart but casual, just a pair of jeans and a floral blouse. She looked lovely. Even her make-up was on point tonight. Fastening her shoes, she knew it was time to go. It was now or never. Harpur stood up from the bed and looked at herself for the last time. It was time to face the family.

"Nana, you look nice," Joseph stated as soon as she walked into the room.

Joanne nodded her head too. "Whit-woo. He's right. That new hair colour really suits you."

Neil was examining her. She was uneasy and wondered if he knew what she was up to. "Yep, my darling wife looks stunning tonight. Come here and give me a great big kiss before you go out."

Harpur looked over to where he was sat. Was he taking the piss or what? Why was he throwing compliments at her all of a sudden? She'd have much preferred him to have said nothing. At least then she could have gone out without a guilty conscience. Harpur walked over to where he was and casually bent down to peck him on the cheek. There was no way he was getting a full-blown necking session. As she placed her lips near him he gripped her and dragged her onto the sofa with him. "Gorgeous aren't you. Why don't you stay in with me tonight and watch a film? We can have a date night. The football's over in an hour so, come back early from Bridget's if you want?"

Was he having a laugh or what? What planet was this guy on? There was no way she was playing second fiddle to a football match, he could shove his date night right up his arse as far as she was concerned. She pulled away from him and she could feel Joanne's eyes all over her.

"Thanks, but no thanks, you watch all the football you want. Tonight's a girl's night."

Neil smacked her arse as she walked away. "Well, don't say I didn't offer."

Harpur snarled over at him. He was getting right under her skin and nothing he could do was right, they were heading towards dangerous ground and sooner or later these two would be separated. "Right, Joseph give Nana a kiss before I go."

The boy ran towards her and swung his arms around her neck. "I love you Nana," he whispered into her ear.

Harpur's eyes clouded over as she looked directly into the child's eyes. "I love you too. To the moon and stars and back again."

Joseph ran to his mother and dived on her. "Can we go to the shop please, can we? Can we?" Joanne was too busy on her phone and pushed him away from her. She never looked at the child once while she spoke. "Yeah, in a bit, just relax for now."

Harpur picked up her handbag and looked around the room one last time. "See you all later, I might be late so don't wait up." Neither Joanne nor Neil even flinched, they were both too busy doing their own thing. She was gone.

★

Bridget filled the glasses up again. It was nearly time to Skype with Dessie. Harpur kept fidgeting in her seat, walking to the mirror, reapplying her pink lip gloss. Her head was all over the place and it was fair to say if she carried on the way she was, she could very well have a heart attack. Bridget was trying to calm her down. "Just chill out. God, it's not like you don't know this guy. You have history together so at least you're not going to be stuck for something to talk about. Just go with the flow, it will come naturally to you once you start talking again."

Harpur swigged another mouthful of red wine and sat cracking her knuckles. She changed the subject. "I'll have to go and see my mam tomorrow too. I know we've had words but she'll be sat on her own."

Bridget smiled gently. "It wouldn't be half as bad if she apologised but she's a right battleaxe and she never gives in does she?"

"You can say that again. Stubborn isn't the word for her. She's just so bitter sometimes, stone-faced. I swear, if I end up like her just shoot me. Put an end to my misery." The girls were laughing and then Harpur looked at her with a serious expression. "I'm sure Joanne is seeing somebody else on our Sam. I just have a gut instinct about her. You know when you know something is going on but you can't put your finger on it?"

Bridget plonked down on the chair next to her and patted the side of her arm. "Stop worrying about what everyone else is doing. Let them all piss off! This is your time so concentrate on making yourself happy for a change. Let them all sling it, you do enough for them all anyway. If they mess up, then leave them to deal with it."

Harpur was staring into space, she was in a world of her own, away with the fairies. Her mobile started ringing, a Skype call from Dessie was alerted across her screen. She swallowed hard, panic set in. Bridget was screaming at her now. "Answer it, bleeding hell, hurry up before it goes off." Harpur held the phone tightly in her hand, debating, worrying. Bridget repeated herself; she was trying to grab the phone from her to answer the call. Harpur shoved her handset back in her handbag. "I'm not ready. I'm sorry, I thought I was but the timing isn't right for me at the moment. If I start talking to Dessie it will only end up in misery. That man has trouble stamped all over him."

There was a text alert. Harpur shot a look over at Bridget but never flinched. "Bleeding hell, the suspense is killing me, see if the message is from him." Harpur reached for her phone and scanned the screen.

"Shitbag, aren't you? Love Dessie X"

Bridget read the message with her and shook her head. "Are you really not going to speak to him? He could be your destiny, the one, everlasting love."

"Oh will you piss off with your predictions, bleeding Mystic Meg. There is no such thing as a happy ending in our world. Give your head a shake and realise once and for all that Mr Perfect doesn't exist."

Bridget spat her dummy out and gritted her teeth tightly together. "Oh, is that right Mrs Negative? He does exist and that's who I'm holding out for. I'll tell you what should I?" She poked her finger into Harpur's arm. "You stay in your little bubble and see how long you last. What, are you going to sit about until you're old and grey and can't move about to do anything about it? Don't say I didn't tell you so when you're a pensioner and I see you still miserable and bitter just like you say your mam is."

These were harsh words indeed and they hit a nerve. Harpur shrugged her shoulders and knew her friend was right. Necking the rest of her wine, she flicked her head over her shoulder. "Right, okay. I'll ring him back. Just back off and let me do things at my own speed." Harpur was sweating, small beads of sweat were forming on her forehead. Sucking in a large mouthful of air, she picked her phone up and went into the bedroom. She was raging inside and had something to prove now. She was still daring and she still believed in Mr Right. "Here goes", she whispered as she dialled the number. Harpur straightened her hair and sat with the phone in a position where she could see her old flame. It was ringing and ringing. Come on Dessie, answer the call. The sound changed on the connection and an image started to appear on the screen. Harpur twisted her fingers rapidly and got ready to see her first love. They both looked at each other for a few seconds and Dessie started laughing out loud.

"So, you finally plucked up the courage then did you?"

"I don't need courage to speak to you, Dessie Ryan." So here it was, their first date, first Skype call. The start of their friendship, their affair.

Dessie moved closer to the screen and examined every inch of her. She could see him digesting her. There was no way she was moving, she was making sure she kept a straight face. "So what have you been up to?" He asked. Harpur just started to talk and it was funny how calm she was when she spoke. There were no nerves, no jitters, she was confident. "Just working I suppose. I'm pretty boring really, not like you living in the sunshine."

Dessie smiled and she melted inside as she started to remember his smile from when he was younger. "I can't imagine you ever being boring. And as for me living in the sunshine, it's not all it's made out to be. I've got a good tan though haven't I?" Dessie yanked his grey t-shirt up and revealed his stomach area. Harpur's jaw dropped low.

The guy was ripped with a six-pack, he was toned. She swallowed hard and tried not to look impressed. "You must be a right sun- worshipper. I bet you're a right poser over there."

Dessie held his head back and chuckled. "Why would I be a poser? I'm pretty shy I am."

"Since when have you been shy Dessie Ryan, stop chatting shit." Harpur covered her mouth with her hand. She was trying her best not to swear but it just slid out. He must have known she was common now and had never bettered herself.

Dessie raised his eyebrows. "I see you're still a straight-talker then. Some things never change do they." These two had chemistry, right from the start this couple clicked. It was like someone had given them a sip of love potion for each of them to drink and they were besotted with one another.

Bridget opened the bedroom door and sniggered. There was no way she was missing a glance off him. She marched forward and waved at the screen. "Are you alright Dessie, long time ay?"

Dessie studied her for a few seconds and burst out laughing. "That's got to be Bridget for sure. Oh my God, you've not changed one little bit."

Bridget blushed and blew him a kiss before she left the bedroom. She got Harpur's attention before she left. "Hottie or what? Get hooked up, arrange a meeting," she whispered. Harpur tried ignoring her best friend and flicked her eyes back to the screen. The pair of them spent around forty minutes chatting and they filled the gaps in the years that had passed. Harpur looked at her wristwatch, she needed to go but she was enjoying herself like she hadn't in years. Dessie lit a cigarette and blew smoke towards her through the screen. Harpur was glad he was still smoking and lit a fag up too, she was gasping for a fix of nicotine. Even the way this man smoked sent her head spinning, he just had something about him that she was instantly attracted to. "I'm home at the end of next month if you want to meet up. We can have a date, a catch-up?"

Oh, she hadn't been expecting this. What was she going to say? She choked, became lost for words. "I'm married Dessie and you have a wife or girlfriend don't you?"

He let out a laboured breath and shook his head slightly. "Ssshhh, stop being a shit-bag. I'm just saying it would be nice to meet up that's all. I'm not saying we will dive in bed with each other," his eyes were wide open and he smirked over at her. "Well, not unless you wanted to and then I'd need to think about it." He roared laughing and she did too.

"Get over yourself Dessie. The days are over when you could have me. You're punching above your weight and you know it." Go on girl, she was holding her own and giving it him back.

Dessie licked his lips slowly and his voice was quiet. "I'm just saying think about it and see if you fancy it. No pressure."

This was getting out of control, she had to end the call, give herself some time to think. "Maybe I will. Maybe I won't. I'll let you know when I've thought about it," she quickly checked her wristwatch. "Dessie, I've got to go. It's been nice speaking to you and I'm glad everything has worked out for you in your life. But it's late." Bleeding hell, what a speech that was, why on earth had she said that. She should have been cool with him, kept him on the back burner, teased him, made him beg her. She cringed and played with the corner of her blouse as he started to talk.

"My life is anything but perfect Harpur. Perhaps I'll explain to you one day when we sit down together. There is some stuff I need to tell you. Can we talk again?"

Harpur just wanted rid of him now. Her arse had fallen out and she was starting to feel guilty. "Let's see. I'll let you know." She looked at the screen and waved at Dessie. "Goodnight, it's been good catching up. Take care. Speak soon." Dessie was about to say something else but she ended the call before he got the chance.

Bridget ran straight into the room and dived on the bed. "You did it. How easy was that! See, what was the harm in a little chat with an old buddy?"

Harpur gasped her breath and rubbed her hot sticky palms together. "It was easy, I just felt at ease with him. I swear he's got me all, erm, oh, I don't know but he makes me feel good and sort of reminds me of the woman I was."

"Come on, did you fancy him, did he give you butterflies?"

"Derr.. did he 'eck. Come on Bridget, I'm not a kid anymore. It will take more than a video call for me to ever be interested in Dessie Ryan again, he's just a friend now. Nothing more, nothing less. Just let's say he made me smile again."

Bridget followed Harpur back into the front room. Her phone was getting lots of text alerts. Harpur was cool and never once looked at her phone. Dessie Ryan could wait, there was no way she was jumping through hoops for him, not now not ever. Harpur kicked her legs up on the sofa. "Come on then, get them tunes on. I fancy a dance." Bridget didn't need asking twice. She pulled out her ABBA

CD and waved it in the air. "Come on then, let's get a groove on." Bridget loaded the music and danced over to her friend, singing as the song began. "Dancing Queen, feel the beat of the tambourine, oh yeah."

★

Later, as Harpur lay in bed looking at the back of Neil's head, she reached over and touched the back of his neck. Was she being fair on him? Was her marriage that bad that she had to find fun and excitement somewhere else? Checking her husband was asleep, she picked up her phone and started to read the list of messages from the night before.

"You looked amazing Harpur. You took my breath away. I didn't expect to feel like this. What the hell have you done to me I can't get you out of my head. Love Dessie X"

There was no way she was replying yet. It was too risky. Neil could wake up at any second. Placing her phone on silent she shoved it back onto her bedside cabinet. Harpur snuggled down to sleep, she had a warmth rising through her body, a feeling she'd not felt for a long time. She jerked her head forward a bit and kissed Neil's back, he never flinched. He was fast asleep. Harpur closed her eyes and started to drift off. Tonight she was at ease with the world, her problems seemed to have melted away. Dessie Ryan must have sprinkled her with love and cured her. All she could think about was him.

CHAPTER ELEVEN

HARPUR DROVE INSIDE the cemetery and headed down the path to where she could park her car up. She needed to talk to her brother, ask his advice, let him point her in the right direction. He always knew what to do in a crisis. Brady had always been good like that. It was quiet here today, there was an eerie silence and a slight chill in the winter air. Harpur plodded along the path and crossed the grass verge to where her brother was laid to rest. She quickened her pace. There were new flowers on Brady's grave, bright blooms of colour. Bending down slightly, she read the small white card sticking out from the flowers.

"Always Melanie XX"

Harpur gripped the card tightly in her hand and squashed it up in a tight round ball. How dare she come here! Why was she coming to see him now he was gone? She'd never seen sight or sound of this woman. Hold on, yes, Sam had mentioned this name to her when she was on a visit with him. Harpur needed to find her, find out what she knew. It was obvious she thought a lot of Brady, otherwise why did she come to his grave and bring him flowers? Harpur inhaled deeply and plonked down on the floor near Brady's headstone. It took a few seconds before her words began to flow. "It's a mess our kid. I need your help. I'm just getting myself in deeper and deeper but I can't stop myself anymore. You know Neil will always just be Neil don't you? Well, I need more. You said yourself that he wasn't my type when I met him but I thought I knew best and ignored you. For crying out loud, what's happening to me? I should just be happy that I have a man who adores me." Harpur started laughing and touched the headstone with her fingers. "You said I needed a bad lad, a gangster, someone who kept me on my toes. Bloody hell, it was the last thing I needed after that lunatic I was with, wasn't it? Do you remember when you attacked that idiot for me? Orr, he was a big bastard too wasn't he. I can still see you now jumping on him, throwing punches. You were only a kid too wasn't you? But I loved you for that Brady. We were there for each other no matter what, through thick and thin," she held her head to the side, thinking before she spoke again. "I ask myself do I even love Neil any more and I don't know Brady. Honest, it's sad but true. Everything he's doing lately is just getting under my skin. He's bugging the life out of me and he knows it. Sex is like watching paint dry too," she smiled gently and made sure nobody could hear her. "We can talk about stuff like that me and you can't we? We can tell each other anything." Harpur paused and just looked down at the soil beneath her. Was he really gone, was her brother really lying underneath her? "I'll never forget how you always stood by me our kid, especially when nobody else would. Thick as thieves we were. And I suppose you were the sister I never had. Do you remember jumping on our mam's bed with me when we were younger, flying kicks and all that? The way I bounced that high I nearly went through the bleeding ceiling. They were the good old days weren't they?"

Harpur looked up at the sky above and her eyes clouded over. "I think you have been coming to see me haven't you? I lay in bed this morning and I woke up smelling you. It was the Lynx body spray you used to wear. I swear to you I could smell it all over my pillow. It's nice of you to visit me, it shows you still care." Harpur looked at her surroundings and started to pull the dead petals from the flowers. "I'm going to see mam soon, she does my head in too. You know what she's like when she sees her arse. Can't you send her a new man or something, anything to cheer the miserable cow up. She's kicked off with me again, no surprise there. As you know she always starts on me when nobody else is about. I wanted to rag her about. Honest Brady, she winds me up so much. Every day is a struggle with her lately and I'm sure she blames me somehow for you not being here." There was anger now, frustration, bitterness. "I need to find out what was going on though, Brady. I just know you wouldn't have left me without saying goodbye first." A tear streamed down her cheek as she continued. "I miss you so much our kid. I play your Talking Heads CD a lot too. It just reminds me of you. There is a track on it called Heaven, it just makes me cry when I listen to the words of that song."

Harpur started to sing softly and the tears were coming now, she was sobbing. "I've started talking to Dessie Ryan again Brady. Don't go mad at me, just try and understand me. I just needed a bit of something to help me through this bad time. And he does, honest, he takes me away to a place where there are no problems, no misery. I can see your face now saying, 'Why him, he hurt you once before, don't give the tosser the time of the day,'" her fingers touched her brother's face on his small photograph on his headstone. "Orr, you sat with me nearly every night after Dessie cheated on me didn't you? Wiped my tears away you did. I'm just going to see what happens and to tell you the truth, if it helps me through the day then I can't see what harm it is doing can you?"

Harpur stood and stretched her legs, she was getting anxious. "I'm scared Brady. I can't remember your face anymore, brother. It keeps fading and I panic. Nobody knows what I'm going through but you. I need you to guide me, help me get my life back on track. I've got my counselling appointment later today too. I'm sure he thinks I'm a lunatic. You should see his face when I tell him stuff about my life. He's gobsmacked, you can tell he's never lived in the real world like us." Harpur got a text alert on her phone and she smiled at her brother's headstone. "That will be Dessie, here, look at his photograph and see what you think." She flicked to Dessie's profile picture and held it to face her brother. "What do you think? He's not changed much has he?" She read the message out aloud.

"I loved seeing you last night. My heart has been pumping all day thinking about you. Can we do it again? Love Dessie X"

"See what I mean, Brady. He makes me feel alive. I've never felt like this before in my life. He makes my heart skip a beat. Even when I met Neil I never had this kind of feeling inside me. This man takes my breath away." She covered her mouth with her hand. Had she really just said that? Harpur sat back down and folded her arms across her chest. "Okay, I'm going to come clean and tell you how he makes me feel. It's like a warmth riding through my body when I think about him, I get butterflies. He feels like home if that makes sense." Harpur was pouring her heart out here and she shocked herself that she was talking so openly about her feelings. This was her secret though, only her and Brady would ever know how she truly felt. Her heart needed to be protected. Dessie Ryan had already broken it once before and she could never let him do it again. She was older now and a lot wiser. Or so she thought. "I've got to leave you now. I will call again soon. And if you are coming to visit me again, please don't do any spooky shit to me, you know that I hate anything like that," she smiled and looked at his photograph one last time and smirked. "No, seriously. Don't mess about with me. Just send me some white feathers, that's enough for now." Harpur stood and straightened the flowers in the pots nearby. She kissed his photograph and stood looking at his resting place for a few more seconds. "I love you, our kid. I miss you so much." Harpur was gone.

Harpur sat in the car and flicked the engine over. She looked at her phone and smirked. She was in this now and there was no backing out. It was a do or die situation. Her fingers were itching to get started. She began to type her reply to Dessie.

"Hi there, I enjoyed our chat too. I can't say my heart has been pumping about all day though like yours has. You have always been a bullshitter and I never believe a word you say to me. I'm immune to you I think. You're a player Dessie Ryan and that will never change. Love Harpur X"

She pressed the send button and stared at the screen for a few seconds. Harpur knew this was wrong but what the hell, she had to get her kicks somewhere didn't she? She checked her wristwatch and sighed. Harpur had fifteen minutes to get to her appointment with Mark. Pulling out onto the main road, she joined the traffic. Neil had said earlier that it was a date night tonight too and he was going to put something together for tea. He must have sensed that she wasn't happy with him. Too little too late she thought. He should have done something months ago. This was all his doing.

Mark sat facing Harpur and he seemed a bit moody today. Perhaps he should have had some therapy, help ease his own troubles, the miserable get. His tone was different too. He was speaking as if he just wanted to get this session over with; he was snappy, rushing, not digesting anything. Harpur shot a look over at him and spoke in a low tone. "Is everything alright Mark, you seem a bit stressed today, a bit down even." How funny was this? Here she was with troubles of her own and she was the one doing the comforting.

Mark crossed his legs and he was doing his best to be as professional as he could, but his own dramas were taking over. "Oh, just ignore me Harpur. I've just got out on the wrong side of bed today that's all. It will all sort itself out anyway."

Harpur dipped her eyes and sniggered to herself and tried to hold a straight face. Mark coughed to clear his throat and told her the usual confidentiality rules. Harpur sat back, she was relaxed today. Her words seem to flow and she had no difficulties opening up. Mark sat back in his chair and chewed on the end of his black biro as he began speaking. "So how are you feeling? I must admit you do look a bit happier than the last time I spoke to you."

Harpur nodded and smiled. "I suppose you're right. I seem to be coping with stuff a lot better than I normally do." Mark began to take a few notes and he continued to listen to her. "Mark, I think I might be a bit closer to finding out what happened before my brother's death.

There is a girl who might know more than she is saying. Once I find her I'm sure she'll tell me what she knows and then I can put all this to bed once and for all. He might have had woman troubles I think."

Mark thought she was pissing in the wind if he was being honest and raised his eyes as he continued. "Maybe you should just leave her be. I mean, say she tells you something that you don't want to hear? Brady was in a bad place from what you've told me and people do things they wouldn't normally do when the need for drugs becomes stronger than anything else." Harpur looked at him and you could see she was getting angry. Why was he judging Brady when he knew nothing about his life? Yes, he was a junkie but he was a human being too! She retaliated. "No Mark, no matter what's gone on I need to know the truth. My mam's like you, she keeps telling me to leave it alone but if you knew our Brady, you would know he would never do anything like this without something pushing him over the edge. He would never have left me without saying goodbye. It doesn't make sense. Night after night I sit wondering if I've missed something, some little detail that would put my mind to rest." Mark let her finish talking. He'd heard all this before and just sat listening. He was getting bored, hiding his mouth as he yawned. Harpur was thinking out loud. "It would all make sense then wouldn't it? It would help us deal with it better. At the moment it's like a jigsaw but nothing seems to fit. Do you know how frustrating that is?" Mark never said a word. She sat thinking for a few seconds and suddenly changed the subject, just blurted it out. "I'm speaking to my old boyfriend too. Is that classed as cheating? I've only had a chat with him on Skype. We haven't had sex or anything. Just chit-chat really."

Mark was interested now. This was something new and not the normal doom and gloom she spoke about. "Obviously you know it's wrong, otherwise why have you just told me about it?"

Harpur tilted her head to the side a little. It wasn't the answer she wanted to hear. Mark needed to loosen up for once and see things as they really were. If she was getting a buzz from chatting to some man, then so be it, what harm was she doing? Harpur sat up straight in her chair and crossed her legs. "For once in my life I want to do something for me. All my relationships in the past have been, well, decided for me if you know what I mean."

Mark was into this conversation and he delved deeper. "Can you explain what you have just said, your relationships have been decided for you? I don't understand what you mean by that."

Harpur sighed and rolled her eyes. "When I met Sam's dad, well, I was sort of on the rebound and I was probably searching for a quick fix, a fling, just some fun. But I got what I deserved and it served me right for being such a dickhead. I should have known better. And the same thing happened when I met Neil. I was broken and he was there to fix me. I suppose I was damaged goods in a way. Well, that's what I think."

Mark tapped his pen on his teeth rapidly. "And this new man, would he be a rebound from your husband?"

Harpur sat forward in her seat and cupped her hands around her knees. "No, there is no rebound this time. My marriage has just gone stale. We've drifted apart. And you can save your words by saying try working at my marriage because I've already tried that. Nothing works. I have to face it, it's over."

Mark was such a do-gooder, he always had to put a dampener on it. "Does Neil know it's over?"

Harpur was sad now, her bottom lip was trembling, her yes welling up. It hurt her inside to even think of seeing her husband upset after all they had been through together. "No, he just thinks we're just going through a bad patch. He doesn't seem bothered really. He tells me he loves me all the time but he doesn't make me feel safe anymore. He's taken me for granted for so long and he just expects me to carry on like everything is rosy in the garden." Harpur folded her arms tightly across her chest, she was on the defensive. "Mark, I've tried for years to make my marriage work. God knows I've tried everything but when it's gone it's gone isn't it? It would break his heart if I left him so I just plod on. Every day is a struggle. But what about me, don't I deserve to be happy?"

"And, this new man. What do you expect from him, can he make you happy?"

"I expect nothing, we're just talking. What would I want from Dessie anyway?"

Mark could see she was getting agitated. "I think you should take things slowly. Don't be jumping into anything too quickly. From what you've told me in the past, Neil is a good man and perhaps you should just give it one last go. I mean, just to see if it is really the end."

Harpur snarled at him and he knew she didn't like what she'd just heard. He was judging her, thinking she was a slapper, a slut who jumped into bed with the first man that came along. She sighed heavily, deflated. "I'm not leaving Neil. I'm just telling you how I feel that's all. That's part of your job isn't it, to listen?" Harpur clammed up straight away and there was no chance she was talking about her dilemma with him anymore.

Mark dipped his eyes and continued. "In our last session, we spoke about the domestic abuse from your ex-partner." Harpur had never told Mark her previous partner's name and even now she would never tell him. Her lips burned with hatred every time she used his name and if she was ever speaking about him, she always referred to him as 'the prick' or 'dickhead'. It was funny because everyone knew who she meant, even Mark. Harpur was losing interest. She didn't want to talk about her past anymore. It would only put her on a downer for the day. At the moment she was just ticking over and she didn't want a dark cloud above her head anymore. The two of them sat talking about everyday life and how her son was set for a new life when he came home from prison. She spoke about Maddie too, she never really saw her anymore. Her daughter just bobbed in every now and then, staying the night when she was bored. Maddie had always been independent, she never needed anyone, she only ever needed money. But something had changed with her lately, she seemed withdrawn. Perhaps her uncle's death had hit her more than she was letting on. The pair of them were close and they got on well. The session came to an end and Harpur picked up her belongings to leave. A waste of a session it was, nothing to report really, no life-changing decisions made.

Just before she left, Mark knew he'd probably been a bit too hard on her regarding her new friend. He stood up and coughed to get her attention. "Harpur, I do believe everyone deserves to be happy. And like you said, this is your time. Just think things through. I just don't want you jumping out of the frying pan and into the fire that's all. Love is a beautiful thing and is sometimes found when you're not looking for it. When it's real, you can't fight it off, it just gets a grip of you and you don't think straight. Just remember that will you?"

Harpur raised her eyebrows. Mark must have known she'd spat her dummy out and perhaps she'd been a bit off with him since he gave his opinion. But anyway, the air was cleared now and they were both back on track. "See you next week Mark, and thanks for listening. I know I do your head in sometimes but I just need to get stuff out of my head every now and then. You do understand don't you?"

Mark sniggered, "Of course I do. Remember, it's my job." Harpur swung her bag over her shoulder and left the room. Mark sat back down in his chair and sat staring into space for a few minutes. Harpur was right, he did have something lying heavily on his mind.

Sheila sat near the back door smoking her head off. The back gate opened and Harpur strolled inside. "What are doing sat there, you never usually move from your chair when the television is on."

"You're a cheeky bleeder you are. Of course I move. Who do you think does all the cleaning in this place?"

Harpur twisted her head back over her shoulder and from the corner of her eye she clocked a pile of black bags in the corner of the garden. "What's all that?" she asked as she walked inside. Sheila stubbed her cigarette out quickly.

"It's all a load of old shite. It's the last of our Brady's stuff. I've rooted through it and there is nothing worth keeping. Just crap really."

Harpur plonked herself down on the sofa and by the looks of her she wasn't happy. How could she just throw his belongings out without talking to her first, she might have wanted something out of it? "Well, I might want to keep some of his stuff. I'll have a look through it myself. You know what you're like for throwing stuff away."

Sheila hesitated, the colour draining from her cheeks. "No love, just leave it alone. I've sorted through it and it's just a pile of shit really, old letters, old socks and trainers. Nothing worth keeping. You know what he was like for hoarding stuff." Harpur could see she was distressed and never said any more about it but she watched her every movement, she was hiding something for sure, she was edgy. Sheila walked into the kitchen and flicked the kettle on. "Do you want a brew, I've got some nice cakes in?"

Harpur looked shocked, she'd never treated her like this before. Her mother was actually being nice. "I'll have a coffee please. I don't want a cake though, Neil's cooking tea tonight so I'll have to leave some room for that."

Sheila walked back from the kitchen holding a white envelope in her hand. "Marion from number six called here before. The neighbours had a whip-round and they all donated some money to help with the funeral costs."

Harpur smiled, "that's nice of them isn't it?"

"It is considering our Brady probably robbed half of them!" Harpur sniggered, her mum had such a way with words, she just said it how it was sometimes. "There's one hundred and sixty pounds here. I was thinking we could buy him a pot to go on his grave, perhaps, another black and gold one to match the others."

"Yeah, that would be nice. I went to the cemetery earlier Mam and there were some flowers on Brady's grave from someone called Melanie. I've never heard of her, have you?"

Sheila popped a fag into the corner of her mouth and walked back into the kitchen. She shouted behind her.

"Oh, yes, I know her. That's nice of her isn't it?"

Harpur was puzzled. "Who is she mam? I've never heard you mention her before. Did Brady know her?"

Sheila came back into the front room holding two cups hooked around her finger. "Quick, grab one of them cups before I scold myself."

Harpur quickly gripped one of the mugs and placed it on the floor near her feet. She needed to get back on the subject of this Melanie girl. Sheila spoke as if she knew her. "Yes, anyway, the flowers were lovely from her. They must have cost an arm and a leg. Did you know Melanie?"

Sheila scratched the side of her head. "I didn't know her as such, but I heard Brady mention her a few times. And she was always speaking to him at night on his phone when he was in bed. Well, that's if he came home."

"Where does she live, is she from round here?"

Sheila shot a quick glance over at her daughter and she must have realised what she was saying. She became cagey and dismissed what she'd just said. "Our Diane's on her way over. Apparently, she's met the man of her dreams and wants to tell me all about it. I mean, what do I want to know about her love life for? I'd rather have a nice pot of tea than listen to her talking about the next perfect man she's found. She's better off staying single if you ask me. Men are nothing but trouble!"

Harpur began to chuckle. "It's about time she met Mr Right isn't it, she's never had any luck with the men has she?"

Sheila let out a laboured breath. "I suppose it runs in the family that bad luck, we're cursed. Look at me, I only attract nutters, not one of them have been normal."

Harpur picked her coffee up and blew at it, hoping to

cool it down. "You and me both then. I've had a share of them too."

"Yeah, but look at what you have now. Some women would cut their right arm off to have a husband like Neil. You could have done a lot worse you know."

Harpur shrugged her shoulders and rolled her eyes. What did her mother really know about the life she was living? All she could see was that Neil went to work and he wasn't out every night on the piss like her men had been in the past. Marriage wasn't just about that was it? A relationship needed to be kept alive, couples should never stop trying. Romance should never die when two people love each other, they should bend over backwards to make each other happy; it was about teamwork, helping, caring, two becoming one. Was this topic even worth wasting breath on? Sheila would never have a bad word said about her son-in-law, she was up his arse, a brown-noser.

The back door swung open and in walked Diane. She smiled over at them both and swept her hair back from her face. "It's official, I'm head over heels in love." Sheila screwed up her face and didn't take her eyes off the television. Maybe she was jealous. It was just something in her eyes that seemed a little bit different. "I swear to you both, this guy is the love of my life, we just clicked. Sheila, he's got a brother if you fancy a double date? Come on, let's see if we can get rid of some of them cobwebs in your knickers girl."

Sheila snapped and from out of the blue she started screaming her head off. Whoa, where was this coming from? "Are you all forgetting I've just buried my son? Do you think for one second that I would want a man all over me while I'm grieving? Have a bit of bleeding respect will you?"

Harpur shot a look over at her auntie. Sheila was bang out of order and she knew sooner or later Diane would give her a mouthful. She would never be spoken to like this. "Sheila, if you take your head out of your arse for a few seconds you would see we all know what you're going through. What, do you expect nobody else to ever be happy again because Brady decided to take his own life? That was his choice love, not ours. I'm sorry he's gone but you can't expect us all to shut up shop and sit crying for the rest of our lives. Perhaps if you would have stood up to Brady a bit more he wouldn't have walked all over you. Don't think I don't know what went on in this house because I do. People talk you know and I've been told all about the way he treated you too. He threatened to hit you, go on admit it." Diane knew a lot more than she was letting on, she locked eyes with her sister. Harpur cringed, she would have never gone that deep into it. But it was all true. Every word Diane said was bang on.

Sheila gritted her teeth and she was ready for blowing. How dare she speak about her boy like that? She would scratch her eyes out if she carried on darkening his name. Diane wasn't scared, she sat down and waited to hear what she had to say. If Sheila wanted a fight then she was ready for her, she was sick to death of hearing it day in, day out about how she was the only one who cared for her son. Well, not today, no more, she was getting told. Sheila was on the war path. "We all have our troubles behind closed doors as you know. And whoever has been gossiping about me and our Brady then go back to them and tell them to keep their bleeding nose out of my business before I start telling all I know about people around here. Oh yes, there would be a few divorces if I let the cat out of the bag I can tell you. Those who live in glass houses shouldn't throw stones." Sheila's back was up alright but she never took it any further, she plonked back down in her chair and tightly folded her arms across her chest.

Diane looked over at Harpur and rolled her eyes. She knew Sheila wouldn't give her any more grief. She'd tear her apart if she did. Diane carried on talking to Harpur and filled her in on the new man she'd found. Every now and then she looked over at her sister and smiled because she knew she was listening in. Stubborn cow she was. Harpur looked at the wall clock and stood to her feet. "Diane, are you staying for a while because I've got to go home. Neil's cooking tea tonight and I don't want to be late."

Sheila piped into the conversation. "She doesn't have to sit with me I'm not a bloody baby, I can look after myself. I like my own company as you both know."

Diane growled over at her. "Oh and don't we know it! Nobody said you need looking after did they, so wind your bleeding neck in. I'm staying for a bit anyway. Well, that's if you shut that moaning arse up for a second."

Harpur smirked and walked to her mother's side to kiss her cheek. Sheila kept her eyes on the TV and never flinched, her cheek was cold, just like her heart really. Before she left she asked Diane, "keep me updated on your love life too. I do hope he's the one. God knows you've waited long enough for him."

Diane nodded. "I know love, go on, you get going before your tea gets cold. I'll be here tomorrow so call and see me if you get a chance."

"I will, right, I'm getting off. Come here and give me a kiss." The two women hugged and Harpur kissed her auntie on the cheek before she left.

Harpur walked down the garden path and looked behind her to make sure nobody could see her. Quickly, she gripped the black bags from the corner of the garden. She headed out of the back gate and slung them in the boot of her car quickly. What on earth was in there? They were heavy. As soon as she got the chance she would go through all her brother's stuff and see if there was anything of interest inside them. If he was hiding anything she would find it for sure. Harpur locked the boot of the car and walked to the driver's side of the car. Lifting her eyes, she could see her brother's bedroom window staring back at her. Was there someone there hidden behind the curtain? She wasn't sure. Eyes squeezing tightly together, she examined every inch of the window. No, she must have been imagining it. There wasn't a soul there. It was probably wishful thinking, hoping Brady would be waving at her from the window like he always used to.

Harpur walked into the kitchen to met by delicious smells of garlic, herbs and onions. Neil was stood at the stove and he smiled at her as she began to take her coat off. "Come on princess. You sit down there and let me wait on you. I'm your loyal servant tonight, my dear."

Harpur shot her eyes around the kitchen. It was a bloody mess, he must have used every single plate and pan in the place. They were all stacked high in the sink. Looking further round she could see the stains dribbling down the front of the cupboards; there was sauces and oil all over the place. He was such a messy bleeder. This was going to take her hours to clean up. Neil wiped the edge of the plate before he gave it her. "Oh, you want romance I'll give you romance." He pecked her on the side of her cheek. "There you go my darling, get stuck into that." He turned around and walked back to the kitchen side. He stood flicking his lighter and lit the vanilla scented candle near him. Harpur was trying to get a glimpse of what he was doing. As soon as she saw him holding her candle from the bedroom she could have dropped down dead. She'd had this candle forever and never once had she lit it. This was a present from Brady, a gift on her birthday. The rage was pumping inside her and she couldn't hold it in.

"Neil, blow the candle out quick, for fuck's sake. You're a right daft bastard. That candle was from my brother. It's just for show, it's not to light."

Neil looked at her as if she was mental. "What, we have candles in the house that we don't light now. Are you for real or what?"

Harpur stood to her feet and moved quickly towards the yellow flame. Blowing hard, she made sure the candle was no longer burning. She gripped it in her hands and you could see by her expression that this meant so much more to her than he thought. Neil just looked at her and said nothing, he was speechless. This romantic night seemed to be over before it had even started. He ragged his fingers through his hair and let out a laboured breath. She'd pissed him right off. "I just can't do right for doing wrong me, can I?" He stomped about the kitchen, slamming doors, launching plates into the sink. He was on one, raging. Harpur stared over at him. Did he really want an answer to that question or what? The man was a clown, a brain-dead idiot who never thought anything through. She sat back down and stared at her food. And, to add insult to injury her husband had put mushrooms on her plate, he knew she hated them. What on earth was he playing at?

Had he never taken one bit of notice regarding her likes and dislikes throughout their marriage? Her cheeks were on fire, she wanted to sling the meal up the wall, smash the plate over his big daft head. Her appetite was gone, there was no way she could pretend everything was alright here. It was a disaster zone.

A text alert from her phone sounded. Neil was still stood at the sink and he'd seen his arse. He was mumbling under his breath as Joanne walked into the kitchen. She'd heard the commotion from the other room and had come in to see what was going on. She loved a bit of drama, she loved that something exciting was happening in her life. Sitting down at the table, she clocked the food on the plate and looked over at Harpur. "Oh, that looks lovely. Have you made this Neil?" She didn't have to wait long for an answer.

"Yes, I did. But you get no thanks in this house. Ungrateful she is. All because I lit a daft bleeding candle. Apparently, we only have candles for show. Who in their right mind doesn't light fucking candles?" Joanne smirked and covered her mouth with her hand slightly. Neil came to the table and pushed Harpur's plate over to her. "You can have it if you want Joanne. No point in it going to waste is there?"

"Yes, you eat it because I won't be touching it. How sad is it when your own husband doesn't know you don't like mushrooms? So much for romance. I think we are way past that don't you Neil? It's more like divorce proceedings we're heading to."

Neil spun his head back around and his eyes were bulging, she'd hit a nerve alright. His true colours were coming out now. "Like I give a flying fuck anymore. If you want a divorce then let's crack on. What's the point anymore. I'm sick of trying with you. Go and try to find someone who will love you like I do. Good luck with it, you'll need it. Hard work you are, draining."

Joanne picked a fork up and started to eat the meal slowly. This girl had no shame, the greedy cow. There was a deadly silence. Come on Harpur, she thought, it's not like you to let him speak to you like that, retaliate, tell him he's an arsehole, say something, put him in his place. She swallowed hard and stood to her feet. Here it was, she was ready to let rip. Placing a single hand on her hips, she moistened her lips. Their eyes locked and he knew she was at breaking point. "You think you're so special don't you. Everyone thinks you're perfect and have no faults. Well, they want to try living with you. You're lazy, selfish, and a tight-arsed penny-pinching bastard. Do you know what, I might just find someone who loves me too because it's obvious all you care about is the bleeding football and the gym. So it works both ways. You go and find somebody who looks after you like I do because as far as I'm concerned, this marriage is dead and has been for a long time. Shove this marriage up your arsehole."

Joanne's eyes were wide open, her jaw dropped. Well, fuck a duck, she never expected this. She always thought these two were strong together. Just wait until Sam rang her, she would fill him in on the family traumas. Neil ragged his hands through his hair and his nostrils flared. He was sorry now, wanted to make amends. He walked over to her and placed his two arms around her neck, looking her straight in the eye. She was wriggling about, trying to move him from her. "I'm sorry love. I just worked so hard all day trying to get everything right for you. I'm sorry about the candle too, I should have asked before I lit it." This man was so manipulating, he had a knack of always making her out to be the bad one. No matter what went on, he always turned the situation around so he looked innocent. He was a twat, end of. Joanne sat watching them, she'd nearly eaten everything that was on her plate, the greedy bitch shovelled it in.

"Take your hands off me Neil. I just need time on my own. I'm sick to death of us and how we are together. We're not in love anymore. Come on, admit it, we just make each other miserable."

Neil was in a panic, this wasn't what he wanted to hear. "Harpur, it's just a silly argument. Come on now, stop overreacting. Why do you just blow everything up so much? Just let it go and let's make friends." She gripped his hands and prised his fingers open one by one. She was serious now and ready to snap. He'd pushed her buttons and there was no way she was backing down.

"I said, I want to be left alone, fuck off away from me. Go on, piss off and go and watch some football. Just leave me alone before I say something I might regret."

Oh, this was real alright, how could he ever come back from this? Okay he'd let his marriage slip for a while and by his own admission, he could have done more to keep his wife happy, but he just got comfortable and took her for granted. He was up shit street for sure. Harpur stormed out of the kitchen. Neil punched the door behind him and plonked down at the table. Joanne reached over and patted his shoulder softly. "She'll calm down, just give her time. You sit here and I'll put your food on a plate. You've worked hard preparing this and there is no point in it going to waste is there?"

Neil smiled over at her. She was so caring and always knew what to say to cheer him up. "Thanks love. You see now what I have to put up with. Fucking crazy she is, a nutter."

Harpur slammed the bedroom door. She flung her shoes off and slammed her body onto the bed. Punching her clenched fist into the pillow, she was having a meltdown. Why was her life so hard at the moment, why was everything falling apart around her? Looking at her phone, she read another message from Dessie.

"Can we Skype, need a chat with you. I'm here when you're free"

Harpur dried her eyes and read the text over and over again. What did he need to talk with her about, she'd already spoken to him earlier in the day? Was he alright, had something happened? She replied to his message rapidly.

"Hi Dessie, yes course we can. Are you alright? Give me about ten minutes though."

The message was sent and she sat staring out of the window. Her head was in bits, was her marriage really over or was this just a bad patch they were going through? Anyway, what was the point in worrying about it, what would be would be, wouldn't it? Checking her make-up in the mirror, she quickly touched it up and straightened her hair. Dessie would cheer her up for sure, nothing else seemed to matter anymore but him. He was just the remedy that she needed. Harpur quickly put her shoes back on and gathered her belongings. Heading down the stairs, Neil was waiting at the bottom for her. Her eyes were wide open, she needed to leave now, go and see Dessie. What on earth was she going to tell him, she needed to think fast, sort it out. "Neil, I'm just nipping to Bridget's, she's got man troubles and needs a chat. Please, don't start on me. My head's banging and I just need to calm down."

Her husband was desperate. "Can we talk when you come back later? I need to sort this out. You said we should get a divorce, what's all that about? Tell me you were just angry and said it in the heat of the moment, go on tell me. Don't make me suffer like this."

Harpur held her breath, she needed to leave and there was no way he would let her go until she told him what he wanted to hear. He would peck her head for hours if she didn't tell him what he wanted to hear. "Neil, just let me go. You make me angry sometimes and I probably overreact."

Neil let out a relieved sigh. That was enough to put his mind at ease. If his marriage was over he would have fallen apart, he would be crippled inside. Harpur and Maddie were his life. At that moment Neil seemed to understand all the things she'd said to him. He rested his hand on her waist. "I'm sorry love. I'll make thing better I promise you. From now on I'll make sure I put you first." He leaned in for a kiss and she cringed as his lips touched hers. She just wanted to go now, put her troubles behind her. Escape her life.

Harpur positioned her mobile phone on the dashboard. She'd parked up in a quiet lay-by and she was nearly ready to make the call. Just a few last tweaks to her lip gloss and she was ready to go. The sound of the phone ringing filled the car and her heart beat rapidly. What on earth did Dessie want to talk to her about? What if he said he didn't want to talk to her anymore, how would she take it? Perhaps that might have been a good thing anyway. Maybe then she would have tried to patch her marriage up and smooth over the cracks.

The call connected and it took a few seconds before she could see his image on the phone. She smiled as he appeared. She took in every inch of him, his surroundings, his hair, his teeth, his clothing. "Hi, there, how are you?"

Dessie raised a smile back but it was obvious something was bothering him. She remained quiet and gave him the chance to talk. "I've got a few decisions to make that's all. But I'm over in England next week and I was thinking if you're not busy we can meet up. Maybe a weekend away together?"

Harpur was shocked, speechless. Her and Dessie spending a full weekend together? She didn't mind meeting up for a few drinks but this guy was asking for so much more. Would that mean sleeping together, spending the night in the same bed, sex? No, there was no way she was up for this, it was too much, too soon. She laughed it off. "Who, me, you and our partners?"

Dessie chuckled loudly. "Derr, me and you, nobody else. I just think it would be nice for us to spend some quality time together that's all. We get on right?"

"Yes, but we're mates Dessie. You can't just say let's go away together. Where is your head at, we're both married are you forgetting that?"

Dessie stretched his arms above his head and smirked at her. "I see you're still the same old Harpur. Where has your sense of adventure gone?" This guy was using every trick in the book now and she was unsure of her answer.

She changed the subject, she wasn't ready to answer this yet, no way, she had to think about it. "I've had a shite day I can tell you. It's just gone from bad to worse. Perhaps a weekend away from life is what I need."

Dessie was listening now and he answered her. "Can I say something?"

"Yes, crack on, you can say what you want, there is no need to ask."

"My life may look all perfect to you because I live out here in the sunshine, but I can tell you now it's not all it seems. I've not been happy for a long time and when you got in touch with me it just put my head into a spin and, well, I…"

Harpur was hanging on his every word, waiting for him to finish what he was saying. "You what?" she eagerly replied.

Dessie swallowed hard and it was obvious he'd let something slip. He tried backtracking. "I kind of like what we have going on here. You make me feel alive again."

Harpur blushed and if she was being honest here, she felt the same. She studied him longer than she should have as he spoke, taking in every expression he made, looking deep into his eyes, getting flutters inside her heart. It was true, he made her feel alive too. "What if we met, would you expect us to be sleeping with each other, having sex?" She just blurted it out, straight to the point.

Dessie choked and smirked at her. "I think you won't be able to keep your hands off me. I'll have to fight you off." The banter had started and both of them were having a friendly pop at each other. Harpur could tell this man anything, she could feel the connection they had. Was it possible that the love that developed so many years ago could still be stored in their hearts? But that wasn't love way back then, surely? It was just puppy love. Not the real everlasting love, her true love? Was Dessie really her destiny, her fate? She wasn't sure. This man was playing havoc with her emotions and she wasn't sure if she could trust herself in the same room as him. Harpur was being drawn towards him though, like a moth to a flame. Their two hearts were becoming one. "So are we up for a bit of fun then? Me and thee, you and I, having a catch up?"

Here it was, she had to decide. Harpur flicked her hair over her shoulder and still she wasn't sure of her answer. "Maybe, maybe not."

"It's just a date Harpur, God, live a little and come and see me."

It was there on the tip of her tongue, the reply, her heart's desire. Without thinking any further she followed her heart. "Alright then, but if you start chatting any shit to me or trying your charm on me it won't be working. I won't be having sex with you, you know that don't you?"

"I never thought for one second that you would. Plus, you're still frigid aren't you."

This man had charm for sure, the gift of the gab, she was like butter in his hands. "Do you mean just because I didn't drop my knickers for you, you think I'm frigid?"

Dessie became serious and he looked her straight in the eye. "No, but you dropped them for someone you didn't even know. I know all about that crank you was with and even now I still can't believe you ended up with someone like him." Dessie dug deep and you could tell by his tone that whatever happened years ago was still lying heavy on his mind.

"It wasn't like that Dessie. Maybe when we sit down together I will explain some stuff to you. Anyway, what did you care? You went with any girl that had a pulse. So much for what we had."

Dessie shook his head and sucked hard on his lips. "Whatever darling, maybe I will explain some stuff to you too."

Harpur checked the clock in the car and realised that she had to go. These two had been gabbing for over an hour now. "I'll text you the hotel details once I've booked. I'm looking forward to it now."

Harpur sniggered and you could tell by her face she was excited by it too. "Bye Dessie, take care."

"Bye gorgeous, speak soon."

The video chat ended and Harpur had to take a few seconds to compose herself. What had just happened? Had she really agreed to meet her ex-boyfriend and spend the weekend with him? Harpur pulled up outside her house and sat staring at it. It didn't mean what it used to to her anymore. In the past she couldn't wait to get home. To look after her family, to make sure all her chores were done and for her husband to come home from work. There were no more cosy nights snuggled on the sofa with Neil anymore, no more date nights, it had all just drifted away from her. Harpur got out of the car and headed to the boot. Dragging the black bin bag out, she headed into the house.

It was late now and just the living room light was on. She peeped inside and Neil was lying on the sofa fast asleep, the football still on the TV. She stood at the doorway and stared at her husband. He wasn't a bad man, he wasn't violent. But was he enough for her anymore? Could he relight the passion in her heart? She wasn't sure. Harpur closed the door slowly. She wasn't going to wake him up, no way. He would only have gone on and on about their marriage if she did.

Harpur sat on the bed in her pyjamas going through

her brother's belongings. There were lots of notes and photographs, scattered about. She read the letters and her eyes clouded over. This was more or less her brother's life in this bag. Why had her mum just launched all this stuff out? There were letters from jail from his mates, little keepsakes that told a story. Harpur picked up a photograph. She closed her eyes and took a while to look at it again. It was a picture of Brady when he was younger, when he was clean from drugs, before his life had gone wild. Her finger stroked slowly across the picture as tears ran down the side of her cheek. "You're still my baby brother our kid. Look at you here all neat and tidy. You were a good-looking lad too weren't you. What happened Brady? Tell me how you became so lost that you just left us all behind?" She was sobbing her heart out, grieving for her sibling, wishing things could have turned out differently. She slowly kissed the photograph and laid it on the bed next to her.

Her eyes shot to a small folded piece of paper near her legs that must have dropped out of the bag. Reaching over towards it, she unfolded it slowly. The writing was small and she was struggling to see the words written on it. "Brady, we need to sort this out. I hate lying to everyone. You need to help me, it's your mess too. Love M X" Harpur held her flat palm against her chest. At last a clue as to what was going on in her brother's life. She read the words over and over again. "I hate lying to everyone." What the hell did this mean? Who were they talking about and who was this letter from? Harpur was confused and she went through all the other letters slowly. There were only two letters left on the bed and she chose the one to the left of her. Her eyes squeezed together as she tried to read the words written there. This was Brady's handwriting, she could recognise it anywhere. Little squiggles.

"Mam, I'm sorry alright. I just got mixed up in it all trying to help. You know I'm trying to get out of this mess but it takes time. I love you and I'm grateful for all you do for me. Please don't judge me. I feel bad enough that you know. All I can say is that I'm trying mam. Love Brady XXX"

This was getting worse by the minute, what on earth was going on here? Brady was involved in something and Sheila knew about it. Why hadn't she told her, put her mind at rest? At least then she could have accepted her brother's death instead of going over it every day in her mind. What a snide cow her mother was, how could she have done this? Harpur folded the letter up and sat thinking. The truth was coming out, she could sense it.

Suddenly there were noises from the hallway, stairs creaking. She held her ear to the door. Nothing, silence, she must have been imagining it. Harpur started to put all of Brady's things into a bag. She kept some stuff out though, private stuff, sentimental to her. There it was again, noises outside. Her heart was leaping about inside her ribcage. Footsteps coming closer to her bedroom door now. The door opened and her heart was in her mouth.

"Sorry love, I thought you would be asleep."

Harpur looked confused. "How long have you been upstairs, I heard the stairs creaking, then nothing."

Neil walked inside the bedroom and sat on the edge of the bed with his head in his hands. "Babes, I don't want to lose you. You're my world. I'd be nothing without you. My head's in bits, can't we just sort it out."

Harpur finished putting the letters into the bag. This was the same script he always used when he was in the dog house. These were just words now, they didn't mean anything anymore, nothing ever changed. There was no pity in her eyes, no feeling sorry for him. She was immune to his bullshit, there was no way he was pulling the wool over her eyes anymore. Once bitten, twice shy. "Just get in bed Neil, it's late. We can sort this out tomorrow. My head's banging. I just need to sleep, to clear my head, please don't go on."

Neil fell onto the bed and he was after the sympathy vote. "Ok love, I'm sorry for upsetting you and like I said before, I'm going to make you happy again." They both lay down in their marital bed and Harpur turned away from him. His finger stroked up and down her spine and he kissed her back. "Goodnight darling, I love you." Harpur never replied, she had too much going on inside her head already. What on earth had her brother been involved in and was she really going to rekindle her relationship with her childhood sweetheart Dessie Ryan?

CHAPTER TWELVE

HARPUR WAS WAITING OUTSIDE the house where Bridget was working. She had a viewing for the estate agents she worked for and she was just showing a couple around the property. They usually met at houses like this, especially if the property was unoccupied, or the owners were away on business. This house was the dog's bollocks; a detached five-bedroom in a prime location. Harpur could never afford anything like this, it was what people like her would have called a dream home. Hold on, Bridget was at the front door of the property with the viewers now, they must have finished looking around the property. Harpur watched her best friend shaking the man's hand. She must have sold the property by the look on her face, clinched a deal. Bridget could sell sand to the Arabs when she put her mind to it. She was good at her job and loved the people she met. Harpur hid away as the couple walked past her. Keeping her head low, she watched as the couple got into a car that was parked not far from where she was stood. Bridget came to the gates of the house and gave Harpur a wave. The coast was clear and they could have a good few hours inside this gaff without anyone bothering them. Bridget waited for her to step inside and jumped about with joy. "They bought it, they loved everything about the place but come on, who wouldn't? Come and have a look around. It's massive."

Harpur went on a tour of the house and her eyes were

wide open. "It's amazing isn't it?"

Bridget jumped on the king-sized bed and lay with her hands behind her head. "Yep, it sure is. Where do these people get their money from to buy something like this? It's up for nearly a half a million you know?"

"Bleeding hell, it is special though isn't it?" Harpur bounced on the edge of the bed and she was dying to tell her best friend all about her plans. "Bridget, you know like you said I was boring?"

Her best friend nodded and giggled. "Yes, I did say that, why what's changed?"

"I'm going to spend next weekend with Dessie."

"Fuck off lying. Stop it."

Harpur lay back on the bed and rubbed her hands together with excitement. "No, it's true. I'm going. I need to put this to bed once and for all and well, it's not like things are good at home is it."

"Are you going to have sex with him?"

Harpur twisted her head to face Bridget. "I don't know. I'm just going to play it by ear."

Bridget sat up on the bed and something wasn't right with her. "You need to be careful with Dessie. Remember, he's a player. They are your words not mine."

"I know, but I need something to take my mind from the shit that I've got going on. It's just a bit of fun, bleeding hell what's changed with you anyway? You're the one who said I needed to have a life, remember?"

"I know, but Dessie Ryan is trouble."

Harpur played with her fingers and melted into the bed. "He makes me weak at the knees, you know. Honest, I just don't have any control over my feelings with him anymore. I keep trying to stop myself thinking about him but I can't help it. I'm cursed or something."

Bridget sniggered. "Oh my God you're going to bang his brains out aren't you. Go on girl, show him what he missed out on, ruin him. Isn't it weird how you two have ended up speaking after all these years? Do you think you two have been set to meet all this time? Like the law of attraction. It's like the universe has made you two come together." Bridget loved the law of attraction and she always believed things happened for a reason. "Where are you going to tell Neil you are going? I mean, you've not been on a weekend away for as long as I can remember, don't you think he will suss something is going on?"

Harpur shot a look over at Bridget. "That's where I need your help. You know I'm no good at lying. I need you to come up with a plan."

Bridget held a single finger in the side of her mouth, nibbling at pink glossed nails. "Okay, let's tell him we are going away on a hen weekend. You can say it's a girl from my works. Neil hasn't got a clue who I work with anyway so it should be fine."

"Will you mention it when you come to our house. You know, as if I don't know?"

She winked at her and smiled. "Yeah, don't worry I'll sort it. Never mind that, that's the least of your worries. You need to go shopping and find an outfit and some nice sexy underwear just in case you want to show the growler."

Harpur burst out laughing. "Stop it you. I'm nervous enough without you giving me other things to worry about. But, you do have a point. I mean, when was the last time I bought any sexy knickers? This is getting worse by the minute, fuck, fuck, fuck. Orr Bridget you need to help me."

"Relax, we can go after work tomorrow. I'll come and drop the bombshell to Neil and then we can say we are going shopping. Since when has Neil batted an eyelid anyway, he'll be watching the footy, he won't even know you've gone."

This was true, Neil had never cared where his wife was. In fact, she could have stayed out all night long and he still wouldn't have noticed she was missing. Harpur reached inside her pocket and passed the letter she'd found in her brother's belongings over to Bridget. This was serious now. "Have a read of this and see what you think."

"What is it, who's it from?"

"I found it in our kid's stuff that my mam was throwing out. Just be quiet and read it."

Bridget opened the letter and her eyes flicked across the page, her mouth was moving but no words were coming out. She kept stopping and looking at Harpur and continued to read. Once she'd finished she folded the letter back up slowly and shook her head. "Something's not right is it? And what does your mam know, because it's clear in this letter that she knows more than she's letting on? What a dark horse she is."

Harpur sighed and finally she felt like she had someone else onside. "I'm going to see her soon. I'll show her the letter and see what she has to say for herself."

Bridget didn't like this, she wanted to keep it on the low for now. "No, just leave her alone. It's not like she's going to tell you anything is it? I say you go and see that girl your Sam mentioned and see what she knows. Yes, start with her and if you get no joy there then go and start asking your mam. It's the way forward I think."

"Perhaps you're right. If my mam wanted me to know

then she would have told me I suppose. I just have a really bad feeling about all this that's all."

"Never mind that. I can't believe you have a real date. It's an affair isn't it!"

These words scared Harpur. She would never have said she was having an affair. It was more just meeting up with an old friend. The girls sat chatting for over an hour and they both agreed to meet later that night. The plan was set to tell Neil about the weekend. Once this was done it would be all plain sailing.

Harpur had already made some enquiries about the estate and she now knew where Melanie Byfield lived. Sam had told her some stories about this woman and she knew she would have to be prepared when she met her. Harpur was streetwise though, she knew the crack and if push came to shove she would rip her head off, punch her lights out to find out the truth. Life living with her ex had taught her a thing or two about fighting and even by her own admittance, she was an animal once she started fighting; biting, punching, kicking. Yes, she had some moves up her sleeve.

Harpur sat in her car watching the house from a distance. Cars kept pulling up outside the gaff and she was sure they were selling drugs there. Each junkie that walked away from the house looked as desperate as the next. Her brother had looked like that sometimes. She'd know that look anywhere; hunched shoulders, sunken cheeks, grey skin. Yes, she'd seen Brady hit rock bottom a few times and this lot reminded her of him. Brady would go weeks without having a wash sometimes and when he was on a drugs binge he was lucky to even brush his teeth. If it wasn't for his mother Sheila, Brady would have starved to death for sure. No matter what state her son came home in, his mother would always make sure she fed him. It must have been hell for her. How hard it must have been to watch your child crumbling away right in front of you? It must have been hell on earth. Why had he turned to drugs in the first place, was he that weak-willed that he didn't know just how his life would turn out and what it would do to his family? It destroyed them. Granted, all kids dabble in drugs as they are growing up but to touch the hard stuff like heroin and crack, he must have had a screw loose.

Sheila always blamed Tony Wallis for her son's addiction. It was never Brady's fault, no, her blue-eyed boy could never do any wrong in her eyes. It was always somebody else's fault. Sheila would scratch anyone's eyes out who said a wrong word about her boy. She could call him and shout at him but God help anyone else who blackened his name. Harpur had seen some horrible stuff when she lived at home. Her brother begging her for money to score, he would do anything when he was roasting for drugs. He'd robbed so much of her own personal stuff too; rings, bracelets, earrings, all presents from Sam's dad, he'd taken the lot and sold them for peanuts, just enough to get a bag of brown. He had no morals where drugs were concerned. Heroin was evil and whatever it did to people, it never let them go, stripped them of all emotion. Gripped them from inside and tortured them. They were prisoners for life. So what happened to Brady to make him turn to drugs.

Harpur's brother was only fifteen when tragedy struck his life. Brady's best pal was called Callum Quinn and they were inseparable. A cheeky kid he was, always laughing.

A loveable rogue some would say. The two of them were always together and many a night Callum would stop over at Brady's house. In fact Sheila used to say that he needed to start paying rent there, he was there that much. In fairness, Sheila had a lot of time for Callum and even though he was a mouthy sod, he had a good head on him. The two friends were never short of money either and whatever they were up to, they kept it to themselves. Ask no questions, tell no lies. It was Brady's idea to go swimming in the locks. It was a warm summer's day and the sun was cracking the flags. The Seven Wonders was a well-known place everybody went to when the weather was good. There were no adults present, no trunks or bikinis, no supervision. The kids there just used to jump in the water in whatever they were wearing, sometimes commando, bare-arsed. Callum had never been a strong swimmer but he could always manage a quick dip in the locks. The other lads used to laugh at him and say he was a wuss because he would never jump from the bridge there. He was terrified of water but only a few knew his weakness. Brady knew of course and offered to teach him to swim properly all the time, but Callum never accepted his offer. He was too cool for that. Brady and Callum kicked their shoes off and they were messing around in the lock; splashing and spraying each other with water. Callum stayed near the side away from any real danger. This was fine until the other local lads came along and started to bomb them both. Andy Morley was their ring leader and he had an evil streak about him. He was a bully and wouldn't have thought twice about ragging you about for nothing. He was bigger than most of them too, a giant. A man child, the kids nicknamed him. It was funny because he never knew what they called him behind his back. Even his own gang members called him it too.

Andy clocked Callum near the side of the lock and stood over him sneering. "Come over here lads and look at this little prick who's scared of the water."

Callum's dipped his head and gripped onto the side with both hands, teeth chattering together. The others joined in and before long, Callum was a laughing stock. There was no way Brady was having this and he stuck up for his friend. "He's no chicken, he would take up any challenge you want to put in front of him."

Andy Morley held his head back and chuckled. He shot his eyes over to the tall bridge to the left of him and pointed at it. "So, why doesn't he prove it and get his bony arse up there and jump from it?"

Callum swallowed hard, what the hell was going on? Brady shook his head and tried to talk his way out of it. He knew this was a big ask of his mate. "Nar, he's not doing it. Pick something else. Nobody you know has done that dare before, so stop chatting shit."

Callum started to climb out of the water and the challenge was accepted. Brady dragged at the back of his jumper and tried to talk him out of it. "Take no notice of the prick, just walk away from him. You have nothing to prove to any of them. They're all wankers."

Callum dipped his head and Brady would never ever forget the words his best friend spoke to him on that day. "If I walk away now he will never leave me alone. I've got to do this for me. To save face."

Brady watched Callum walk to the bridge. He was confident and he was sure he could do this jump without any problems. Plus, Brady was there if he ran into trouble and he could help him out. Andy and the others watched

Callum as he stood on top of the bridge. "Go on chicken, jump, or has your arse fell out. Jump, jump, jump." The others joined in now and they were louder than ever. "Chicken, chicken." Brady looked over at Andy and he was sick to death of this kid. Who did he think he was anyway? He snarled over at him and saw red. Before he knew it he was pummelling his fist into his face, blood splurging all over the place. The others just stood there watching, not one of them tried to break up the fight. Brady dragged Andy up by his neck and booted him right up the arse. "Go on, fuck off and if I see you bullying anyone else you'll get another bunch of fives from me."

Andy was wounded, holding his head and wiping the blood gushing from his nose. The gang had a new leader and they were all patting Brady on his back. This was a moment none of the kids from the estate would ever forget. It would go down in history. Andy Morley's reign of terror was over and there was a new sheriff in town. Brady shot his eyes to the bridge and searched for Callum. He shouted his name more than once. He ran up and down the bank looking for his friend. As he sprinted to the far end he could see Callum's hand just disappearing underneath the water. Brady jumped in, screaming, panicking, but the current was strong and there was no way he could locate him. Brady came back up for air and screamed for the others to go and get help. Up and down Brady swam but it was no good, his own life was in danger too and he had to head for safety.

Callum was dragged out of the water over an hour later. He was pronounced dead. Of course, a kid never gets over something like that and from that day Brady just sank into a deep depression. He blamed himself, he should have been there, watching out for Callum like he always did. Callum's family blamed Brady too. He'd had death threats from one of his mate's brothers and for months he just sat at home, too scared to even go out to the shop. His name was shit on the estate where he lived and no one would give him the time of day anymore. It wasn't his fault. The inquest even confirmed it as misadventure. There was no charge for murder so why was he being victimised?

Sheila couldn't get a word out of her son for months and at one point they were scared of what he would do next. He was a loner with no friends and no life. That's when Brady started to smoke weed. The guy who gave it to him told him it would chill him out, help him sleep, make him forget his problems. And it did for a while but as time went on, the effects didn't touch him anymore and he needed something stronger. At the age of seventeen Brady was introduced to heroin by a local junkie. He was always searching for a high and couldn't turn his back on anything new. A few of the other lads tried it too and even to this day a few of them were still tanning the gear. Two of his old friends had died too, drugs overdose the coroner said, but still it never deterred Brady from taking the devil's drug. None of his family had a clue what he was up to and Sheila just thought he was depressed. It was only when she came into his bedroom one night that she could see exactly what her son was involved in. There was silver foil folded on his bed with dark stains all over it and a rolled tube nearby. Sheila had seen enough TV shows to know exactly what she was dealing with. She was at her wits' end with her son and in fairness, she took him everywhere possible to get some help.

There were times when Brady was clean but there

was always an addict ready to tempt him back into the life he was trying to leave behind. His life was set in stone. There were dark day when crime was the only way to feed the addiction. He had no self-worth. Every day Brady needed to score, to feed his habit, sometimes eighty or ninety pounds worth. He had a raging habit. Robberies, shoplifting, credit card fraud and even trolley dashes out of the local Asda became the norm. The police were always at Sheila's door. Night and day they would be hammering her front door down looking for Brady. He played on the death of his best friend for years. The reason he needed to take drugs was to blank it out. But it was wearing thin now and nobody believed him anymore. Not even his mother. He was a drug addict by choice, no other reason.

Harpur cracked her knuckles and watched as she spotted a woman leaving the house. That must have been Melanie. Surely Brady wasn't sleeping with her, she was rotten. A big fat arse, no teeth and dressed like she was a teenager. Mutton dressed as lamb. Melanie had black tights on and high heels, what a trollop she was. Harpur put two and two together and realised this woman must have been on the game. It was the way she was dressed, the way she kept her head down when she walked, shame making her shoulders hunch over. Melanie was over fifty, she was sure, she looked haggard. Harpur sat up straight in her seat, ready to pounce. Should she get out and confront her now or wait until she was further down the street?.

Melanie was walking away in the distance and she had to make her move soon. Harpur flicked the engine over and pulled out of the darkness. It was now or never. "Excuse me love, can I have a quick word with you." Melanie squeezed her eyes together and bent her head down trying to get a glimpse of the driver. Was it dibble? She wasn't sure. She carried on walking and Harpur knew she would have to park up and chase her down the street. Her breathing was heavy and her heart was racing as she ran behind her. "Can I have a word?"

Melanie turned around and it looked like she was going to make a run for it. "Fuck off, no. What do you want anyway? I'm a busy woman."

"I'm Brady's sister and I just need to ask you a few things." Melanie started to walk off and shouted over her shoulder. "You'll have to walk with me I've got no time to talk, I have to be somewhere soon. Time is money love."

Harpur walked at her side. She digested every little detail about her, she was hanging; old and wrinkled. It was fair to say that this woman had had a hard life, very hard. Her eyes were fierce and you could see she could have ripped your head off if rattled. "You know my brother passed away don't you?"

Melanie let out a laboured breath and nodded her head. "Yeah I know who he is. Not that I'm arsed anyway. The man was a liberty-taker, a cheeky cunt."

Harpur was ready to swing for her but she needed to know the answers to her questions first. "Well, that's your opinion isn't it. I just want to know what happened before he died. It's obvious he was involved in something because he would never have done what he did without something bad happening. It must have pushed him over the edge."

Melanie spat on the floor and wiped her hand across her mouth with a quick movement. "Listen love, I get that you're hurting but I'm the last person you need to be talking to about your brother. It's none of my business what he was into and I want it to keep like that. Life's hard enough without people coming round to my house booming my door in."

"Like who, who are you protecting?"

Melanie stopped walking and turned to face her. "Do yourself a favour love and let it lie. People who talk around here get hurt, so piss off to your pretty little life and put it to bed. Your brother was big enough and daft enough to look after himself and if he strung himself up, it's nobody's fault but his own." Her expression changed and you could see how low this woman was feeling. "I wish I could end it all too but I have a family to take care of. I've got to put food on the table each bleeding night so I do what I have to, to make ends meet."

Harpur was listening, it was a crying shame for her. "Just tell me, a name, anything. Just something to help our family. If you thought anything about him just help me." Harpur was desperate, pleading with her.

Melanie checked around and made sure nobody had clocked her. "I hated your brother for my own reasons which are none of your business. That was between me and him. He knows what happened and the liberties he took, so there is no need for me to bring it out in the open. You know who calls the shots around here so look closer to home. If anyone knows what happened to your brother, it's him."

Harpur was hanging on her every word. "Who, tell me his name. That's all I need, a name."

Melanie chewed on her bottom lip and her eyes were wide open. This woman was petrified, scared of even saying his name. She walked a few steps forward and over her shoulder she whispered in a low voice. "Paul Burton."

Harpur stood frozen. "Just for the record I loved Brady.

He was my man, my rock when I was low."

Melanie rushed away into the shadows. Harpur stood listening to the woman's heels clip along the pavement. She stamped her feet firmly onto the ground. Her fists curled into two tight balls at the side of her legs and she bit hard onto her bottom lip. "I fucking knew it. I knew that rat had something to do with it." She ran back to her car and once inside, she locked all the doors behind her. She wasn't safe around here. This was his patch, where he lurked in the shadows watching everything that was going on. Paul Burton was out of her league. Yes, she could throw insults at him but she knew deep down inside he was dangerous and could have ended her life at the drop of a hat. There were rumours about this guy. Dark, seedy stories about how he treated people who crossed him. He must have had a weak spot though, a jugular. This was her quest now, she needed to catch this prick unaware and bring him down. Her head rested on the steering wheel as her eyes closed slowly. This was a whole new ball game now and she needed a plan, some way of making sure Paul Burton told her everything she needed to know about her brother's death.

All Harpur could hear was the ticking of the clock, tick tock, tick tock. Neil had been in bed when she arrived home and she knew the moment she went upstairs he would want to talk to her regarding the state of their marriage. The sound of the front door slamming shut was heard. Harpur sat up straight and shot her eyes to the living room door. She thought everybody was home. Her heart was pounding inside her chest. Had Paul Burton seen her in the area and now he'd come to her home to make sure she never set foot on his turf again? He wouldn't thought twice about booming her front door in, putting a gun to her head, terrorising her husband. Slowly, she reached over and grabbed an empty bottle of beer from the table at the side of her. If he wanted trouble she'd give him trouble, she would gouge his eyes out with it, stick it deep into his chest and make sure he never breathed again. The door handle moved slowly down. Harpur stood up and she was prepared to fight, white with fear.

"Bleeding hell Mam, what an earth are you doing with that?" Maddie asked in an anxious voice.

Harpur was trembling, her hands shaking. "I thought you were an intruder. For crying out loud what are you doing here at this time? I thought you were staying with Diane?"

"Mam, I live with Diane but as you know, every now and then I like to come here and stay in my old room. Has it ever crossed your mind that I might miss home sometimes?"

Harpur collapsed back down in her chair and she was still shaking. She always thought it was strange that Maddie had moved in with Diane because she was a home bird, she liked her home comforts, familiarities. "A phone call would have been nice. You know, just to say 'Mam, I'll be home later' or something."

Maddie took her black leather coat off and hung it on the back of the chair. This girl was all skin and bone. Why on earth wasn't she looking after herself? Harpur blamed the media, all those photos of stick insect models who were borderline anorexic. Maddie rubbed at her arms, she was freezing. "Where's my dad, is he in bed?"

Harpur raised her eyes to suggest he was. "I've just got

in. I think he might be watching television in bed. Don't be going up there and disturbing him if he's asleep. What's up anyway, why do you want him?"

Maddie was edgy, she stretched her arms above her head and yawned. "Nothing really, I just wanted to know where he is?"

Harpur looked at her daughter and knew there was something more to this than she was letting on. If Maddie wanted to see her dad it was usually for money or a lift somewhere. Her daughter had been distant for a while now and after Brady's death she'd made the decision to go and live with Diane. It was a weird thing to do really when she should have been around people who loved her, but she left anyway. It was likely that she hated how Joanne was living there with Joseph – kids weren't really her thing, she had no patience for them. Maddie looked tired, her hair tied back in a scruffy bun. Her daughter's hair always used to be styled; shiny and bouncy.

Harpur lit a fag up and sat chugging hard on it. She could feel Maddie watching her from the other side of the room before she spoke. "Joanne said you and dad are at war, what's going on this time?"

Harpur sighed and dropped her head low. "Just the usual love, nothing for you to worry about. She's got a right gob on her anyway. Why's she telling you without speaking to me first, she's a right busybody?"

Maddie was alarmed, frustrated. "Because I'm part of this family that's why. Anyway, our Sam's home next weekend so hopefully she'll be finding her own place. She's been here too long now and she should be sorting stuff out, the scruff."

Harpur nodded, it was hard having her son's girlfriend

living with her and she wondered if that was one of the main reasons she'd been arguing with Neil. Perhaps they could have had more romantic nights in, talked more, become closer if they were alone. Harpur studied her daughter further, it was strange that she was getting on Joanne's case, she thought they were good friends. She delved deeper. "What's up with Joanne being here anyway, you were a big fan of her when she first moved in with us. You two spent loads of time together. 'The sister you never had' you said, what happened to that?"

Maddie mumbled something under her breath before she spoke. "Things change Mam and the sooner she's gone from here the better. Our Sam can do a lot better than her anyway. I don't trust her, she's a wrong-un. A dirty sweaty cow."

"What do you mean by that? If you know something about her don't beat about the bush, just tell me."

Maddie kept schtum, whatever she knew she was keeping close to her chest. Harpur had her doubts about this girl too but as of yet, she had no evidence to prove she was right. Maddie kissed the side of her mother's cheek. "I'm knackered. We can have a catch-up in the morning. Come on, I'll help turn everything off."

Harpur stopped her dead in her tracks. "No love, I'll be up soon. I'm just chilling on my own for a bit. My head's been mashed lately and I just need some me time." Maddie rolled her eyes and left the room. There was no way she was getting into any long conversation about what was bothering her mother. More than likely it would all blow over anyway. It always did.

Harpur began to turn all the electrical appliances off. An hour or so had passed and she was more than ready for some sleep. With any luck, Neil would be asleep and she could rest knowing he wasn't pecking her head all night long. Climbing the stairs, her eyes were drawn to a crack of light coming from Joanne's bedroom door. As she stepped up the last few stairs she paused. She could see Joanne texting on her phone. Every now and then she would take a snap of her breast and start to giggle. Harpur smirked, she must have been on the phone to Sam. She knew her son had an illegal mobile inside the jail. Lots of inmates had them and after bang up, the prisoners would pull their phones from their secret stash and phone their loved ones.

Harpur lay in bed and as predicted, Neil was snoring his head off, grunting like a pig. Her mind started to drift to meeting Dessie in a few days and her breathing was getting faster, she had to stop it, try and relax. What on earth should she do? Dessie was trouble in her eyes but the attraction was strong and there was no way she could back down. Say he was the one, say after all these years he was the man she was destined to be with? He did give her butterflies, he did make her laugh and whatever the connection was, it felt good. What was her alternative anyway? To live a life she would never be fulfilled in and be unhappy? Or to take a chance on a man she knew nothing about?

And then there was Paul Burton. What was her next move with him? Sam knew a few hard cases in the area and if needed, she would pay them to avenge her brother's death. Yes, she'd do whatever it took to see justice served. This was street law now. Paul's days were numbered and the clock was ticking. But for now, she had to plan her weekend away. Looking at her mobile, she clocked a message from Dessie. Peering over at her husband, she began to read it.

"Harpur, I'm so excited about this weekend. There is

so much I want to say to you but I'll wait until we are face to face. We will have a laugh me and you. I can't wait. Have a great day tomorrow and keep smiling. Always Dessie X"

Harpur felt a warmth rush through her body. It started in her toes and went right up to the top of her head. Her fingers typed a reply.

"Me too. It will be good to catch up. Love Harpur X"

Wait a minute, he might read too much into that. He might think she loved him…

She erased the message and stared at the screen, hesitating. After a few seconds she retyped "Love Harpur X" What did it matter anyway, it was only a word.

CHAPTER THIRTEEN

BRIDGET WAS SIPPING COFFEE at the kitchen table in Harpur's house. The plan was set and she was ready to deliver the news to Neil about the girls' weekend away. Harpur was a dithering wreck and you could see the fear in her eyes. Neil walked into the kitchen and as soon as he spotted Bridget, he mumbled something under his breath. "Good morning Neil. I see you're as pleased to see me as I am you?"

This woman was so straight, she held nothing back. Neil raised a false smile over at her and let out a sarcastic laugh. "Yep, it's always a joy to see you Bridget. What's happened to you to be here this early in the morning, have you shit the bed or something?"

Here it was, the chance to deliver the killer blow, to make his jaw drop. "I've come to ask Harpur if she's allowed to come on a hen do this weekend. You don't mind do you?"

Neil shot a look over at his wife and acted like he never stopped her from doing anything. "She's free to do whatever she wants. She doesn't need my permission. My wife knows that without even asking."

Bridget raised her eyes over at Harpur, this was a lot easier than she first thought. "There you go love. I wish I had an understanding fella like Neil." He turned to face her and he knew instantly she was taking the piss out of him. But he was already in the bad books and he would have been hung drawn and quartered if he'd tried to throw any abuse at Bridget. Harpur made some small talk about the weekend away and acted like she wasn't really in the mood to go. Bridget pretended to work on her. "Come on, when was the last time you had some time for yourself? It will be a laugh, the girls are a right scream and to tell you the truth I could do with the company."

Neil was pottering about the kitchen and they knew he was listening to every word they said. "Right, okay. I'll come. I've got nothing to wear though. God knows when I last bought anything new."

Bridget smirked and folded her arms tightly across her chest. She knew she was pushing it here but went ahead anyway. "I'm sure Neil, being the kind-hearted soul that he is, will treat you to a new outfit. Isn't that right Neil?"

He swallowed hard and you could see the tight-arse didn't want to part with any cash but the pressure was on, he was on the spot. "Of course I will. How much is a new dress love, twenty quid will cover it won't it?"

Bridget burst out laughing. She would teach him a lesson. "Are you having a laugh? She wouldn't get a pair of tights for that much. You need to dig deep in your pocket and pull at least a oner out. And that's shopping on a budget, trust me I know."

Neil's cheeks were bright red, he was actually sweating as he opened his wallet. If things had been different, and he wasn't trying to save his marriage, he would have told her straight that she was getting twenty quid and that was her lot. Take it or leave it. Neil passed the money over to his wife and kissed her on the side of her cheek. "What my wife wants, my wife gets from me Bridget. How are you doing finding a man by the way, are you still single?" What a wanker he was, he knew this was Bridget's sore point. "I mean, time's ticking now surely? You need to be thinking about whether or not you're ever going to have kids or not."

This was below the belt, fancy saying something like that to a woman. Bridget saw red and there was no way she wasn't giving him a mouthful. "Well you see Neil, I won't get married to any old prick. I want to meet the one, perhaps Harpur should have waited around a little longer and she might have found her Mr Right too."

Neil was ready to throw Bridget out of the house, he was seething. How dare she talk to him in his own house like this? He looked over at his wife for some support. After all, he'd just bunged her a right few quid, surely she must have had his back. Instead Harpur never said a word, she turned to face the sink and sniggered to herself. That would teach him to think he could have one over on her best friend. Bridget stood up and flicked the invisible dust from the top of her shoulder. It was game, set and match in her eyes. She was the winner and Neil would have to walk away and lick his wounds. "Right, I'm off to work. If you want, we can meet at lunchtime and go look for something to wear?"

"Yeah, that would be brilliant. You have more fashion sense than me anyway." Bridget left the room after a quick kiss on her friend's cheek. Before she left, she checked where Neil was and winked over at Harpur. The mission had been successful. Neil stomped about the kitchen and it was obvious he'd seen his arse. Was it because she was going away for the weekend or was it because he'd had to fork out some money for his wife's dress? She wasn't sure.

Joanne walked into the kitchen and Joseph followed closely behind her. Joanne looked like she'd been crying.

Joseph barged past her and stood facing his nana. "My dad said Mummy is a slut and he's going to shave her hair off when he gets home."

Harpur was distraught and she quickly picked her grandson up and placed him on her knee. "Daddy would never hurt mummy. He is probably having a joke or something like that. Take no notice of him."

Joanne burst out crying and sat down at the table. "He's not lying Harpur. Someone has told Sam that I've been sleeping about and he said I need to pack my stuff and get out of here before he comes home."

Neil butted in, "Well, just ignore him. How dare he say stuff like that to you. And since when have you been sleeping around, you never go out?"

Harpur was thinking, her eyes dipped and even though she should have kept her mouth shut she spoke her mind. "Well, you do go out. What about when I mind Joseph? In fact, you were out a few weeks ago and God knows what time you fell in here."

Maddie entered the kitchen and joined the conversation. "If Sam heard it in jail then it must be true. Let's face it Joanne, it's not like you've not been around the block a few times. What do you expect when you have had more nob ends than weekends?"

Joanne turned to face Maddie and she was ready to knock her out. Who was she to judge her anyway? She hissed over at her and pointed a single finger in the air. "Listen Maddie, I know he's your brother but he's wrong about this. Yes, we all have a past. You know that more than anyone and we all have secrets we like to keep, but as for sleeping around I'm innocent this time."

Maddie backed down almost instantly. What was going

on here? Her daughter was gobby and this was so out of character for her. Harpur clocked the look between the girls. They were staring each other out, ready to fight. They had hate in their eyes. Neil came over and patted Joanne on top of her shoulder. "Dry your eyes, you can stay here as long as you need to. Sam needs to grow up. Where does he think you're going to go at such short notice? You have his son to think about too. Is he forgetting that?"

Harpur pulled a face. He was always having a snide pop at her son and she was sick of it. She fought his corner. "Sam must have his own reasons for this. He wouldn't just say something like that for nothing would he? There is no smoke without fire." She looked at Maddie for back-up but she never said a word. "Anyway," she said glancing at the clock, "I'm off to work, you can sort it out yourselves. I think a shaved head would suit you anyway Joanne so it's not all bad is it. See you later."

This was so harsh, where was the sympathy? Harpur picked up her handbag and left the room. Neil ran after her. Joanne turned to face Maddie and snarled. "Oh, so you think you're Mrs Innocent now do you? You forget who I know so I'd watch what you're saying if I was you. We all have skeletons in our closet don't we?" Maddie looked like she was going to be sick, the colour drained from her and her legs buckled. There was something wrong here for sure.

Neil marched back into the kitchen and ragged his fingers through his hair. "For crying out loud, that woman will be the death of me. Nothing is ever good enough for her." He looked over at Maddie and he could see her eyes clouding over. "Come here love, don't you be getting upset. I know it's upsetting but we will get through this. We're just all a bit stressed at the moment." Neil looked closer at his daughter as he wrapped his arms around her. She was still his baby, always would be, no matter what. Joanne sat at the kitchen table staring into space. Sam would be home soon and she knew her days were numbered. He was a mad head and she knew she'd have some serious explaining to do to make him believe her story. She was sick to death of people interfering all the time. Why the hell didn't they keep their big noses away from stuff that didn't concern them anyway?

Harpur sat behind the reception desk. It was boring today and the phone had hardly rung at all. Sitting back in her chair, she felt her mobile phone vibrate in her pocket. Quickly, she checked the message.

"Show us your tits then. Love Dessie X"

Harpur sniggered and her cheeks were beetroot. What kind of woman did he think she was? She sat thinking for a few seconds before she nipped to the toilet, she held a mischievous look in her eye. She'd show him how game she was. Harpur was excited and up for a laugh. Before she knew what was happening she'd lifted her top up and took a snap of her red lacy bra. This would shock him, teach him a lesson. He would fall down dead when he saw a glimpse of her breasts. Without any further hesitation, she sent the snap over to him with a message attached to it.

"There you go smart-arse. Now let's see something from you. Maybe a cock shot. Love Harpur X."

The message was sent and she didn't care anymore what he thought about her. All was fair in love and war. She was excited and alive and that was all that mattered at this moment. This had really got out of hand, there should have been boundaries set. Okay, chat to an old friend every now and then, see how life is treating them but this was on another level. Harpur went back to her desk and she was smirking. She felt liberated, full of confidence. Proud that for once in her life she'd done something without even thinking about it first. "Hello gorgeous," a voice shouted from behind her. With a quick look she spotted Donny. Her mouth wobbled and it took her a while to reply.

"Good morning. I didn't know you had ordered any parts."

Donny walked straight towards her and leaned over her desk, maintaining eye contact. "I haven't, I was just passing and thought I'd nip in to see you. No crime in that is there? Do you fancy coming out for dinner? Come on, it's nearly lunchtime anyway. And I bet you're only stuck in here eating a daft Pot Noodle or something like that. I'll take you for a top scran."

Harpur smiled and shook her head. "Sorry, I'm meeting my friend in a bit, we're nipping into town to see if I can find a new dress. Female bonding."

Donny was deflated. "So you're blowing me out again, really?"

She twisted her blue pen in her fingers and looked him up and down. This guy was a dish, a prize catch for any woman. Why on earth was he bothering with her when he could have had the pick of any woman he wanted, she was flattered. "Maybe some other time. I've told you already I'm married right?"

Donny gasped his breath and shook his head slightly. "God blimey, I said I would take you out for a bite to eat. I've not said I want to marry you have I?" He smirked at her and she realised that perhaps he was just after a bit of friendship. Anyway, what harm would it do to keep her options open, plan B maybe? Dessie was just a friend and no different from Donny. She thought about it for a few seconds, not wanting to hurt his feelings.

"I'll come out with you tomorrow. But on my life, today I've already made plans."

Donny was impressed with himself and leaned over the counter so she could feel his warm breath on her cheeks. "I wouldn't mind marrying you too if I'm cutting to the chase. I've not fancied anyone in years but you just take my breath away. It's like you have put me under some kind of magical spell or something. I'm mesmerised by you."

Harpur froze; was he being serious or what? She'd only met the guy a few times and here he was declaring his undying love to her. Was this a wind-up or something, he couldn't be serious. "You don't even know me. How can you say stuff like that?"

Donny held a flat palm over his heart and delivered his words. "I know what I feel in here and you have been playing havoc with my head. I can't stop thinking about you. What's all that about never ever feeling like this before?" Harpur burst out laughing and so did he. Of course, he was bullshitting. "So, I'll meet you here tomorrow at this time. I'll take you somewhere nice. It will be better than eating some of that crap you eat anyway." Donny pointed at her sandwich. It was curled up at the sides and soggy.

Yes, he was right, anything was better than eating a crusty old sandwich that she'd made early that morning. Donny whistled as he walked from her desk. She checked him out and for the first time ever she imagined what he would be like in bed. He looked like he'd be fun between the sheets, adventurous. Harpur pressed the numbers on her phone and sat back in her chair. "Hi Bridget, you never guess what," she paused before she continued. "That Donny I told you about has just offered to take me out for dinner tomorrow." She listen eagerly to whatever Bridget was saying to her. "If you be quiet for a second I will tell you. I said yes." Harpur held her hand over her neck that was turning red and blotchy. "I know, what's up with me lately? I think I'm having a mid-life crisis. First Dessie and now Donny, I'm like a man magnet at the moment." Harpur arranged to meet Bridget to go shopping and the call ended. Staring into space, she seemed in a world of her own, a world where anything could happen.

"We're not shopping in the old-codger shops. You need something bright and sexy. If Dessie Ryan sees you in a frumpy outfit he will run a mile and make a laughing stock of you. Come on, I know a few shops that will have just what you need."

Harpur stood on the spot, not sure of anything anymore. "Bridget, I don't want a latex dress or something slutty. I want to look nice, not like a prostitute."

Bridget grabbed her by her arm and dragged her into a nearby store. There was a sea of colours; red, blue, green. Her eyes were all over and she didn't have a clue what she was looking for. Bridget loved shopping and now she had a project she was walking around the shop picking up dresses and blouses. The music in the store was upbeat and Harpur found herself singing along to the tune. Bridget piled a load of outfits into her hands. "Right, grab these and start trying stuff on while I look around and see if there is anything else. Go on, I've not got all day." Harpur wobbled into the changing rooms and was met by an assistant. Once her items were counted she was given a card and shown to a free changing room. Harpur stood looking in the full-length mirror as she started to get undressed. She wasn't fat, in fact she was pretty good for her age. A lot of women would have been envious of her body. She stared into the mirror and examined every inch of her body. Nobody had seen it in years, well, only Neil. How would she feel if she decided to have sex with Dessie, would she crumble, be shy? No, if the date went that way she would give him the time of his life and show him what he'd been missing all these years. She knew she had a sexy side and although she'd not used it for a few years, she knew it still existed. She pushed her breasts up, sucked her stomach in and turned to the side. Yes, she would show him what she was all about for sure. Any woman could be a porn queen when they put their mind to it.

Bridget's big gob could be heard from outside, screeching. "Have you tried anything on yet?" Harpur put the first dress on and opened the door. Bridget screwed her face up. "Hanging, take it off and try another one on. You look like a school teacher in it. Harpur went back inside and checked the dress on herself again in the mirror. Nope, it looked like a bag of rags, nothing like the look she was trying to achieve. The next dress seemed more her style. Red was her favourite colour and as she slipped the garment over her head, she knew then that this was the dress for her. Opening the door, she met Bridget's eyes. "Check you out, turn to the side. That's the one, you look mint, slender and most of all sexy." Harpur twisted her body about and walked up and down. A few of the other customers checked her out too and she knew by their expressions that the dress was the one she would be buying. Bridget smiled and seemed proud that she'd picked a nice outfit for her friend. "So, we just need some underwear now and a few things to wear in the day."

Harpur pulled a sour expression. "I've got some alright knickers at home, it's not like Dessie will be seeing them is it?"

Bridget sniggered and spoke out in a loud voice. "Always be prepared love. Never say never. It's always the way. You think you're not having sex and before you know it you're already regretting that you don't have any decent knickers on when things get out of hand. Trust me, I know."

Harpur gasped and headed back into the changing room. "You're a barm-pot, Bridget, a couple of butties short of a picnic."

The looked around the store. Harpur held a pair of briefs up in the air, examining them. "This pair of knickers has no underneath in them Bridget. How do they expect a woman to wear something like this. Her flower would be freezing?"

Bridget took them out of her hand and examined them further. "Derrr... they're crotchless that's why you geek. You don't need something like this. You need something that says I've not made an effort and all my underwear looks like this. For fuck's sake, can't we tell you've been married for years." Bridget had this dating thing boxed off for sure. Harpur must have been living in a bubble for most of her married life. She was so behind the times in her fashion sense and even her underwear choices. Since when did passion killers turn a man on? They wanted filth; red lacy numbers, black sexy lingerie. Bridget pulled at the back of Harpur's skirt trying to get a look at her knickers. "What are you wearing at the moment, Brazilian, thong, what?"

Harpur raised her eyes and smirked. "Will you get off me," she started to giggle. "Manchester knickers they are. I didn't know there was any other kind. What the hell are thongs anyway?"

Bridget howled laughing and crossed her legs tightly. "Orr, stop it I'm going to piss my knickers with you. Are you being serious or what? Don't tell me you don't wear a thong."

"No, I don't even know what it is so don't make fun of me, just bleeding help me. I've been married for years and well, I've not been interested in sexy underwear. You know how it's been. So, instead of taking the piss, help me put it right."

Bridget could see she'd embarrassed her friend and tried to make amends. "Come on, I know just the place. You can get a few pairs of knickers for a decent price there. Sexy ones too, not like them tents you're wearing."

Harpur was walking along swinging her bags when she halted suddenly. "Quick, get over here. There's Joanne. Bleeding hell, that's all I need is her seeing me. She's a right gobshite and she'll want to see everything I've bought." They hid in a shop doorway and peeped out. Harpur stretched her neck and watched as Joanne stood on the opposite side of the shopping centre. Bridget was hung over her shoulder and she was checking her watch. "We need to be heading back, love. I've got a viewing to sort out and I can't be late. Here, give me your bags. She's not going to ask me to see what I've bought is she? Just say you've come with me. There, problem solved."

Bridget took the bags from her friend and they headed over towards Joanne. Hold on, who was this talking to her?

Harpur quickened her step and within seconds she was stood next to Joanne and her new man friend. "Hello there, fancy seeing you here. Who's this then, aren't you going to introduce me?" Harpur stood facing the man and looked him up and down, waiting on an answer. Bridget could see she was ready for kicking off and tried to calm her down. Joanne began to stutter, small beads of sweat forming on her forehead. "This is Bradley, he's an old friend. I've just bumped into him."

What on earth was going on here? Did Joanne think Sam's mother was green or what? It wasn't rocket science to work out what was going on, she was cheating on her son and was caught bang to rights. Harpur made sure Joanne knew how angry she was. "Oh, what's your name? I'll tell Sam when he comes home next week that you two have bumped into each other."

Joanne swallowed hard and stuttered. "I'll tell him myself,. Harpur. Why are you making a mountain out of a molehill? Just stop being so suspicious and concentrate on your own relationship instead of mine."

Bridget shot a look at Joanne and she was ready for punching her lights out too, the lippy cow. How dare she give any back chat to her friend after all she'd done for her. She was getting told. "Oi, less of the mouth. If you're just meeting an old friend then there's no problem with Sam knowing is there?"

The man was edgy and this was the second time he'd heard Harpur's son's name. The colour drained from his cheeks and he spoke in a low voice. "It was nice seeing you again Joanne. Tell Sam I was asking about him. Catch you soon." The man walked off and Harpur was ready for throttling Joanne. She didn't believe this story for one second. She was up to no good and she'd been caught in the act. She hissed over at her. "I'll see you when I get home. You can explain this then can't you!"

Bridget eyeballed Joanne and sucked hard on her bottom lip. "I wouldn't like to be in your shoes," she whispered under her breath as she started to leave to follow Harpur. Joanne stomped her feet and whatever she was mumbling under her breath couldn't be repeated.

Harpur was furious as they headed back to work. Bridget was doing her best to try and calm her down. "How dare she mess about on our Sam? I mean, she's living under my roof too! The barefaced cheek of her. I swear, she's lucky I never twatted her all over the shopping centre. And I would have you know. She'll soon see what I'm about if she thinks she can treat our Sam like this."

Bridget reached over and patted the middle of her arm. "Bleeding hell, when it rains it pours in your life doesn't it. Come on, cheer up. You've got this weekend to look forward to so don't let anyone piss on your parade and steal your thunder. Be happy remember."

A text alert was heard. Harpur quickly scanned her screen and rammed her phone back into her pocket. "Bleeding hell, that's my mam. I'll have to call there tonight after work. Will you do me a favour and take my new underwear home with you? If Neil sees them he'll think it's his birthday and moan until I put them on for him."

Bridget sniggered and held her head to the side. "Do you two still have decent sex or what?"

Harpur let out a sarcastic laugh. "Sometimes he thinks he's a porn king and we have a bit but that is few and far between. Those days are long gone and I'd rather watch paint dry if I'm being totally honest with you. I swear, it's the same every time. Nothing changes. Boring it is. Wham, bam, thank you mam." "Have you told him what you like in the bedroom?" Bridget asked. "Of course I have. I've been married for years not months. He doesn't listen and thinks I'm having a go at his male ego. Sex has never really been his good point if I'm being honest, it's just a basic in and out if you get what I mean?" "Yeah, I know the script well. It was the same with Gary, that was one of the main reasons I carted him. I used to watch the television when we were having sex. It was boring as hell. Anyway, now's your chance to do something about it. If I was you I'd shag Dessie's brains out. Have a one-night stand, have great sex and walk away. No harm done is there?"

Harpur gasped. "I was thinking along the same lines you know. It might even save my marriage if I have a fling."

The girls sat in silence for the rest of the journey. When they parted they kissed and hugged each other. Bridget could see Harpur was still stressed and gave her a few words to make her smile. "Things happen for a reason, love. Never be scared of change." Harpur smiled and walked away. Her shift was nearly over at work and once she got home she was going to have a serious chat with Joanne. Was this the pot calling the kettle black though?

★

The two sisters were arguing, there was a heated debate. "It's always been the same with you Sheila, you knew what was going on and you were part of it just like I was. There's no point in regretting it now is there? We were just trying to help her that's all?" Diane shut up as soon as she saw Harpur stood at the door. Sheila bared her teeth over at her sister and it was obvious the conversation they were having was now finished. Diane was in a mood and whatever had been said between these two it was far from over. Sheila's cheeks were bright red and she was scratching at her neck just like she always did when she was angry.

Harpur plonked down on the sofa and you could have cut the atmosphere with a knife. "What's up? Are you two arguing again. What's happened now, come on, who started it this time?"

Diane closed her eyes slightly and bit hard on her bottom lip. Whatever had gone on here was something so serious that neither of them wanted to talk about it. Diane twisted her gold earring in her ear and tried to calm down. She changed the subject quickly. "How's your day been cock, you look tired, are you sleeping alright?"

Harpur rubbed at her eyes and stretched her mouth open wide as she yawned. "I'm exhausted. My home life is shit, but ay, I'm not going to bore you with it all. I'll deal with it myself."

Sheila let out a laboured breath and shot her eyes over at her. "We all have shit to deal with, just get on with it like I have to."

What was going on here, why was she having another pop at her when she'd just walked through the door? She was well out of order. Harpur was sick to death of the way she was being spoken to and in fairness she'd had enough crap today to last her a lifetime. "Mother, stop being a miserable arse. What shit do you have to deal with, go on tell me that?"

Why didn't she just keep her big mouth shut, Sheila was ready to bite her head off. She twisted her head to face her and went to town on her. "I'll tell you should I? I have to sit in this bastard house every day and remember what our Brady did here. I was the one who cut him down after he hung himself. How do you think that feels ay, to see my own son swinging about like a fucking piece of meat on a hook upstairs? Don't you ever tell me you've had shit to deal with when every night I close my eyes and I see him there, swinging about, his eyes, his mouth. He was my son for crying out loud."

Harpur swallowed hard, this was all too much to hear. She clenched her teeth together and for once she was telling her straight. So what, Sheila had been through a lot, but so had she. Brady was her brother and she was hurting just like she was. "You made a rod for your own back, mother. You let our Brady get away with murder. Go on, ask your sister she'll tell you the truth. You hid stuff from us all so what did you expect to happen when it all fell apart? Go on Diane, tell her that she hid the truth from us and we never knew the half of it."

Diane wafted her hand in front of her face and she was having a hot sweat or something, her lips were trembling and fear was in her eyes. "Harpur, come on now. We've all been through a lot. Pop the kettle on and let's all just have a nice cup of tea and calm down."

Harpur couldn't believe what she was hearing. Where was the back-up, the support? Why wasn't Diane fighting her corner like she usually did, something was wrong. Sheila was just about to blow when her sister stood up and screamed out at the top of her lungs. "Listen, just be quiet the both of you. We're all hurting here and it's nobody's fault what happened to Brady. Your mam is right; she has been through a lot. So, let's agree to disagree for now. People do things for different reasons, so let it lie for now. Bleeding hell Harpur, just make a cup of tea for fuck's sake and let's all chill out."

Harpur marched into the kitchen and punched the kitchen worktop. So much for her auntie backing her up! She froze and held her ear towards the doorway. She could hear whispering from the other room. Her heart was racing and she was having a full-blown panic attack. Grabbing a small plastic bag from the side, she gripped it tightly as if her life depended on it and started to blow into it. Her skin was turning blue and she was banging her clenched fist on her chest trying to free her breath, she was suffocating, panicking. Harpur sprinted to the front door and open it with shaking hands. A small crisp breeze circled her body and Harpur sucked in hard and blew her breath into the bag. She was in control now, her breathing returning to normal. She hung her head over the garden fence and inhaled deeply, gagging for air. A passer-by walked past her but she just kept her head low. She needed to go back inside now, get things back to normal. Harpur continued waiting for the kettle to boil, it seemed to be taking forever. Pulling her mobile phone from her pocket, she tried to take her mind from what was going on inside her body. Harpur's eyes were wide open and she twisted her screen one way then another, she swallowed hard. Dessie had sent her a photograph of his private parts with a message attached.

"I think it's grown since you last saw it. What do you think, can you work with it or what? Love Dessie X"

Oh my God, this was filthy, what on earth was she doing? If Neil ever saw this on her phone he would file for divorce at the drop of a hat. Surely she was going to reply now and tell him this had got way out of hand and it must stop. Her fingers started to type.

"Dessie, it looks more or less the same size as I remember it. I think a hobbit may have a similar sized one. And as for working with it, are you having a laugh or what? I'm coming for a chat with you, just so you can see what you missed out on, nothing more, nothing less. Love Harpur X"

The message was sent and she smirked. Harpur turned around and nearly jumped out of her skin. Sheila was stood right behind her and she wasn't sure if she'd clocked her sending a message. "Do you want a brew mam? You need to stop having a go at me all the time it's doing my head in. We should be helping each other to cope, not fighting each other." Sheila grabbed her cup of tea from the side and never said a word, she just marched back into the front room. She was such a stubborn cow. Harpur looped the two mug handles around her fingers and headed back into the front room. Maybe she should have kept her mouth shut but things were lying heavily on her mind and she wanted some answers. "Oh yes mother, that bag with our Brady's stuff you sorted out. I took it home to have a root through it and I found some letters."

Sheila never flinched, she just kept her eyes on the television. "I told you that was for the bin men. Why don't you ever listen? How dare you take stuff from here without asking me first!"

"Are you for real? You've just said yourself that it was going into the rubbish bin so what harm is it if I've took it? Sometimes you amaze me with your ways. You're not right in the head."

Diane knew this was going to kick off again and sat forward in her seat. "Harpur, for now, just let's not talk about Brady. Everyone's raw so don't ask any more questions please." Diane had changed her tune, since when had she been the mediator? Usually she would have stuck by Harpur and put her sister in her place without a second thought. Harpur was ready for breaking down. She slammed her cup on the table and went out of the room. As she headed upstairs a cold wind slid over her body, the hairs on the back of her neck were standing on end, goosebumps appearing on her arms. One by one, she climbed the stairs until she faced her brother's bedroom door. As if it held an invisible magnetic force, it seemed to be dragging her inside. Harpur looked around the bedroom, the smell, the coldness, the memory of her brother was still in this room. Slowly, she crept over to his bed and sat on the edge of it, scared to move, afraid to look behind her. "Brady, I need you to help fix this mess. I don't care what you were involved in, I just want an end to this nightmare. You know I'll find out sooner or later so you better come clean." Harpur looked up at the ceiling and held her tears back. "Don't say you can't hear me because I know you can. Your big sister can still make you cry," she whispered under her breath. The tears flooded her eyes as she remembered the toy fighting with her brother, pinning him down on the floor and making him say, "My big sister still makes me cry." She closed her eyes and she could see the two of them rolling about together as children. Brady had a contagious laugh and once he started, there was no stopping him. The bond they had was strong and no matter what, they could always find something to laugh about, no matter how hard times were. Even in her darkest hour her brother could still make her laugh.

Harpur opened her eyes and looked to the top of the bed. Her fingers stroked across his white pillow. "I would give anything in the world to have you lying here with me one last time. To see your face, to tell you my troubles, to bollock you for whatever you'd been up to. Why can't I just let go Brady? I need you to help me. I've always been there for you and when I'm having the worst time in my life you decide not to be around anymore." These words came from the heart and as she wiped her tears away she stood up and looked out of the window. Brady had stood at this window so many times, it was like his perch. If anyone came into the garden, he would always get a glimpse of them first. It would give him a chance to get on his toes if it was the dibble or time to shout to his mam to say that he wasn't in. There was always someone knocking at the house for Brady. Mostly for money he owed, or someone who wanted to buy knock-off stuff. Yes, this was a busy address when he was alive. Harpur moved the curtain from the window and looked at the silver moon in the night sky. It seemed so far away tonight, she placed her finger on the window and drew a heart shape on it. With the end of her finger she wrote a few words. "I miss you our kid." Her heart was heavy and the thought of never seeing her brother again dug deep in her heart.

Diane stood and walked to where her coat was on the side of the chair. "Sheila, I'll call tomorrow after I've been to Asda if that's alright?" Sheila didn't reply.

Harpur stood up too. "Mam, I'm going. I'll see you tomorrow after work." There was still not a sound from her. Diane and Harpur shot a look at each other and left the house together.

Sheila waited until she heard the back gate slam shut and peeped out of the window. She looked at her son's photograph nearby and pointed her finger at it. This woman was angry, raging. "See what you've bleeding caused. Didn't I tell you this would all come back to bite us on the arse. Didn't I tell you? Mother always knows best, son. She does, she always knows best." Sheila carried on watching the television. She turned the volume up and every now and then she looked over at her son's photograph, shaking her head.

Harpur walked into the house and as predicted, Joanne was waiting for her. She knew she'd be there, trying to talk her way out of being seen with another man. She walked straight up to Harpur and before she could get a word in, Sam's mother held a flat palm up to her. "Don't waste your breath. I'm going to bed. I'm in no mood for bullshit so save it for someone who gives a shit because I don't." These were harsh words and maybe she could have put it another way but she just turned her back on her and headed straight upstairs. Joanne's jaw dropped and for the first time she was stuck for words. Usually, she could talk Harpur round, make her believe her but she'd not even given her the chance tonight. Joanne was up shit street for sure now. There was no way she wanted Sam to find out about this. He would have ragged her about for sure. She needed a way out, something to get her out of the shit.

Harpur stripped off and got straight in bed. She could hear Joanne coming up the stairs and going into her bedroom. Neil was still downstairs and that's how she liked it, peace and quiet. Once she was in bed, she started to look at Facebook on her phone. It was great on this social media, she could find out all the gossip, catch up with old friends, see what was going on in other people's lives. Yes, she was nosy, but wasn't that what Facebook was all about? People dished the dirt on here, ended relationships publicly, told the world that a father had not paid a penny for his children in months. Yes, it was all going on, on there. Harpur was reading through her newsfeed when she spotted Dessie's status update. "I can't wait for this weekend, catching up with old friends." She read it over and over again. Did he mean her? Was the status aimed at her? What on earth was he doing? This rendezvous was supposed to be hush-hush. What if someone put two and two together and knew it was her who he was meeting? Suddenly there were noises outside, the stairs were creaking. And then silence.

Harpur woke up and shot her eyes over to Neil lying next to her. Today was D-day. The start of her weekend away with Dessie Ryan. Her insides were shaking all over. She felt sick in the pit of her stomach. Neil reached over and his fingertips ran slowly over her lips. "I'm going to miss you this weekend. They say absence makes the heart grow fonder. Who knows, you might even come back and be madly in love with me again."

Harpur looked deep into her husband's eyes. Did she still love him, was this all just a big stupid mistake? Why on earth was she risking her marriage for a man she hardly knew? The lies just rolled off her tongue and there was no going back now. "I just need some me time Neil. I need to figure some stuff out on my own. It's only a few days away. You're going on like I'm leaving you forever."

"It will feel like a lifetime, honest darling, without you I'm nothing. You're my world." What the hell was he playing at? Why now, when she was moving on with her life had he decided to declare how much she meant to him? Before this he hardly ever said how much he loved

Karen Woods

her. Okay, he'd send her text messages every day saying he loved her and a kiss each morning before he left for work, but that meant nothing, she wanted more. Harpur rolled over on her side and stared at him. Was she having second thoughts, was she going to bail out of the weekend away? Neil reached his head over to hers and placed his warm lips on top of hers. He was after some early morning sex. Harpur checked the clock again and jumped up out of bed. There was no chance of hanky panky, she was on a mission. Her suitcase was already packed at the side of the bed and all she needed to do now was get herself ready. The date was in two hours and she had to be in tip-top condition for the first time she met Dessie. Bridget would be here soon and she'd go berserk if she wasn't ready.

Neil looped his hands above his head and watched her applying her make-up. "So, who's hen do is it? You never said?"

Harpur flapped, she wasn't expecting to be interrogated so early in the morning. She had to think fast. "Oh, it's one of Bridget's friends from work. I don't really know her. I'm just going for a rest. They say a change is as good as a rest and I'm hoping to be relaxed and chilled by the time I come back." Neil was thinking, she could see him through the mirror. She sprang to her feet and left the room. Phew, that was close.

All too soon, Bridget arrived honking her horn outside the house. Neil stood and flicked the curtain back from the window. "Gobshite is here. Why does she need to make so much noise?" Neil pulled a sour expression and walked back to the sofa. Harpur was rushing about, she was stressed.

Joseph watched her and held his head to the side.

"Nana, where are you going? Can I come too?"

Neil didn't give her a chance to answer. "No, Nana hasn't got any time for us this weekend mate. We can do something though, leave her to go and enjoy herself with her friends." What an absolute wanker he was! Why now, what was he playing at? She walked over to her grandson and bent down. She gently held his face in her hands. "I'll be back before you know it. Anyway, won't it be nice for grandad to get up from the sofa and take you to the park to play some football? When was the last time he did that, ay?" Touché! That would teach him to be smart with his mouth. Neil was speechless and he knew Joseph would never shut up now until he'd been to the park. Joanne was sat on an armchair nearby and she spoke to Joseph again. "Perhaps your mother will take you down to the shops too and buy some cake mixes. She's always promising you to bake cakes so I think you're going to have a busy day after all." This was hilarious and she smirked as she picked up her suitcase. That would teach them both. "Enjoy, see you all in a couple of days. Don't miss me too much." Harpur left the room and she could hear Joseph asking his Grandad when they were going to the park. She chuckled to herself as she opened the front door. Bridget was stood at the car and she was checking her wristwatch. "Don't you ever call me for being late! Ten minutes I've been sat outside here. Get in, come on, hurry up." Harpur placed her small grey suitcase on the back seat and sat down next to Bridget. She looked at her home one last time before they drove away. "Are you shitting yourself?" Bridget asked.

"Actually I'm quite calm. Don't get me wrong, I've been sat on the toilet all morning but I'm fine now. It's just a meeting. Me and an old friend catching up that's all."

"You look amazing. He's going to drop down dead when he sees you. You look mint."

Harpur pulled the mirror down and ran her fingers across her lashes. "I'm looking forward to seeing him. I wonder if he looks the same?"

"You've spoken to him on Skype you lunatic, you know what he looks like!"

"No, I mean in the flesh. Face to face."

"It's a bit late now to be having second thoughts isn't it? Even if he's a minger you will have to take one for the team. Don't do all this for nothing!" Bridget was laughing her head off as she continued. "And what he may lack in the looks department he might make up for in the bedroom department, so it could even things out if you're lucky."

"Bridget, you have sex on the brain. Are you on heat or something?"

"I might be you know, the last leg over I had was with that guy I met in the pub when you were there. I've not heard a word from him since. In fairness though I was steaming drunk and I must have just lay there when we were having sex. I bet it was like shagging a sack of spuds for him, no wonder he never rang me for another date."

Harpur burst out laughing. "How long is it before we get there? I'm going to have a quick fag I think." Bridget turned the music up in the car and she was singing her head off. Harpur got a text alert and she pulled her phone out from her handbag. As she started to read the message the corners of her mouth started to rise at the corner. "Orr, look what he's just written to me. He said he has never been this nervous in years. He's asking for me to be gentle with him."

Bridget carried on driving and turned her head slightly.

"What time did he fly in? Was it last night or has he been here a few days?"

"He landed last night. He texted me in the early hours to say we were both in the same country now."

Bridget was being inquisitive. "Doesn't his mother still live in Manchester?"

"Yes, that's where he's staying he said."

Bridget was thinking, she held a finger in the corner of her mouth. "I wonder what he's told his missus? Do you think she's come over here with him?"

"That's nothing to do with me love. I'm just spending a bit of time with him that's all."

"I know that but if your fella goes to another country you'd be with him wouldn't you? Don't you ever ask him anything about her?"

Harpur went bright red. "I do not. God Bridget, you're proper nosey you are. All I know is that he's been with her for years. I don't know anything about her."

"Well, things can't be all rosy in the garden if he's eager to see you. It's not rocket science. If he was all loved up at home he wouldn't be sneaking to a hotel to meet you now would he?" Bridget coughed to clear her throat and tapped her fingers on the steering wheel. "Say you two fall in love, what will happen then? Would you leave Neil? More to the point would you leave Manchester?" Her friend just asked too many questions and none of this was relevant to her situation at the moment. For the last time, this was a meeting of two old friends, nothing more.

The girls pulled up outside the hotel. The Gabrielle song 'Out of Reach' played softly in the background. Harpur swallowed hard and she rubbed her hot sweaty palms together. Bridget turned the engine off. "It's showtime, love. I hope you're ready for this!"

Harpur was silent for a few seconds. Her heart was pounding inside her chest and she was anxious. Her nerves were shattered and small droplets of sweat were forming on her forehead. "Oh, I don't know if I can do this. I think I've not thought it through."

Bridget held a serious expression and poked her in the arm. "You're not changing your mind now, no way in this world. I'll drag you there myself if you don't start making a move." There was another text alert. She shot her eyes to her screen and read the message out loud.

"I'm here. I'm sat in reception waiting for you. Hurry up before I have a heart attack. Love Dessie X"

Harpur inhaled deeply and closed her eyes. "Right, I can do this. I can do this. If I turn back now I'll regret this for the rest of my life won't I?"

Bridget reached over and hugged her. "Go and have the time of your life. Ring me as soon as you get chance. I'll be in hiding for the next few days anyway so nobody will see me. I mean, that's the last thing you need is Neil getting suspicious isn't it?"

Harpur touched the door handle and gritted her teeth together tighter. This was a leap of faith. Another deep breath and she finally opened the door. Harpur reached on the back seat for her suitcase. "Wish me luck! I'll ring you as soon as I get chance."

Bridget never replied, she just wanted her gone. As she watched her heading towards the hotel she quickly typed a message to Harpur. "Remember take one for the team if he's a minger." She sent it and watched Harpur in the distance looking at her phone. She could see her laughing. Bridget started the engine up and drove slowly from the car park. This wasn't even her date and she was more excited than her best friend was.

Harpur reached the top of the stairs and stood for a few seconds to get her bearings. The sign for reception was right in front of her. Her feet moved slowly and when she got to the door she pushed it open with the palm of her hands. He would be able to see her now, where was he? Harpur twisted her neck about, eyes flicking one way then another. As she stood looking at her phone, a message appeared. "You look gorgeous." He must have been able to see her, he was looking at her right now. She was just about to reply when a firm hand landed on her shoulder. "Hello sexy. It's been a long time hasn't it?"

Her body shook from inside, heart racing. She knew that voice anywhere. It was Dessie Ryan. Turning slowly, she smiled as she met his eyes for the first time. "Hello Dessie, at last we meet again." The two of them looked into each other's eyes. Not a word was spoken. "I've already been up to our room. Should we go up so you can put your case in? If you like we can have something to eat in the hotel restaurant. I've just been to have a look at the menu and it looks impressive." Harpur nodded. Her legs were like jelly and she felt sick. Dessie took her case from her and made his way to the lift. She was checking him out. He was dressed casually but he looked smart. His hair could have done with a good cut, but apart from that he looked like he did on the video chat. The pair of them stood looking at each other in the lift. Dessie was nervous and his eye was twitching. She was digesting him. Every inch of him. She wasn't sure, she didn't know if she fancied him anymore. Of course he was handsome but she wasn't sure if he was, well, the man she'd imagined he'd be inside her head. The lift opened and he smiled over at her. "What have you got inside here, it weighs a ton." Harpur blushed, he was right it was heavy and she'd probably brought lots of things that she didn't need. Okay, she'd panicked and over-packed. Dessie walked along the small corridor and he was whistling. She checked his bum out in his Levi's Jeans and smirked. He'd always had a fit arse and it was one of her favourite things about him. Dessie slid the card into the door and it opened. Here it was, there was no going back now. Everything they'd joked about, everything they'd planned was about to happen.

Harpur walked into the room and shot her eyes about. He'd done them proud. It was such a lovely room with all mod cons; Flat screen TV, mini bar, and a king-sized bed. This was an awkward moment. She couldn't just stand there like a spare part, she had to do something - talk, anything but stand there looked like an idiot. Harpur walked over to the bed and pressed down on it with her hand. "Bed seems comfortable."

Dessie burst out laughing and made his way over to her. "Do you want a drink? They've got anything you want in this place. Just say the word and it's yours." Harpur nodded. Yes, this would calm her down, she would have had a bottle of vodka if he'd offered her one. "Can I have a vodka and lemonade please?"

"Of course you can sexy." Dessie kicked his shoes off and opened the mini bar. She could see him necking a small bottle of gin as he poured them both a drink. He was as nervous as she was, the poor sod. Harpur started to relax and she was ready to make conversation. "So, Dessie Ryan. What have you been up to since you landed in Manchester?" She pulled her shoes off and climbed onto the bed making herself comfortable.

Dessie popped his head from around the door and answered her. "Nothing really, I've just been at my mam's. I've not had time to do anything yet. I've come straight here to see you. I'm going to meet up with a few of the lads early next week though. Have a few pints and catch up with them." Dessie walked over to the bed and joined her. He passed her drink over and stared at her.

Harpur was uncomfortable and wondered what on earth he was looking at. She stroked the side of her cheek and nose, just to make sure she had nothing stuck there. He still stared at her. "Why are you looking at me like that. Do you fancy me or something?"

Dessie licked the bottom of his lip slowly. He moved in closer to her. She could feel his warm breath on her skin. "Can I kiss you? Just once for old time's sake." Harpur giggled and pushed him away. She wasn't sure she wanted anything like this at the moment, it was too soon. "Stop it, you said we were just meeting as friends nothing else. Don't start all that with me."

He rolled on his side and chuckled. "Still a shy girl I see then." Why could he still make her feel like this even after all these years. She'd show him now. Watch this space Dessie Ryan, watch and learn. She grabbed his head in her hands and pulled him down until their lips touched. Now, she was ready to kiss him. They both looked deep into each other's eyes and without any control over their bodies, their lips connected. Was this really happening? What was she thinking? What happened to just catching up with an old friend? Oh, there was passion here, chemistry, lust. They both wanted it as much as the other. This was a memorable kiss for sure. Harpur was the one who ended the moment.

He was getting to her. She pulled herself away and lay smiling at him.

Dessie let out a laboured breath and smiled over at her. "That was heaven. Just how I imagined it to be." He was such a charmer. He always had a way with words and there was no way she was letting him get into her head with his bullshit.

"I hope you enjoyed it because you won't be getting another one." The banter was in full swing now and after a few hours of catching up, they'd drained the mini bar. Dessie kept bursting into song and dancing about the bedroom. "Shall we go out to the pub or go out and get something to eat?"

Harpur's face dropped. She was a married woman, what if someone saw her, reported back to Neil that she was not where she said she was? Dessie could see by her body language that she was struggling. "Or we can have a drink in the bar downstairs and have a meal." She nodded. It was alright for Dessie, his wife was out of sight and he could go and see who he wanted. Whereas she, on the other hand, had to keep a low profile. She supposed that was what happened when two people were having an affair, ducking and diving. Was this an affair? It was just one kiss; you couldn't really call that grounds for a divorce could you?

The pair of them sat at the table and read the menu. Dessie didn't take his eyes from her and she kept catching him admiring her. There was chemistry between these two, it was like they'd never been apart. They seemed at ease with each other, familiar. Harpur was well on her way now and even though she shouldn't have asked, she did. "So, tell me about your wife and kids. I hardly know anything about you or your life. You said when we met you would tell me all I need to know about you."

Dessie swallowed hard, his head dipped and you could see this wasn't something he wanted to talk about. Yes, he'd tell her about basic things but there was stuff he wanted to keep to himself. Anytime she'd mentioned his wife he always clammed up, changed the subject. Harpur ran her finger around her wine glass and looked over at him. She never gave him a chance to answer her. "It's been nice seeing you Dessie. And I'm glad we have finally set the record straight after all these years. Well, you finally admitted cheating on me with that Wendy O'Malley, so I suppose I can forgive you now. I just really hated her guts and for you to risk losing me for someone like her, well, it was heart-breaking. She was a right slapper too, a proper dirt bag."

Dessie's eyes were wide open and his mouth was moving but no words were coming out. She'd shocked him for sure with her comment. He changed the subject quickly before she carried on delving into his past. "So, I hear you had a bad time with that guy you ended up with? A few of the lads told me he was a right bastard with you."

Harpur's head dropped and she sat playing with her fingers. "It was hard and yes, he was a wanker. I suppose I was young and didn't know any better. I had Sam with him and the rest is history. I've not seen him for over twenty years now and I want to keep it like that. He was a crank, fucked in the head."

Dessie reached over the table and touched the top of her hand. "Don't talk about it if it upsets you. I know more than you think about him. You don't need to explain anything."

Harpur raised a smile and lifted her glass up. "I'm stuffed. I don't think I could eat another thing. Shall we leave desert? You've spoiled me tonight and I'd like to say thank you for such a lovely time. And thank you for making me smile again."

"It's not over yet. Just you wait until I get you back to the room." He held the bottom of his stomach and sniggered. He was such a cocky fucker, full of himself he was.

Harpur was drunk and she was ready for some fun. She'd show him, she'd wipe that smile right from his face. "I'm glad you've said that because I'm feeling ever so horny. It's the wine, it always makes me feel like that. I think I'm going to ruin you Dessie Ryan, so drink up and get your arse back in the room." This did the trick, his jaw dropped and he wasn't as confident anymore. He'd shit a brick. Harpur smirked over at him and raised her eyes. "Not so loud now are you Dessie?" He stood to his feet and came and stood behind her, helping her to pull her chair out. As he bent down slightly he kissed the side of her neck, his warm breath floating down her shoulder blades. She turned back to face him and her nostrils flared. He was arousing her; she knew she wanted him now. Harpur stood and took hold of his hand before leading him to the exit. The two of them were nearly running to the lift. Once inside he dragged her to where he was stood and kissed her passionately, gripping her hair tightly, biting her neck, ravaging her body.

The pair of them couldn't get their clothes off quickly enough. This was bad, they were both married. But neither of them seemed to care. The wine had taken over now and Harpur was like a lioness as she sank her nails deep into his back. There was passion, filth, sensual touches, it was all happening. There was no going back, they were caught up in the moment. Dessie looked down at her and he paused, his body remaining still. He brought his head down slightly and kissed her hot lips slowly. "You know already don't you, so I don't need to say it." Harpur wasn't listening to a word he was saying. This was the best sex she'd had in years and nothing was going to stop her enjoying it. He needed to stop talking, she was near orgasm. Was this actually the same woman? This wasn't the Harpur that everyone knew. This woman was confident, controlling and she was the one calling the shots. Dessie was just her sex slave, obeying every word she said to him. What happened to just meeting an old friend, chatting, having a bite to eat? The sin had been committed now and both of them had committed adultery. There was no going back, the deed was done.

Harpur lay on Dessie's chest after the sex was over, panting for breath. He stroked her hair back from her face and kissed her forehead. "That was heaven. Honest, I don't know what you've done to me but I'm totally besotted with you. Wow, incredible sex. The best I've had."

She tickled the sprinkle of hairs on his chest. "See, I'm not frigid am I?"

He sniggered and tickled the side of her waist. "I only ever said that to wind you up. Can I say something to you please?"

"Yes, why do you keep asking? Just say what you have to."

Dessie took a deep breath and laid his heart on the line. "Since we've been chatting I've not been able to get you out of my head. It's like you've cast a spell over me and I'm mesmerised by everything that you do. I think..."

Harpur reached up and placed a single finger on his lips. "Go to sleep Dessie. It's a good job I don't fall for all this bullshit isn't it? Imagine if I did, you'd have me wrapped right around your little finger wouldn't you?" She let out a little giggle and snuggled deep into his chest. "Once bitten twice shy, goodnight Dessie." Harpur closed her eyes and her breathing became slower. Dessie was wide awake. His hand gently stroked the top of her neck. He was infatuated with this woman. This wasn't bullshit, she had his heart and he knew it. He was never letting her go, not now, not ever. He'd fight for her if he had to.

The weekend was coming to an end and Harpur was packing the last of her belongings into her suitcase. Bridget would be here soon and she needed to be ready. Dessie was sat on the edge of his bed and he kept dragging his hands through his hair and looking over at her. Lifting his head up, he had to get it off his chest. The words he had to say were strangling him. "Can we just have a quick chat before you have to go rushing off?"

Harpur had her back towards him and she was just zipping her case up. "Yeah, two minutes. What's up?"

Dessie coughed and patted the edge of the bed. "Come and sit down for a few minutes. It will take me a while to get out what I have to say."

Harpur joined him. She was ready to go now. Looking deep into his eyes, she held her head to the side. "What's up? Are you going to tell me or what?"

Dessie sat cracking his knuckles, he was so nervous. "I'm in Manchester until the end of the week. Do you want to meet up again before I have to go home? I'd spend every day with you if you'd let me," this guy was getting emotional as he continued. "You feel like home Harpur. Honest, my heart beats when I'm with you and I've not felt like this for as long as I can remember. It feels so right to be with you."

Was he being serious or was this just part of his plan to get her hooked? There was no way she was falling in love, this was a bit of fun, something to save her marriage. But how could she word this without making him feel like a complete idiot? She didn't know how she felt about him anymore. Last night was good, but she was pissed and perhaps she just needed to get it out of her system. Okay, he made her excited, but was this any real reason to end her marriage? Neil was a dickhead every now and then but he was her security blanket. She couldn't throw all that away just because Dessie Ryan had turned up and declared that he loved her after all these years. Where was he when she needed him? He had been nowhere to be seen, she owed him nothing. Her voice was low and she treaded carefully so as not to hurt his feelings. "Dessie, we've had a great time me and you. This weekend is something that I will remember forever. You're a married man and you're just probably feeling a bit unloved at home at the moment. I'm not what you want. We've just had a fling that's all. You enjoyed it right?"

Dessie's shoulders sank low. "I was hoping for more if I was being honest. I was thinking we would fall madly, passionately in love with each other and run away together to live happily ever after."

She couldn't help but laugh, what had happened to him, where was his banter? "Dessie, can you hear yourself? Don't be sad. And as for feeling how you do, I'm totally flattered. But, I can't allow myself to get involved with you. I have responsibilities at home, a husband." Harpur's phone started to ring, it was Bridget. "I just have to answer this." She held the phone to her ear and turned her body away from him. "Hi Bridget, are you here already? Okay, I'll be down soon, give me five minutes I'm just packing the rest of my stuff." The call ended and Harpur stood up from the bed. She didn't look at Dessie once. She had to hurry up, leave without any more complications.

Harpur stood at the door and placed her suitcase down on the floor. Dessie was standing looking out of the window. She walked back to him and placed her arms around his waist. She couldn't leave him like this. He was a mess. "Dessie, if things were different I'd have loved to get to know you better. Maybe our time has been and gone and we have both already chosen the paths we are taking. I'm sorry I can't offer you anything more. If you're free we can go for a coffee through the week. Are you up for that?" He turned round and pulled her closer to his body. He bent his head slightly and kissed her. Harpur was caught up in the moment and she kissed him back. This time the kiss meant so much more, he took her breath away, made her heart beat faster than normal, a warmth rising throughout her body. This was so scary and she knew if she stayed any longer she would be lost in the moment forever. His words were still running through her head, he said he loved her. She could feel it too. But did she love him? Pulling away from him, she never said another word, she just walked to the door. Harpur was gone.

Bridget reached over and opened the car door. "Come on, tell me everything. Did you sleep with him? Tell me, tell me." Harpur's heart was heavy and whatever had just happened in that room had scared the life out of her. She kept looking at the hotel, numb, not knowing what to do for the best. Bridget playfully punched her in the arm. "So, spill, how did it go?"

Harpur popped a cigarette into her mouth and sucked hard on it as she opened the window. "It was really good. We got on well. He makes me smile, he's off his head really. Bridget, he's said some stuff to me and well. It's done my head in. He's told me he loves me."

Bridget huffed and opened her eyes wide, completely shocked. "What, just after a weekend away together? Mind you, it can happen in an instant. It only takes a minute to fall in love, one look, one kiss, so it could be true. When you think about it you two have been chatting for ages now and the video chats too, so I suppose a relationship could have been forming without you both even knowing. Do you have any feelings for him?"

Harpur sucked hard on her fag. This was the big-money question. "I didn't think I did but something just happened to me in that room before I left him. The kiss, it changed, it was like he sucked my heart out. Honest, I've never felt like this before. I can't describe it."

Bridget looked closer at her best friend. Was she falling in love or was this just lust, a bang, a quick leg-over? Bridget was driving now and from the corner of her eye she could see Harpur thinking. She was receiving endless texts but never once did she look at her phone. She was in some sort of trance, numb, not taking anything in. Bridget was getting worried. "Harpur, you need to shake this off. Neil thinks you have been on a girl's weekend away. Sort your face out and try smiling. Bleeding hell, this is a nightmare. Pull yourself together before you get home. You're so on top you are."

Bridget watched Harpur walking down her garden path. She'd hardly spoken a word on the drive home. Bridget waved to her as she left. "Ring me if you need me," she shouted after her but still, there was no reply. Neil sat up as his wife entered the room. He was smiling and you could tell he'd missed her. He pulled her down on the sofa and cuddled her in his arms. "I've missed you so much babes, honest, I've not slept properly since you've been gone. I've done some thinking too and you're right, I need to start pulling my finger out of my arse and helping you in the house. I'll take you away on romantic weekends too."

Harpur could have burst out crying there and then. She felt guilt, betrayal and she needed forgiveness for the sin she'd committed. She held her husband tightly in her arms and squeezed him with all her might. "I'm sorry too Neil. This weekend has made me realise a lot of things too. I know you love me and I should just accept you for the man you are."

"No love, things are changing. As from today you will see the change in me. And anything you want, you can have. I don't care anymore. You're the most important thing in my life and I never want to lose you, ever." The couple shared a kiss and it looked like the weekend away had saved their marriage.

Sometimes, you don't realise what you have at home until you risk losing it all. As far as she was concerned now Dessie Ryan was in her past, and that's where he was staying. He was out of her system now and she'd done what she had set out to do. Joanne walked into the room and Harpur smiled at her. She wasn't going to judge her anymore, how could she when she'd been away with a man who wasn't her husband and had hot passionate sex? No, she was forgiving her right here right now. "I'll order takeaway for us all. Joanne, where is Joseph, tell him he can pick what pizza we are having. I've missed you lot, I've missed this mad little family.

Neil and Harpur spent the evening cuddled up on the sofa. Joanne had gone out and Joseph had just fallen to sleep on the chair next to them both. Neil was holding his wife in his arms and every now and then he was kissing her. She was loved tonight, back in the arms of the man she loved. What a foolish woman she'd been. Her mobile phone had been switched off and when her head was a bit clearer, she would message Dessie and tell him she would not be chatting with him anymore. The film was almost over and Neil was itching to watch the highlights from the football match. She could tell, he kept checking his wristwatch. Harpur looked over at Joseph and spoke. "I'll take him up. Joanne should be in soon so he won't be on his own for long. I'm going to go to bed love. I'm absolutely knackered. I've not slept properly for days. You know what the girls are like when we're all together.

Harpur stood and Neil squeezed her bum cheeks tightly. "No worries love. I'll be up soon anyway. I'm going to watch a bit of the match if that's alright?"

"Yeah, I'll be asleep as soon as my head hits the pillow anyway." Harpur scooped her grandson into her arms and headed upstairs. When she was halfway up she could hear Joanne in the hallway. "I'm in early Harpur. It was a shite night out anyway. I'm sorry I bothered."

Harpur shouted down to her. "No worries, I'll put Joseph in bed anyway." Joanne was back in her good books at last. Sam was home the following week and she was relieved his mother was going to keep her big mouth shut. Thank God for that.

Harpur lay in bed and looked at her phone. She knew the moment she switched the power back on there would be endless messages from Dessie. She placed her phone back in her handbag and lay on the bed. Her eyes were already closing when she heard Joanne going into her bedroom. At this time of the night she usually spoke to Sam until the early hours to keep him company. At least she was home now and she could stop worrying about her. Perhaps she'd been wrong about her all along, maybe she did love Sam and she was faithful to him.

Harpur had been asleep for what seemed like hours. A barking dog nearby had woken her up. Her eyes flicked to the clock at the side of the bed. It was two o'clock, shut the yapping fucker up for crying out loud. She folded her pillow under her head and tried to get back to sleep, punching at the pillow, kicking her legs about, unsettled now. There were noises from outside the bedroom, stairs, creaking, then silence.

This was doing her head in now and she wanted to know what the commotion was. For months, weeks, she'd heard this sound. Once and for all she had to see what it was. Slowly, she twisted her body out of bed and crept to her bedroom door, there wasn't a sound. Perhaps they had mice, there had been an infestation of them in some of the houses on the row and the tenants had already had letters regarding the vermin entering neighbour's properties. She tiptoed cautiously and stood at her bedroom door with a shoe held in her hand, ready for attack. She'd squash the little fucker to death if it was out there. Rubbing her knuckles into the corner of her eyes, she held her breath.

Her eyes were wide open, her heart leaping about in her chest. She could see something at the other end of the landing. Her windpipe tightened and her fingers curled tightly around the weapon she was holding in her hand. Why was she still stood there? Quick, get it, pummel it and sling it outside before it ran off. Harpur closed her eyes as she heard Joanne laughing inside her bedroom. Bleeding hell, she was going to scare it off. Harpur had to make sure she was seeing this right and she wasn't still asleep. No, her eyes were not letting her down this time, it was real. All so real. She could see the shadow of a man bent down looking through the gap in the bedroom door, his hand was moving, he was masturbating. Harpur gritted her teeth tightly together and she crept up slowly behind him. This was her husband, her other half, what the hell was he thinking, the dirty bastard? Neil never heard a sound, she could hear him grunting, deep rapid breathing. This was real and there was no way she was imagining this. Taking a deep breath first, she confronted him. "You dirty no-good bastard, what the fuck do you think you're doing?"

Neil turned around slowly and quickly pulled his hand from down the front of his black shorts, his jaw dropped low. He'd been caught bang to rights. How on earth did he ever think he could get away with this? He was in his own home, the marital home with his wife. He was a pervert, a dirty no-good pervert. Harpur saw red and grabbed his hair and dragged it down to the crack in the door. She squashed his face up to the yellow light seeping from the door. "Let's see what you're looking at ay." Harpur nearly collapsed when she looked through the gap in the door. Joanne was lying in her underwear on the bed and it was obvious she was having phone sex with her son.

The grip on her husband loosened and she ran back into the bedroom gagging for breath. She couldn't touch him anymore, he was diseased now, filthy. She wiped her hands on her pyjamas as she entered her bedroom. No, this wasn't happening, he loved her, he said she was his world. He told her how sexy she was and how much she turned him on, even now after years of marriage.

Neil stood frozen, he walked one way then another, his game was up. He ran in the bedroom after his wife. "Love, it isn't what it looks like. I just heard her laughing and thought I would see if I could find out who she was talking to. I mean, to see if she was cheating on Sam. You said yourself that you didn't trust her."

Did he think she was green or what? He'd been caught in the act. For crying out loud, didn't he have any respect for his wife's intelligence here? Harpur sat on the bed and stared at him, shocked, speechless, eyes burning into him. Taking a deep breath, she pointed at the space next to her. "Sit here, just sit down while I get my head around this." Neil hung his head low and sat facing her. She looked deep into his eyes and snarled over at him. "Please, don't insult my intelligence. If you do, then God knows what I'm capable of at this moment in time. Tell me what's been going on because this is not a one-off. I've heard the creaking noise on the stairs for ages now and I thought we had mice when it was you all along. How could you do this to us? This is sick and twisted, like something you read about in magazines!" She sucked hard on her lips as she continued. She had to remain calm, get this out. "Now, think carefully before you answer me Neil. Tell me the fucking truth before I flip out and knock you that far into next week it will take you two weeks to come back, you slimy cunt." He stuttered and he was about to deny his guilty pleasure. Harpur clenched her fist tightly together and smashed it into his face.

Neil tried to hold her hands because she was ready to cause World War Three. "Love, just calm down. Please, I'll do anything just be quiet." Her eyes were dancing with madness and she was ready to have the house up. Oh yes, she would have named and shamed him to the neighbourhood if he denied this. She'd drag him out onto the street and let everyone know his dirty little secret. Her voice was getting louder with every word she spoke.

"Then tell me the fucking truth. You owe me that at least." Neil fell to the floor and curled up in a tiny ball, his body shaking. Harpur knew then that it was all true, her stomach was in knots and she wanted to be sick. She stood over him and spat down at him. "I know what's just happened and if you ever try to deny it I will make sure it's the last breath you ever take. I said, for the last time tell me the fucking truth!" Neil lifted his head up and drew his knees close to his chest, rocking, blubbering, lips shaking. "You was peeping at her weren't you. And it's not the first time."

There wasn't a sound. Neil rested his chin on his knees and spoke. "Yes, I've done it a few times that's all, I promise you love. I swear. I'll never ever do it again. I don't even know why I did it. I don't fancy her or anything like that. It was a mistake, I'm sorry, please say you will forgive me."

Harpur shot a look outside the window and sucked hard on her lips. Everything made sense now, his late nights downstairs watching films. The way he always came to bed shortly after Joanne did. What a fool she'd been, why didn't she see what was happening right in front of her? In her own home for crying out loud. Her voice was calm as she spoke to her husband. "In the morning you will pack your things and leave this house. We are done. I'll never forgive you for this, ever. It's sick Neil, perverted." He jumped to his feet and tried to put his arms round her. She stood tall and flicked his arms away from her body. "Move you dirty bastard, those grubby hands will never touch my body again!"

Joanne must have heard the commotion from her bedroom and came out of her room. She cautiously walked to Harpur's bedroom. Her head dipped inside the door. "Is everything all right, I heard shouting?" Harpur shot a look at her husband and growled. Why should she keep his sordid little secret? She owed him nothing. She would reveal him for the twisted man that he was. "No, everything is not alright love. My husband here has been watching you at night through the crack in the door. Probably while you are having phone sex with my son. Yes. He's been wanking over you. That's right isn't it Neil?" Joanne was gobsmacked. She pulled her housecoat tightly around her body, shocked. "Go on, tell her Neil that you have been getting off on her for weeks, months even."

What could Joanne say to this, nothing, she was horrified, you could see it in her eyes. "This is nothing to do with me Harpur. I swear to you now. I didn't know a thing."

"I know you didn't, love. It's all his own doing. He must like young girls, he's fucked in the head. Anyway, he's leaving now so you'll be safe. I should report the nonce to the police. He's a dirty scumbag."

Harpur snapped and ran at her husband, she launched her fist into his head as she screamed at the top of her lungs. "Get out of my fucking house. Go Neil, before I do something I might regret."

Joanne stood with her back against the wall as Neil scarpered. This was bad, a nightmare. His feet thundered down the stairs. The front door slammed shut and Joanne ran to Harpur's side. "I'm so sorry. Orr... look at the state of you. Please, just sit down and I'll go and light you a cigarette. Just stay right there, you're in shock. Look at you shaking, for Christ's sake this is all fucked up." Joanne left the bedroom in a hurry. Harpur's body folded in two and she howled out like an injured animal. How could he do this to her? She trusted him, loved him. He'd broken everything they'd had together, destroyed it. There was no going back after this. How could she ever be with him again, he knocked her sick. Joanne came back into the bedroom and passed Harpur a fag that she'd already lit. She placed her arms around her and rocked her gently. "I'm so sorry, I'm so sorry. I never knew a thing."

Harpur blew a cloud of thick grey smoke from her mouth. Her hands were trembling and she was struggling to hold it together. "Go back to bed Joanne. I'll be fine. I just need to be alone." Joanne left the room after a few minutes. She had to make sure she was going to be alright, this was disturbing, even to her. Harpur stubbed her cigarette out in an ashtray and collapsed onto the bed. This poor woman was crying her heart out. What was going to happen to her marriage now? Could she ever forgive Neil? Or was it karma after her night of passion with Dessie?

CHAPTER FOURTEEN

HARPUR HAD HARDLY SLEPT a wink all night. Her eyes were red raw and she'd been smoking like a trooper, stressed, not thinking straight. The vision of her husband was still running through her mind. She could still see him, hear him. She pressed the button on her mobile phone and turned the power back on. There were text alerts, ten, twenty, thirty messages all from Dessie. Harpur opened the texts and began to read them. A fat bulky tear rolled down her cheek onto her lip. His words were so sweet, endearing.

"Harpur, please don't end it before it's even started. If you're being true to yourself you will admit that you feel the same way as me. I need to see you. Can we talk? Why are you ignoring me? Please Harpur, I need to say some stuff to you. If after we've spoken and I mean nothing to you, well, you can walk away. I love you Harpur. There you go, I've said it. I love you more than anything I've ever loved in my life. Please get in touch. Love Dessie X"

Wow, did he really feel this strongly about her or was it all just an act to get into her knickers again? He'd had what he wanted so why didn't he just leave her alone to get on with her life? And as for loving her, was he even capable of love? He was cheating on his wife for crying out loud. This should never have happened. Harpur read over the messages again and again. There was no point in blanking him. She started to reply.

"Hi Dessie, sorry for not replying sooner. My head

has been mashed. No, I mean really messed up with
everything that has gone on. I've got so much shit going
on in my life at the moment, it wouldn't be fair to you
to even think about starting a relationship with you at
the moment. Dessie, I'm damaged goods. I need fixing,
repairing. Honest, you don't want to get mixed up with
my shit at the moment. Hope you are okay? Love Harpur
X"

The message was sent. Harpur shot her eyes over at the
wardrobe. She held a sour expression and bolted up from
the bed. Dipping her head low she dragged out a large
navy blue suitcase from underneath the bed. She needed
him gone, anything that reminded her of her husband had
to go. Like a mad woman she opened the suitcase and
started to fling all his clothes out from his wardrobe. Her
fingers barely touched his clothes, she hated him, the smell
of him, the sight of him, she detested him. There were tears,
lots of tears, her emotions were high and every now and
then she collapsed onto the floor and sobbed her heart
out. She was punching into anything she could get her
hands on. Somebody was coming up the stairs, she shot
her eyes to the door and wiped the tears away. "Mam, it's
only me, where are you?" Maddie stood looking about the
bedroom. Her jaw dropped low as she walked into the
room. "Mam, what's going on. What are you doing with
Dad's stuff?" Harpur was lost for words. How could she
tell her what had happened? It would break her heart into
a thousand pieces, this was her father for Christ's sake, the
man she looked up to. Maddie was anxious and in fairness
she didn't look too clever herself, she looked pale, stressed
out. "Mam, what's going on, where's Dad?"

She'd always been straight with her daughter and she'd

never lied to her if she could help it. Okay, she'd told her that her dog ran away when it was a puppy, but what else could she do, the animal was chewing everything in sight and shitting everywhere? That was a white lie, a fib, something all parents did. Harpur swallowed hard, her eyes were closing slowly as the truth made its way onto her lips. "Maddie, come and sit down here for a few minutes. Please, don't ask me what has happened because I don't want to lie to you. All you need to know is that he won't be setting foot in this house again."

Maddie let out a stunned gasp. "You can't say that. It's his house too! Where do you expect him to go? Whatever has gone on it will blow over, stop overreacting."

Harpur opened her eyes and looked at the ceiling. She had to tell her, otherwise her daughter would just think it was her fault. She could never see any wrong in her father. He was her protector, her safe place. "Maddie, something happened here last night and believe you me, you don't want to know. He's finished with me. I wouldn't piss on him if he was on fire."

Joanne was here now and stood at the door. Joseph followed closely behind her and she needed to make sure he didn't see his Nana like this. "Son, you go downstairs and put the television on. I'll be down to do your breakfast as soon as I've had a little talk with Nana. Go and put Horrid Henry on the television." Her voice was animated and she watched as Joseph headed down the stairs.

Maddie looked over at Joanne and snarled. "I suppose you know what's going on don't you?"

Joanne looked over at Harpur and held a blank expression. Was she going to tell her or what? Harpur sucked in a large mouthful of air and held her daughter's hands, stroking at them, rubbing them softly. "Last night I caught your dad peeping through the crack in the bedroom door perving on Joanne." Maddie twisted her head slowly to look at her brother's girlfriend. Joanne nodded her head to confirm it was true. "It's not the first time either, he knocks me sick in the pit of my stomach."

Maddie cringed, shook her head. "What, my dad was looking at her? Why would he look at that scruffy mess when he has you?"

Joanne was about to defend herself when Harpur stood up and cut her short. "It's nothing to do with Joanne. She's the innocent one in all this. Don't be starting with her over it. You two used to be so close, whatever happened to that ay?"

Maddie dropped her head, she stuttered. Joanne knew something and by the look on her face, she would have told the world and his wife given the chance. "Shit happens doesn't it. Joanne knows why we don't get on anymore but that's for us two to sort out, not you. Where is my dad now? I need to speak to him."

Harpur was raging, there were no hugs for her, no sympathy, her daughter just brushed the incident under the carpet as if it meant nothing. "He was the man I loved. I thought I knew him. Don't you dare take sides in this Maddie. He's in the wrong and you know it."

"Mam, he's not had sex with another woman or anything here. He's just had a look at what was on show. Come on, Joanne walks around this place practically naked most of the time, what did you expect?"

"Listen you. Keep your snide remarks to yourself. I'm with your mam on this. Like she just said, he's her husband. And I'm her son's girlfriend."

"Not for long if I have anything to do with it," Maddie muttered under her breath. Joanne stood back as Harpur ran past her, heading for the toilet. She slammed the door behind her and they could hear her gagging behind the closed door.

Joanne walked over to Maddie with caution. She checked behind her to make sure nobody was listening. They were nose to nose now. "Listen you dirty little skank. We both have secrets don't we. I think you will have more to lose than me if all this comes out, so I'd keep that big mouth of yours shut if I was you. What's up? Are you jealous because he didn't want you anymore?"

Maddie's knuckles were turning white, she was going to give her a bunch of fives for sure. She stepped closer to her brother's girlfriend and squared up to her opponent. "Blood is thicker than water bitch. And for your information, he did want me. It was me who didn't want him. Why do you think he's shagging dirty little sluts like you?" This was war, for Christ's sake these two were ready to come to blows.

Harpur stormed back into the bedroom, "What the hell is going on here? Maddie, Joanne, is one of you going to tell me what's happening?"

Maddie's nostrils flared, there was no way she was backing down. Joanne started to walk away, mumbling under her breath. "Those who turn and walk away live to fight another day."

She smirked back at Maddie. This girl was no threat to her. Whatever she knew had a strong hold over her though for sure. Maddie rushed past her mother. "I'm going to find my dad. For all you care he could be lying under a bus somewhere."

"Like I give a flying fuck where he is Maddie. If you see him, tell him from me not to waste his breath coming round here. If he turns up, God help me. I won't be responsible for my actions." Joanne crept out of the bedroom, Harpur needed time alone, time to get her head round things.

There was a text alert on her phone. It was a message from Dessie. Harpur plonked on the bed and started to read the text.

"I'm so glad you replied, all sorts of things were going through my mind. Can we meet today or tomorrow? Just a few hours are all I need. I don't care if you're damaged goods or not. You're the woman I love and that's all that matters to me."

Harpur gasped her breath. What did she have to lose now? She owed Neil nothing.

"Dessie, I will meet you tonight at the bar on Deansgate. I will be there at eight o'clock. Love Harpur X"

She sent the message. Was this all a front? How could she even think about seeing another man when her marriage was on the rocks? Shouldn't she have been sat down with her husband trying to work things out, finding out why he did what he did? Harpur started to get ready. She needed some fresh air, to go for a walk, to clear her head before it exploded.

★

She went back to the place where she always came when she had problems. The cemetery was bright and sunny today, as if all the spirits in the sky were holding candles over this resting place. Harpur walked down the path humming a song. It was a song she used to sing to her brother. 'Fix You' by Coldplay. Brady cried when he first heard the song. The words had so much meaning to them both and the lyrics touched his heart. Harpur was always trying to fix her younger brother, always planning to make him normal again, get him clean, free him from drugs. Yes, the words of this song meant so much.

Harpur started to remove the rubbish that had landed on Brady's grave; papers, leaves, crisp packets. She hated that his place of rest was not clean. Once it was done, she sat down on the grass and touched her brother's photograph with her index finger. "So, what do you say about what's happened? I know you know. He's disgusting isn't he? You always said he was too good to be true and I should have listened to you when you said you had a gut feeling about him. Your gut was always right wasn't it Brady?" The noise of the traffic on the nearby road could be heard, the roaring engine of a bus parked up at a bus stop. People were sat on the top deck just staring at her. Brady would have liked his burial spot. It was close to the road and not as quiet as some of the other graves. She waited until the noise subsided and continued talking. "I'll never forgive him for what he's done Brady. How could I ever forget what I saw? Every time I close my eyes I can still see him looking through the door, touching himself, getting off on the image of another woman. It's over as far as I'm concerned," she sighed and shook her head. "I don't know why I'm telling you. It's not like you can help is it? And then there's our Maddie. I don't know what's up with her lately, she's just not herself, she seems troubled, as if she's got something on her mind constantly."

A man was walking past at the other side of the

cemetery. He was whistling and seemed happy. How could anyone be cheerful in a place like this? It was doom and gloom. How could anyone be happy visiting someone who had passed away? Perhaps he'd watched his loved one suffering. Maybe now he was at peace knowing they were in a better place, without pain. But who said heaven was a better place? Nobody knew that for sure. It was just some wise people who had told the world that when our lives end, we go to meet our maker in the sky. Harpur believed in God and all the wonderful things he'd done, but sometimes she wondered if he was so great and powerful, why were people sad in the world? Why didn't he make everybody happy? Equal? We are all his children, so how could he pick who deserved to be happy and who deserved to be sad? There were so many questions in her head regarding this. If God could have seen her now, he would have sent her brother back to her. He must have seen the tears she'd shed, felt the aching in her heart. Been with her when all she prayed for was her brother to be there with her. He was too young to die, he had years left in him. All she had now was the hope that they would meet again one day in heaven, in a place with no rich, no poor, no sadness; only happiness. Would he be there waiting for her when she took her final breath? Would he take her hand and guide her to a place everybody spoke about?

Harpur tapped her fingers on the cold, damp soil below her. "Brady, I'm going to start thinking about me from now on. Dessie has asked me to meet him again and I'm going to take a chance on him. I want to regret the things I did, not the things I didn't. And if it all turns sour, what do I have to lose? Nothing. I'm going to see my mam before I go and see him. She's doing my head in you know. How you sat in that house with her all day long is beyond me. The woman never shuts up moaning." Harpur chuckled and looked directly at Brady's photograph. "You must have had the patience of a saint, I'm telling you. She is so bitter it's untrue. And now you're gone, it's like the world is against her. I don't know what's going on but Diane and my mam were arguing the other night. I mean really going for it. It must be something bad if Diane is losing her rag. She's usually so calm isn't she?" Harpur started to sing the song again and her head touched the side of the headstone. "I'd better go our kid. I've got a lot of things to sort out. Don't forget, send a bit of help my way if you can." She stood and kissed the photograph. As she left the grave, she twisted her head back and blew a single kiss over her shoulder. "I love you our kid."

Harpur entered her mother's house through the back door to be met with her mum asking "What's up with you, you've got a face like a smacked arse?"

Harpur sat down and pulled her coat off. "Don't ask, it would make your toes curl."

Sheila carried on cleaning and dusting near where her daughter was sat. "Nothing would shock me love. Trust me, I've seen and heard it all."

Harpur went ahead and blurted it out. Maddie would have filled her grandmother in anyway so what was the point in hiding anything. "Neil has been carted and he won't be coming back home either before you start. I'm done with him."

Sheila stopped her household chores and looked over at her. "What, you've already kicked him out?"

"Yes, I caught him last night peeping through the crack in Joanne's bedroom door. Watching her, touching himself, getting off on her."

Well, this was a first, Sheila was speechless, not a sound. She carried on cleaning after a few seconds, she chuckled. "Men will be men love. They all do stuff like that. It's in their blood. I don't know what all the fuss is about, it's not like he's cheated on you or slept with another woman is it?"

Was Harpur the only one who saw this as it really was? She snapped and was ready for walking out. "Mam, imagine if that was your husband. Come on, you would have cut his balls off by now and made a necklace out of them."

Sheila grabbed a cigarette from the side and popped it into her mouth. Her voice was calm and endearing. "Harpur, sometimes you just need to see things for what they really are. There are a lot worse things happening in the world than your husband peeping through a doorway at a woman. Trust me, I know. I get that you're hurt and disappointed but is it really worth ending your marriage over? Neil is a good man, he adores you. He loves you more than anything."

"If that's true then why is he looking at another woman? Honest, I can't even think about him without feeling sick. It's all been lies; our marriage is one big fuck-up."

Sheila sucked hard on her fag. "I'm just saying, it's not as bad as you're making out. I'll say it again. Men will be men won't they?" Sheila was in a good mood today, what was up with her? Harpur watched her carefully cleaning her brother's photograph and froze when she saw her kiss it and start singing to it.

A little later Maddie walked into the house and she was bright red. She stood in front of them both with her hands placed firmly on her hips. "My dad is in a right state. You need to sort this out you two. He can't stay at his brother's forever, he's a right mess."

Harpur never had to say a word. It was Sheila who answered her. "Who do you think you're talking to lady? Your mother doesn't have to do anything she doesn't want to. Yes people make mistakes as you know, but it's the people you love who are the ones who suffer. Come on Maddie, you know that more than anybody don't you?"

Sheila stared at her a lot longer than she needed to. Maddie swallowed hard. There was no way she was back-chatting her nana. Sheila would have knocked her block off. Harpur folded her arms tightly across her chest as her mother continued. Go on Sheila, you tell her. It's about time you stuck up for me. "If your father has been doing what he's been doing, it's nobody's fault but his own. If he's in the doghouse, then it's up to him to sort it out. It's not your problem, so you keep your bleeding nose out of things that don't concern you. This is between man and wife." Maddie dropped her head. That was her told, there was nothing more she could say. Sheila went towards the kitchen and flicked her eyes towards Maddie to follow her. Harpur was busy on her phone, texting Bridget telling her all about her husband. There was whispering from inside the kitchen. Harpur held her ear to the door but couldn't make out what they were saying. Sheila was probably bollocking Maddie. Dessie was texting all the time now. Every two minutes they were texting each other. Harpur needed to pull herself together, get her hair done and her make-up. There was no way she was meeting her fancy man the way she was. Harpur decided to leave now and shouted in to her mother. "Mam, I'll ring you later. I'm going to have a lie down. It was only a flying visit anyway.

I'll ring you later." There was no reply. Maddie was still in the kitchen with Sheila yapping about something or other.

Harpur decided to walk home. It wasn't far and it was a bright day with a fresh, crisp wind. She made her way through the streets to save time. After a few seconds she squeezed her eyes together to make sure she wasn't seeing things. She could see Joanne talking to Paul Burton in the distance. Dipping back behind a wall out of sight she carried on watching them. What the hell was going on here then? That bastard was the one who sold the drugs to her brother and here was a member of her own family talking to him, flirting with him. He was touching her hair, squeezing her arse. No, there was no way she was having this, what a liberty. Harpur stormed over to where they stood.

Paul was one cocky fucker, he never flinched. Joanne knew her game was up and backed away from the drug dealer. Caught in the act again she was. "Why are you here talking to this deadbeat?"

Joanne stuttered, how was she going to answer this? It wasn't like it was the first time she'd been caught bang to rights. "I was just asking him something that's all."

"What, and he needed to touch you too did he? I've just seen his hands all over you."

Paul Burton flicked his cigarette butt into the distance and blew smoke into Harpur's face. "You need to back off. Everywhere I look you're watching me and to tell you the truth, you're doing my head in now. Do you know I could have you and your family wiped from the face of the earth if I wanted to?"

Harpur spat near his feet, she didn't fear him whatsoever. "You don't scare me you daft ferret. You know that I know you're involved in this one way or another and sooner or later, you will slip up and I'll be there to watch you fall."

Paul went head to head with her, ready to smash her head in, spark her. "Oh, is that right? Maybe I'm a lot closer to you than you think. It's you who should be watching what's going on around you, not me."

Harpur was confused, what on earth was he going on about? Joanne wanted to get on her toes, she was anxious and in bad books again. Harpur looked him straight in the eye and clenched her teeth tightly together. "The truth will come out and when I find out, I'll make sure you get slammed for years. Let's see how you cope when you're taken away from the people who love you, just like my brother was."

Paul looked her up and down. Oh, he was one smarmy bastard. "Blah de fucking blah love. Do whatever you're doing. It will be me who has the last laugh, trust me."

Harpur scraped her hair back from her cheeks and tucked it down the back of her coat. If he wanted beef she'd give him beef. Joanne tugged at her arm. "Harpur, come on. Let's get you home. You need to chill out. Come on, for fuck's sake, this isn't the time or the place."

Paul kicked at the floor and nodded his head at her. Before she left he made sure she heard what he had to say. "It will be me who has the last laugh love. Just like I always do. Ask anyone round here who knows me. Nobody gets one over on me without getting hurt."

What was the point in wasting her breath on such a lowlife? His time would come, he would get what was coming to him, she would laugh and enjoy every moment of his downfall.

Harpur's phone started to ring. She quickly grabbed

the handset from her pocket and saw Neil's name across the screen. He could take a running fucking jump if he thought she was speaking to him. She ended the call and rammed her phone back in her pocket. Joanne walked along with Harpur in silence. The women started approached the front door and Joanne's eyes opened wide. "Harpur, Neil is sat on the doorstep waiting for you." They froze and stared at him, he'd seen them now and stood up to his feet.

"Is he right in the head coming back here or what?" Harpur marched forward and she was already planning her attack on her cheating spouse. Joanne hurried behind her. What a bleeding day this was turning out to be. It couldn't get any worse. "What are you doing here? I'll get your clothes to your brother's house. How dare you darken my door. I can't even look at you anymore. Just leave Neil before I ring the police."

Neil was desperate, he pleaded with her. "Harpur, just listen to what I have to say, please."

Harpur was trying to get her key in the door, hands trembling, steam coming out of her ears. "Just leave me alone. We are done. Just go, for crying out loud." The front door opened and she hurried inside. Joanne followed her and closed the door in Neil's face. Harpur didn't look well, her face had drained of all colour. She was hysterical, her hands ragging through her hair as she crashed to the floor in the hallway. "Tell him to go, tell him to leave me alone! Please, I can't take much more of this. I just need him away from me!"

Joanne opened the front door and found Neil folded over in two in the corner of the garden. He lifted his head and his eyes said it all. Joanne licked her dry cracked lips and delivered the message from his wife. "Neil, you need to leave. Honest, I know it's hard but she just needs some time to get her head together."

"I've ruined it all. She'll never forgive me for this ever. Joanne, don't look at me as if I'm a dirty old man. I just had a look, it is nothing like she's making it out to be. I thought you was cheating on Sam and I was listening to what you were saying on the phone that's all."

What a lying fucker he was! Why was he not telling her the truth? Joanne was uncomfortable, what had he seen anyway? She knew that night she was having phone sex with Sam. Did he see what she was doing with her hands, had he seen her privates? Her cheeks blushed. The sooner this was all forgotten about the better. There was no way in this world she wanted him telling anybody about what he'd seen. "I'll have a chat with her Neil. Maybe she might ring you later. It's all up in the air at the moment. She just needs time to think." Neil held one hand on the wall and tried to straighten up. The shame he was carrying was breaking him in two. What was going to happen to him now? Was his married life finally over?

It was time to meet Dessie. Harpur had tried her best to look good but there was no way she could hide the tears she'd shed today. Should she cancel the date for when she was feeling better? But he was leaving soon, flying back home to Spain. Harpur listened as she heard someone coming in the front door. It was Bridget's voice. She was coming up the stairs. She inhaled deeply and her bottom lip started to tremble. The door flung open and there was her best friend, standing there with tears in her eyes. "Oh, babes, I don't know what to say. Come here and let me hug you. I hate what's he's done to you. I hate him with a passion, he's a twat."

Bridget was actually crying more than Harpur, she was genuinely upset. "I'm fine now I've had a good cry Bridget. It was the shock of it all I think. You never know do you? I had Neil down as a lot of things, but a pervert? I never saw that one coming."

"I just can't get my head around it Harpur, why would he do something like that? Watch porn, read fanny magazines, but don't ever cross the line like he's done. He's knocked me sick. Do you think he's ever watched me getting changed over the years? I mean, the chance has been there hasn't it."

Harpur smiled gently. "Has he 'eck you daft bleeder. I honestly think it was just something he got wrapped up in and couldn't stop. It was his kink. Anyway, it is what it is love. One door closes and another one opens. I'm going to meet Dessie now. I've got nothing to lose anymore have I?"

Bridget stood tall. "No, you go and have the time of your life. Run away with him for all I care. Do what you have to do make yourself happy. I've got the keys for a lovely house in Didsbury if you need to use it. I've got a viewing tomorrow so it will be empty, no one will be there. You can go there and spend some time together in private without anyone bothering you."

Harpur nodded. "Thanks love. I will if you don't mind. I can't be arsed ducking and diving."

Bridget searched in her handbag and pulled out a bunch of keys. There was a brown card on them with the address of the property. "Come on, I'll drop you off. Once again, all I can say is I'm sorry. I could never imagine what you are feeling right now. But, as my old grandmother used to say, what makes you ill makes you better. So get your swag back on, put a smile on your face and get yourself back out there in the mix. Nobody would blame you now anyway, so crack on and do what you're doing. Men are bastards, I can't be arsed with them anymore. I'm going to buy a budgie, they're less trouble."

Harpur stood and looked at herself in the mirror. Bridget was right, she needed to dust herself down and get back on the horse so to speak.

As Harpur and Bridget left the house together, Maddie came out of her bedroom and stood outside Joanne's bedroom door, hesitating. The crack in the wood was staring straight at her, she bent down slowly and peered through it, before shivering as the hairs on the back of her neck stood on end. She could see Joanne lying on the bed reading through a letter Sam had sent to her. Now was the time to confront her, to say what she had to say, to put this to bed once and for all. She pushed the door open with the palm of her hand and stood sneering at Joanne. "Can I have a word. Me and you need to sort a few things out don't we?"

Joanne casually flicked some invisible dust from the top of her shoulder and sucked on her bottom lip. "Come in then, let's hear what you have to say. Don't be starting with your attitude either because you can fuck right off if you think I'm listening to you talking shit."

Maddie cautiously entered the bedroom and sat on the edge of the bed. Taking a few seconds to compose herself, she began to talk. "So, what do you know about me and Paul Burton?"

Joanne rolled onto her side and stretched her arms over her head, cocky she was. "I know enough that's all."

Maddie knew this was like getting blood out of a stone. So she put her cards on the table and blurted it out. "I know you've been sleeping with Paul behind my brother's back."

Joanne sat up now but she didn't seem that bothered that her secret was out. Here it was, the killer blow, this would shut her up once and for all. "And I know you was sleeping with him for months before me. What's happened to the baby you were carrying, did you get rid of it?"

Maddie's head sank low, her heart was racing. It was true she'd had a fling with the man her family hated. She swallowed hard and kept her eyes low. Here it was, the shame, the betrayal. It was all Brady's fault, he was the one who had introduced her to him. He made sure Paul was getting what he wanted from his niece and as his reward, he was kept in a good supply of free drugs to keep his big mouth shut. But Joanne had said something about her being pregnant, was she being serious or what? Maddie kept a poker face and looked her straight in the eye, she was ready to fight her corner.

Joanne had nothing on her and she called her bluff. "Who said I was having a baby? It's all bullshit. If I was pregnant then where is the baby?" She opened her jacket and patted her stomach with a flat palm. "Does it look like there's a kid in there or what? Don't listen to gossip, you know what people are like around here."

Joanne was puzzled, nothing made sense. There was no baby, no bump, no pregnancy. "It was Paul who told me anyway. He was twisted and off his head when he said it so he might have been chatting shit. He mentioned something about your Brady too but he must have been lying if there is no baby."

Maddie needed this sorting out and quick. It was a stalemate. They both had secrets they wanted to keep but who was going to make the first move? Maddie cracked her knuckles and continued. "So where do we go from here? As I see it you can tell my mam about Paul and then I will tell Sam about you sleeping with him too. Is that what you want to do?"

This was clever, she put the ball in her court. Joanne twisted her hair around her finger. In two days Sam would be home and if he got a whiff of her being unfaithful he would make her life a misery, batter her until she was black and blue, tell everyone about her. There was no way she wanted that. She held her hand out towards Maddie and opened her eyes wide. "If you keep quiet, then so will I. It's up to you. We can shake on it if you want?"

"That's fine with me because either way we would both suffer. There is no love lost between us but I'll be civil to you for my brother's sake, that's all. Just keep your big trap shut."

Joanne agreed. "It's fine by me."

Maddie left the bedroom. So that was the secret she was hiding. What a dark horse she was. Harpur would have strangled her if she ever found this out, she would have disowned her. But for now, their lips were sealed and their secrets were safe.

★

Harpur sat in the taxi with Dessie. They were heading to the house Bridget had sorted out. Dessie had hold of her hand in the back of the car and every now and then, he lifted it up to his warm lips and kissed it. Considering what this woman was going through, she was doing, well to hide her true feelings. Any other woman would have been on the floor, never getting back up. They arrived at their destination and Dessie paid the fare. Harpur casually walked to the front door of the house as if she owned the property. This gaff was situated in a lovely area and it all seemed so peaceful and quiet, tranquil. The lovers entered the house together and the minute the door closed, Harpur grabbed hold of Dessie and kissed him passionately. This was their time, nobody else's. Inside these walls, anything could happen and they could be whoever they wanted to be. This was hot and passionate lovemaking. Two bodies eager to feel each other's touch, ravishing every inch of skin; kissing, touching, caressing. The need to be loved, fulfilled. There was no bed needed. The sex was all over the house, stairs, kitchen, floors. If this night ended right here, right now they would never forget the time they'd shared here together for the rest of their lives. These two had chemistry, passion, lust, love, an aching for each other, never wanting to let this moment go.

Harpur lay next to him in the king-sized bed, stroking her finger across his firm toned chest. Was he her destiny? Was he the one? Her eyes held so much sadness and it looked like she was going to break down crying any second. Dessie swept her hair back from her forehead and twisted her to look at him. "Harpur, you know I love you don't you?" Did she? In her head this was fun, a bit of slap and tickle but now they were face to face, he'd confused her by saying he loved her. This wasn't ever part of the plan, she had just wanted a bit of fun. How had she ended up like this? She supposed if you play with fire you always get burnt, no matter which way you look at it. It was time for her to confess, tell her lover all about her troubles.

"I caught my husband spying at my son's girlfriend, Dessie. I've flung him out and I'll never ever let that man near me again."

He swallowed hard and asked her to repeat herself. He wasn't sure if he heard her correctly. Once she told him again, he froze. What should he say, what should he do? His grip tightened on her. "I'm so sorry. How could he do that to you?"

"It doesn't matter anymore does it. It's done. They say things happen for a reason and I believe I'm no longer meant to be with Neil."

This was music to his ears. This meant she was free, single, could do whatever she wanted. He was getting excited. "Come and live with me. Come to Spain and let's start a new life together. I promise you Harpur, you won't regret it."

She thought about it. Yes, it would have been a great idea, an amazing time. But this was his life, his dream, not hers. "Dessie, I hardly know you. Okay, we knew each other when we were younger but things change. I've changed. Anyway, you're married. You have commitments."

Dessie raised his eyes and ragged his hand through his hair. "There is some stuff I haven't told you. The timing for us is perfect. My marriage is over too. The moment I started talking to you again I knew where my heart was. Wendy is not who I planned to spend the rest of my life with. She made me lose the only girl I've ever loved."

Harpur started to fidget about in the bed. He said his wife's name, this made it real now. This was too much for her. Her heart was racing, head all over the place. Why was he saying all this stuff to her now? The years had gone by and if he loved her like he said he did, why didn't he ever try coming to look for her? She was frustrated, confused. "Dessie, don't say any more. You left me for the hanging slapper when we were younger. You could have come and tried to put things right with me but you never did. No, you carried on with your life and probably slept with a hundred more women. So, don't lie to me about always loving me. It's just lies and it makes my blood boil."

Dessie sat up, he was fighting his corner now, he had tell her how it was. "You were with him, that tosser. I was going to come and see you but the next thing I heard you were pregnant. What could I have done then, ay?" This was getting heated. Dessie was quiet for a while and he dropped his head. "There are some things you don't know about me and I need to tell you some stuff before I leave."

Harpur was drifting off to sleep and she'd switched off. "Go to sleep love, I'm just so tired. Talk to me later. I feel like I could sleep for a year."

Dessie stared into space. His hand stroked the bottom of her back. He'd lost her once before and he was never losing her again, no way. As soon as the morning light cracked through the curtains he was going to tell her everything, the truth.

CHAPTER FIFTEEN

HARPUR LEFT DESSIE still sleeping. She had so much to sort out, so many problems to solve. It was a good job she had an appointment with her counsellor today because she needed some help, somebody to listen to her, to tell her everything was going to be alright. She started to walk down the street. She didn't really have a clue where she was going but once she got to the main road she would gather her bearings. A car honked its horn in the distance. A man was waving over at her.

"Oi, sexy. Where do you think you're going?" It was Donny shouting from across the road. Harpur pulled her coat tightly around her. This was the walk of shame for sure and there was no way she wanted Donny to know she'd not been home all night. Harpur walked over to his car, perhaps he could give her a lift home? "Morning, what are you doing around here?" he asked in a curious voice.

"Oh, it's a long story. Any chance you can give me a lift home?"

Donny opened the passenger door. "For you my lady, anything." Harpur liked his style, he was so confident and there was just something about him. Okay, she'd been out with him for dinner but that was as far as it went. He was too good looking, a pretty boy. Why on earth did he want her when he could have had any woman he wanted? Perhaps he was looking for a mother figure; a cook, a cleaner, someone to look after him? The two of them drove onto the main road and she could feel his eyes all over her. "So you were out last night then? I mean, I can tell a woman who's stayed out after a night on the beer a mile away."

She giggled and knew the game was up, she had to come clean. "Yeah, I was at a friend's party and I must have got that pissed that I fell asleep on the sofa."

Donny examined her and held his head to the side. "And, your fella, he doesn't mind you not coming home all night?"

She should have kept her mouth shut really but she was flirting and didn't care anymore. "I'm single now Donny. So I can come and go whenever I want."

Donny was gobsmacked, he rubbed his hands together; his day had just got better. "So you're free to come on a night out with me then?"

"If I wanted to but at the moment I'm just chilling. It's been years since I've been single and I don't want to jump into anything so soon."

Donny sniggered, "I wouldn't mind you jumping into bed with me love."

Harpur smirked, this guy made her laugh and if things had been different, she would have given him a chance. But, no, she wasn't going to lead him on. "Donny, you're bloody gorgeous. But you need to find someone your own age. I'm too old for you and I have to be honest. Me and you are never going to happen."

Donny was shocked. "What, ever?"

She smiled and replied. "Not ever."

"Can we still be friends then? And if you ever fancy a hot steamy sex session, you know you can always give me a call right?"

She reached over and patted the middle of his arm

as he carried on driving. "Donny, if I ever need some sex I'll make sure you're the first person I call." These two were good friends now and she knew if she ever needed a friendly ear to bend, he would be on her list. He was sweet and caring and just what she needed at this moment in time. Donny took directions from Harpur and headed home. He turned the music up and wound the windows down as he danced about in his seat. He was so lively, so full of life.

As Harpur walked into the house, Maddie stuck her head out of the front door. "Mam, who was that who dropped you off?"

"Just a friend love, no one you know."

Maddie slammed the door shut and marched behind her mother into the front room. "Have you just spent the night with him?"

Harpur sniggered and brushed the comment off. "No, he's just a man I know from work that's all. I stayed at Bridget's and he gave me a lift home. It saved me getting on the bus didn't it? Piss off anyway interrogating me. I'm the mother here not you."

Maddie was on one and she ranted as she continued following her about the room. "Don't think you can go sleeping about now with random guys just because my dad isn't here. Angela's mam started off like this and now her name is shit around here, don't end up like her."

Harpur stopped dead in her tracks. Who did she think she was talking to? She wanted to learn some respect for her elders. She stormed back and pointed her index finger in her daughter's face. "For your information sweetheart, if I want to drop my knickers for the whole estate I will. Don't you ever think you can dictate to me! When I need your advice I'll ask for it, so until then, keep your mouth shut."

Maddie knew she'd overstepped the mark. "I'm just saying that's all. God, you can't say anything in this house anymore without somebody biting your head off. Everybody needs to calm down and chill out."

"Don't say anything then and we'll be fine. If anything, you should be round at your dad's telling him about his late night affairs, not pecking my head."

"Mam, he made a mistake. One lousy mistake and you're going on like it's the end of the world. Our Sam's home tomorrow, what are you going to tell him, ay? Have you even thought about the trouble it will cause in this family? He'll snap with Neil. Kick his head in, is that what you want?"

Harpur snorted and sneered over at her. "If Sam finds out then so what? I'm not protecting his dark seedy secret." Harpur left the room and headed upstairs. She was late for her appointment already and she had to rush.

Mark was checking his watch as Harpur hurried through the door. "Late again Harpur. You'd be late for your own funeral you would."

Obviously Mark had a sense of humour today, he was smiling. Harpur dragged her coat off and blew warm breath onto her hands. "That funeral may be sooner than you think Mark, when I tell you what's been happening."

He sat forward in his seat. He loved this woman's life, there was never a dull moment. There was a text alert on her phone but she just ignored it. Mark sat eagerly listening to her story, he'd never heard anything like it in his life. This was a drama for sure. She told him about Dessie too and now she was waiting on his wise advice. "Should I go and live with Dessie? I mean, give it a go?"

Mark had to think about this and took a few seconds to gather his thoughts. There was no way he could make the choice for her, she needed to do it herself. "So, this Dessie says he's always loved you?"

"That's what he said but I'm not sure. If that was the case then why has he never tried to contact me before now?"

Mark nodded, she made a good point and he knew she had her head screwed on. "What is your heart telling you to do?"

Harpur had to think about this, she wasn't sure. Since her brother's death her heart was in a right state, it wasn't working properly anymore. It just ached twenty-four hours a day and she wasn't sure what she felt anymore. Was she feeling anything in her heart for Dessie, was this real love or just an escape from her stressful life? Mark could see she was struggling with an answer. "I think you need time alone to figure out what you really want. If this man says he loves you then he will wait forever for you won't he?"

These were wise words and she knew he was right. Her head wasn't in the right place at the moment and she shouldn't be making such big decisions where her life was concerned. Today was her last appointment with Mark and she wasn't really sure if he'd helped her in any way. Yes, he'd listened to her problems and probably helped her deal with her past, but had he really got her over her issues? Maybe it did help to talk to someone about the problems, or maybe it didn't.

As they finished, Mark stood and held his hand out towards her. "I wish there was more funding to keep you here for a few more months Harpur but the NHS cuts have hit us all hard. I've really enjoyed getting to know you and I wish you so much happiness in the future. If it's any use to you, I'd follow my heart. It's never let me down before. You get one chance at happiness, so take it with both hands and enjoy it."

Harpur choked up, this was emotional. This man knew her darkest secrets, her fears, things that made her happy. She felt like she was saying goodbye to a dear friend. It wasn't professional but she grabbed him closer and hugged him tightly. "Thanks for everything Mark. I know I've been a handful at times but thanks for the time and effort you took trying to fix me." Harpur looked at him one last time before she left the room. It was up to her now, she had to be the one who made the choices.

As Harpur walked towards her car in the car park she could see a man in the distance looking in all the car windows he was passing. Her pace quickened, heels clipping along the pavement. This man was a thief, she knew the signs and he was definitely ready to smash a car window to get whatever he had clocked inside the vehicle. Harpur froze, eyes squeezing tightly together, it was him. She sprinted towards the man and gripped him by the back of his hood. "Gotcha, you little rat."

The man was trying to break free but when he saw who it was, he held his hands up and fell back onto a parked car. "Harpur, what the fuck are you doing, I shit it then. I thought I'd been lifted?"

This was no time for small talk, she wanted answers. "You know what I want from you and let me tell you something Tony, if you don't tell me what you know, then I'll make sure I get you nicked. I'll say you attacked me," she watched his jaw drop. "Yes, you'll be in the cells for hours rattling.. You know how that feels don't you Tony? So, what is it going to be then?"

Tony gulped and his Adam's apple was bulging through his thin grey skin. A night in custody was more than he could bear, just the thought of it made his toes curl. "Nar, Harpur. I'll tell you anything I will. I've just been busy that's all."

Harpur knew she had him by the short and curlies. Her plan had worked. "Right, get in my car. I won't keep you long. Ten minutes, tops."

Tony shot his eyes about, he was cornered and there was no escape. He opened the car door and plonked his scrawny body inside. Harpur made sure he was safe and pressed the button for the central locking, he was going nowhere. The smell from this man was putrid, he stunk of horse shit. She opened the window slightly and moved her body away from him. Popping a cigarette into her mouth, she passed one to Tony. "You know what I want to hear so don't make me waste my breath. Tell me what went on with Brady, cut the bullshit too, I just want the truth."

Tony dropped his head and turned the cigarette round in his yellow stained fingers. This wasn't easy for him; he was grassing his best mate up. Bubbling on him. "It was Paul who got him involved. He fancied her from the moment he first saw her and he was constantly ringing him trying to get him to sort a date out. She is gorgeous, everyone fancies her. She was like the forbidden fruit to him. He gave him free drugs, tablets, food, everything to keep him sweet. Honest the guy was besotted with her. What did you expect him to do?"

Harpur was puzzled. What the hell was he going on about?

"Maddie liked him too and that's when the trouble started. Paul had a girlfriend and she was only ever going to be a bit on the side. Brady tried to sort it out when it went pear-shaped but Paul was too big for him. The prick didn't care about Maddie once he'd slept with her and he threatened Brady that if she grassed him up to his girlfriend, he was going to put him in a body bag. Brady was fucked, how could he have done anything? Maddie was heartbroken and then she told him about…"

Tony stopped talking, he'd said too much already. Harpur scratched her head. This wasn't sinking in. Did he say her daughter's name or was it someone else? "Who's Maddie?"

Tony was sweating now, agitated, ready to leave, his hands pulling at the door handle in a mad panic. "Your Maddie. Come on now Harpur, I need to go. I've said too much. I made a promise to Brady that I would never say a word about this to anyone. Melanie knows more than me, go and see her."

Harpur pressed the button to open the door. There were no goodbyes, Tony sprinted off into the distance. Harpur dropped her head onto the steering wheel. "NOOOOO!" she screamed at the top of her voice. Her fingers trembled as she tried to turn the engine over, legs shaking. She needed to find her daughter as soon as possible. She needed answers, she needed to know the truth. The car raced out of the car park. She was driving like a lunatic, weaving in and out of the traffic. This couldn't be true, her own daughter, her own flesh and blood had deceived her. There was yet another text alert on her phone. She ignored it again. There was only one thing on her mind right now and that was finding Maddie.

Harpur rushed in through the front door and flung her handbag onto the floor. Her sleeves were rolled up and she was ready to kick some arse. "MADDIE! Where the hell are you? Get your arse here now!" She was hysterical. Harpur stomped around the living room, throwing things, launching cushions about the room. She sprinted to the bottom of the stairs and yelled out at the top of her voice. "Maddie, get down here now! It's urgent." There wasn't a sound, she burst up the stairs and booted her bedroom door open. Her eyes flicked one way then the other. Not a sign of her.

Joanne appeared at the door, she'd been asleep and her hair was stuck up all over the show. "What time is it? Is it time to pick Joseph up from school yet?"

Harpur went nose to nose with her and slammed her body up against the wall, holding her by the throat. "Where is she?"

Joanne was struggling to breathe. "I... I... don't know, I've just woken up!" Her warm breath was in her face. She could smell the stale tobacco on her breath.

"Tell me what you know about Paul Burton and my daughter." Joanne's eyes were wide open with fear, not knowing what would happen next. Was she going to tell her what she wanted to know or keep schtum? Harpur screamed at her again. "Tell me Joanne, for fuck's sake, tell me the truth before I twat you all over this house." There was no need for that. It was Maddie she was furious with, not her. It was do or die time for Joanne. Her own neck was on the line if she didn't tell her what she wanted to know. But, in fairness, she had no other choice, Harpur had a right to know. Joanne had watched Harpur crying and upset about her brother for months and all she ever wanted to know was the truth about his death. It wasn't a big ask, she just needed closure.

Joanne gulped, she closed her eyes and made the decision. So what, her own infidelity would be revealed too. Harpur had done so much for her, she owed her this as a thank you for all her help and support she'd given her. Here it was, the truth at last, no more secrets. "Yes, I know about it. But I've only known for a few months." Harpur's heart stopped beating for a second. So it was true after all. Her body folded in half and her legs couldn't take the stress anymore. She was gagging for breath, windpipe closing up, she was suffocating, sweat pouring from every pore in her body. Joanne knelt down near her and tried to calm her down. "Maddie said she was going to her nana's. You need to sit down and speak with her. It's her web of deceit, not mine." There were so many tears, desperation, anxiety. What the hell was happening to this family? This was her baby girl, how could she hurt her like this, betray her? And with him, that no-good bastard!

Neil had been ringing Harpur for over two hours now. She kept blanking him and he was now sending endless messages. He was begging her to speak to him, to forgive him, to let him try and make it right. She lay in her bedroom with the curtains closed in complete darkness. Her body was curled up in a tight ball. Harpur looked at the picture frame near her bed, she gripped it with her hand and looked at Brady with hateful eyes. "So, you kept this from me. You sold me out for drugs. Maddie is my daughter and I thought you loved her like I do. No wonder you ended it all." Her knuckles turned white as she clenched the frame and slung it at the wall facing her. "You mean nothing to me anymore. I thought we had each other's backs. You bastard, I'll never forgive you for this!" All night long Harpur lay waiting for her daughter to come home, but she never did. Joanne must have told her she was on the war path. She was such a double agent. Harpur checked the clock, she needed to go and find her, bring her home.

Melanie Byfield was stood at her front door smoking as Harpur drove past. It was like the car brakes were pressed for her, she had no control over them. The vehicle skidded and made Melanie look over towards the car. Harpur regained her composure and sat thinking for a few seconds. This woman was always with her brother and it was time to pay her another visit. She parked the car and made her way over. Melanie saw her straight away and rolled her eyes as she began to speak. "I don't suppose you've seen our Maddie have you? We've had murders and she's not come home yet?"

Melanie was wrecked and stank of alcohol. "I knew that kid was nothing but trouble. But how can you tell someone they are wrong when they think they've got it all figured out?"

"Tell me about it," Harpur replied, "she knows I hate Paul Burton with a passion and yet she's been going behind my back with him."

Melanie must have taken it for granted that the big secret was out and carried on talking. This woman was pissed and swaying about. "Brady did all he could to help her. He got the money together she needed you know, well eventually. You know what he was like with any money he got. I went mad at him when I found out he'd spent it and if it wasn't for your mam and her sister, I would dread to think what would have happened. Paul nearly killed Brady when he spent the money he gave him for the abortion. And I can tell you now, he wasn't proud of it either. He cried his heart out to me you know. He knew he'd fucked up big time and he hated himself for it." Harpur had to pretend she knew all about this, she never flinched, her heart was beating in her ears, taking in everything she said. "I had a couple who were willing to buy the baby if she decided to keep it too. You know me, I'm always here to help. Do you know they even gave us a grand as a deposit for the kid when it was born?" Harpur sucked hard on her bottom lip and shook her head slowly. "Brady done that money in too. Yep, on my life he took it right from under my nose. And he spent every bleeding penny of it. He's lucky I didn't kill him. I swear, I was going to shoot him in the balls. He knew what he'd done and I can tell you something for nothing, it pushed him over the edge." Melanie coughed and banged her clenched fist on her chest, she was choking. A big ball of phlegm came flying out of her mouth, landing on the floor near her. She took a few deep breaths and continued with her story. "Brady watched Maddie crying for days, it broke his heart how much he'd let her down. I suppose he let us all down. But it was her he cared about, her that pulled on his heartstrings."

How could she just stand there and take all this? Harpur was as cool as a cucumber and kept her face straight all the way through the conversation. Melanie shook her head and her eyes clouded over. "I loved him you know. I know he had his faults but he kept me sane. He picked me up when I was down and always supported me. He knew I was on the game too yet he never turned his back on me," the tears started to fall now and she was sobbing her heart out. "I think about him every day and if I'm being honest with you, I may as well be dead with him because part of me died too when he left me here alone. Nothing means anything anymore. He kept me going."

Harpur choked up. She had to stay strong, she'd done so well so far. She had to show no emotion, say goodbye and walk away. "We all loved him Melanie. The past is the past isn't it. If you see our Maddie will you tell her to come home please."

"I will love, she won't be far. She's got a good head on her that girl has, don't be too hard on her, she's had a bad time lately. She's just been mixed up that's all." How could she talk about her daughter like that? How could Harpur not have seen what was right in front of her? No wonder Maddie moved in with Diane, it all made sense now. The cunning bastards had it all planned out. Maddie had told her she wanted more space and to get away from Joanne, when in fact she was pregnant and hiding it away from her. Was she so caught up in her own troubles that she'd let her daughter down? Harpur's head was up her arse, she clenched her fist into tiny balls and started the car up. Sheila knew all along and had kept it a secret. What else wasn't she telling her? There was only one way to find out, she was going to confront her.

★

Sheila's house was in complete darkness, only a dim yellow light seeped from her bedroom window. Harpur sat outside in the car, scanning the area. Her mind was in overdrive and she wanted to calm down before she got her mother out of bed. This was one conversation she was going to have tonight for sure. So what if it upset her mother? It needed sorting out! Heads were going to roll!

Harpur locked the car and walked into the garden, slamming the gate behind her knowing Sheila would be up at the window any second. Her mother was a light sleeper and at the slightest noise she was up out of bed at the window, checking it out. Brady had made her like this, he was like an alley cat, in and out of the house all night long. Harpur stood back looking up at the window until she saw the silhouette of her mother appear. Sheila was squeezing her eyes tightly together trying to focus. "It's me. Open the door." Two more lights came on in the house and Harpur prepared herself for war. She'd already texted Diane to meet her here, saying it was an emergency. Sheila opened the door and was just about to start moaning.

Harpur pushed her out of the way and barged into the living room. So much for being calm. She growled over at her mother and pointed her finger towards her chair. "Sit yourself down there. You have some explaining to do and there is no way you're talking yourself out of this one. No fucking way in this world. I want answers. Diane is on her way too. I want to see the whites of your eyes when I ask you both some questions."

Sheila sighed as she sat down. "Have you been drinking? Are you pissed or something? What time is it anyway? I need to go back to bed." Sheila tried to get up from her chair but

Harpur rammed her hand into her shoulder and made sure she stayed put. "It's truth time mother. That's what fucking time it is. Time to cut the bullshit."

Sheila looked at her daughter and she was frightened, she'd never seen her like this before. She backed off and fell into her chair. "What's going on? Just tell me, you're scaring me now. Is Neil alright? Don't tell me you've done him in?"

Harpur sat down and pulled a cigarette out of her packet. She didn't say a word, she just kept her eyes firmly fixed on her mother. How could she have done this behind her back? How could she betray her? She was a fucking Judas. After a few seconds, she walked to where her brother's photograph was and picked it up with both hands. Sheila watched her carefully, what the hell was she doing? Was she going to smash it over her head? She was anxious, shaking. Harpur's voice was calm as she spoke to her brother's image. "So our kid, it's truth time isn't it. I know you're here somewhere in this house so you sit down too and listen to what I have to say," her head spun around and she made sure she had her mother's attention. "You two are a pair of no good, dirty, lying bastards."

There was near silence, only the ticking of the clock on the mantelpiece could be heard. Sheila's eyes were wide open. This poor woman looked like she was going to have a heart attack. Here it was, the lie, the deceit that she was covering up. "So, mother, when were you going to tell me that Maddie was pregnant?" Sheila gulped, her eyes were all over the place, fidgeting. Harpur repeated herself and this time she sat facing her mother. "Tell me what you know, you lying old cow. I know you and Diane know about this so cut the crap."

The back door sprang open and Diane came flying inside. "What's up, what's happened? Are you alright Sheila, is it your breathing again?"

Harpur let out a menacing laugh and held her head back. "Oh, here she is, your partner in crime. Take a seat, the show's just about to start."

Diane was just about to talk when Sheila spoke. "She knows that we helped Maddie." Diane's eyes were wide open and she sat down on the sofa. The shit had hit the fan for sure. "Harpur, the girl needed help, how could we tell you? We just did what we thought was best that's all."

Harpur hissed and clenched her teeth tightly together. "She's my fucking daughter. Didn't you think I had the right to know if she was knocked up?" Sheila tried to touch her arm but she shook her away. "Don't touch me you traitor. After everything that has happened, I really thought me and you were strong. How could you do this to me?" Diane was trying to hush her up but she was just adding fuel to the fire. "Just calm down and I'll tell you what happened. I mean, we'll explain."

Sheila coughed and cleared her throat. "This is my family. He was my son, so I'll tell her."

Sheila picked the photograph of Brady up and placed it so everyone could see him. The small grin on the portrait seemed to fade now. Brady's eyes seemed to be full of sadness. "This is your mess and you'll sit here and see the hurt you've caused. How many times did I tell you what the drugs were doing to you? You've hurt everyone who ever loved you." Harpur looked over at her and bit hard on her lip. Sheila played with the cuff from her beige nightie as she began to reveal the truth. Diane's head sunk, she was ashamed of her actions, regretting ever being a part of this. "Brady told me when it was too late. Maddie was head over heels in love with that Paul fella. And even though at first he thought it was a bit of fun, Brady told her to back off from him. That evil cunt knew his weakness though and kept on ringing him, promising him drugs to bring her with him. Brady was weak where drugs were concerned and when I say the drugs had a hold of him I mean, they really had a hold over him. He was in a bad way and he would have done anything to score. It was the worst I'd ever seen him. I'm not sticking up for him here, he was a mess." Diane closed her eyes as the tears started rolling down the side of her cheeks. The story started to unfold. This was some dark secret. How could they have kept this from her? They weren't ever to be trusted again. This was her family, people she loved and trusted. There was so much pain in this room; regrets, grief, lies, betrayal, they were a broken family.

Harpur listened to every detail and she never flinched. Once Sheila had confessed all, she stood up and shot a look at them both. There was nothing left to say. How could she ever talk to either of them again? Harpur picked up her belonging up and trudged slowly to the back door. Her hand gripped the handle with force, her knuckles turning white. "I'll never darken this door again. You two are finished with me. You've done some things to me mother, but this, even for you, has topped it all."

Diane tried to talk, to try and make her understand, but Harpur left and never looked back once.

★

Harpur's phone hadn't stopped ringing. There were endless texts from Dessie, calls from Neil and long messages from him begging her to let him come home. Where on earth was this girl's head at? Where was she going to go? Everyone she had loved had hurt her, deceived her, took the piss out of her. It was past midnight now and there wasn't a soul on the streets, not a sound, silence.

Bridget opened her front door and sighed. "Come in love, get inside. You look perished. You should have come here earlier and I would have come with you. You don't need to face this on your own," Bridget was holding her hand as she came inside the house, guiding her. "Has Maddie been in touch, has she come home yet?" Bridget held her arms tightly around Harpur, hugging her, feeling her emotions rising. This was a bond nobody could break. Bridget was always there for her no matter what. She'd never judge her, she had her back. Not like that shower of shit she'd just left behind.

Harpur snivelled. "I've been everywhere looking for her Bridget, nobody's seen sight or sound of her. I just want to hold my baby. How could she have gone through all this on her own? Her head must be a mess."

"I know love, come on, let's get you in bed. You look like you're going to drop down where you're stood. Have you eaten anything today? I'll make us some toast and a brew."

Harpur was in some kind of trance and it would be fair to say she was on the edge of reason, she looked like she could blow at any second, snap, lose the will to live. Bridget escorted her to the bedroom and left her alone while she went to make something to eat. She had something to tell her, some news she'd just found out. But was this the right time? Oh, she didn't know anymore, fuck fuck fuck. Harpur found a t-shirt lying about on the floor in the room. She bent down and picked it up and dragged it over her head. She fell back onto the bed and just lay staring at the ceiling. She didn't move a muscle, she just remained totally still. Bridget came back into the bedroom holding a plate with toast piled high on it and a cup of tea in the other hand. "Harpur, come on, get a few slices of this. It might make you feel a little bit better. I bet you've not eaten all day have you?" She placed the food on the side with the drink and lay next to her best friend. "Come on girl, you've survived worse things than this. Everything will look different tomorrow. Sam's home too so that will take the edge off it. You know what he's like, he'll make sure he gets to the bottom of it."

Harpur was shell-shocked. She couldn't speak. Bridget lay next to her and something was lying heavily on her mind. There was no way she could hold it any longer. She'd found out by accident but she was sure that once Harpur knew what she had to tell her, Dessie Ryan would be carted, history, a thing of the past. "Harpur, I was on Facebook today and got talking to our old friend, Josephine Dillon, you remember her don't you?" Bridget may as well have been talking to herself, there was no response. "Well, Josephine was talking about Dessie and well, she told me who he was married to." Bridget paused. Could she tell her? Would it break her heart all over again? She looked over at her and noticed she was asleep. She sighed. This would have to wait until the morning, bleeding hell, this was getting worse by the minute. Bridget could hear a text alert, she reached over and took Harpur's phone from next to her. Clocking the screen, she started to read the message from Dessie. Sat looking at the phone, she scratched the top of her head. He was a twat, he didn't deserve her, not now, not ever. How could he not have told her? Bridget flung the phone across the bed. She cuddled up to Harpur and pulled the quilt over her cold body. Slowly, she stroked the top of her head. "Ssshhh, everything is going to be alright. I'm here for you always, we'll get through this.

Trust me we will."

What a loyal friend Bridget was, just what she needed right now. A loyal person, someone she could trust. Where the hell was Maddie though? Someone should have reported her missing? This was a young girl out on the street at such a vulnerable time in her life. Phone the police for Christ's sake, somebody do something.

CHAPTER SIXTEEN

HARPUR OPENED HER EYES and looked around the room. Where the hell was she? She bolted up from the bed and held her hands around her neck. Bridget jumped up, what was going on? "Harpur, what's up? Come on lie back down, get some rest."

"How did I get here? I need to go."

Bridget was panicking. "Just hang fire and I'll come with you. I'll take you wherever you need to go. Just take a few minutes."

Harpur looked at her wristwatch and closed her eyes. "Our Sam will be on his way home. I need to get there before he arrives. For fuck's sake, hurry up and get ready Bridget. I need to be there for him." Bridget was still half asleep, there was no time for make- applied this morning, no time to comb her hair, she was on a mission.

Harpur sat at the window with Joanne and Bridget. "Oh, he's here!" Joanne yelled at the top of her voice. She sprinted out of the front room and ran to the front door. Joseph was at school and the plan was to pick him up later with his father. It was something Joseph had craved in his life, to see his dad come to school, to show all the other children that he really did have a dad and he wasn't lying. It must have been so hard for him not to have a father living at home with him, like most of the other children in his class. Harpur choked up as she spotted Sam walking down the garden path with his holdall swung over his shoulder.

She'd missed him so much, her heart ached as he smiled at her through the window. Joanne swung around his neck as she greeted him. Perhaps she did really love him? Maybe the time spent alone and the loneliness had caused her to act the way she had. Prison does that, it makes women seek attention elsewhere. It's hard to lie alone each night with nobody to love, nobody to kiss, nobody to talk to.

Bridget smiled as she looked at Harpur. "He looks well doesn't he. What have they been feeding him on, he looks hench?"

Harpur turned to face the doorway. He'd be here soon, back in the arms of the people who loved him. Prison changed people, made them paranoid, lose trust, lose confidence. Sam was loud as he strolled into the living room. "Come here Mam, give me a great big hug." Bridget fanned her fingers in front of her face, she was blubbering. This was all so emotional. Harpur squeezed her son in her arms. No words were needed, they both felt the love.

"Where's our Maddie?" Well that was quick, he'd not been through the front door two minutes and she was having to tell him the truth about what had happened. There was no way she could lie. Sam shot his eyes around the room and everyone hung their heads, something was wrong, he could tell. Sam sat down on the sofa and flung his belongings behind him. He patted the cushion at the side of him and knew his mother was upset. "Has she been giving you lip again? I told you ages ago about her attitude."

Harpur sat down next to Sam. Joanne sat at the table facing Bridget. How could she find the words to tell him everything that had been going on? Taking a deep breath, she began to tell him everything that had happened. As she told him about Neil spying on Joanne, he shot a look over at her and snarled. Maybe she had encouraged him, he wasn't sure. Now it was time to drop the bombshell, the biggie. "Maddie has been knocking about with that Paul Burton. Brady introduced them both in return for drugs and well, he got her pregnant, and she's had an abortion with the help of Nana and auntie Diane."

Sam cracked his knuckles and closed his eyes slowly. "So, what's going to happen now? Is he getting knocked the fuck out or what. Has anyone been to see him?"

Harpur shook her head as Bridget joined the conversation. "Your mam has just found out about it all. Sam, there has been enough heartache in this family lately, just you keep out of it or you'll end up back in the nick."

Sam's nostrils flared, he was raging. He put his arms around his mother. "And Neil, do you want me to go and see him? I'll kill the cunt for upsetting you like this."

"No, I just want you to keep out of it. You're on probation now so the slightest thing you do they'll have you back in prison. You know that more than me, don't you?"

Joanne hadn't said a word, she knew by the look her boyfriend had given her that sooner or later, he'd blame her for it all. "I'm going to dive in the shower Mam and get some decent clothes on. Please don't worry about Maddie. I'll find her, I'll sort it out." Sam looked at them all and no one said a word. It was like a morgue here today; cold, silent, eerie.

Harpur was sat with Bridget in the front room. A text alert on Harpur's phone. She pulled it out and read the message.

"*I just love you. I can't help it. Let's be together. Love Dessie X*"

Harpur raised a smile and held her flat palm over her heart. "Bridget, he just melts me. I'm going to be with him. I've decided. Things happen for a reason and he must be my soul mate, the one. I've tried fighting it but I can't anymore. I just love him. Honest, he takes my breath away."

Bridget cringed as she watched her typing her reply to him.

"Dessie, I love you too. Meet me later in the pub on Deansgate. I'm coming with you. Love Harpur X"

Was she really packing up and leaving? What about her family, the people who loved her? Harpur looked over at Bridget. "I'm going to Spain with him. We have a chance together and if I don't go now I'll regret it for the rest of my life."

Bridget snapped, she had to tell her before she ruined her life for this deadbeat. "He's a lying fucker Harpur. Has he mentioned his wife to you?"

"Of course he has, he just told me that things haven't worked out. He said he will explain some stuff to me when we're face to face but as I see it, it's nothing to do with me. Let's face it, I will never have Neil back will I?"

Bridget needed to tell her what she knew before it was too late. This woman was giving everything up for this wanker. "I was talking to Josephine Dillon the other day on Facebook and she told me some stuff."

"Oh yeah, I remember her. How is she?"

"She told me Dessie married Wendy."

"Wendy who?"

Bridget opened her cigarette packet and lit two of them. Once she'd passed Harpur one, she prepared herself to deliver the news. "He married Wendy O'Malley."

Harpur's jaw dropped. "What the same Wendy

O'Malley he denied cheating on me with?"

"Yes, the same one love."

This was bad, this was the girl who'd split them up when they were younger. Dessie had always denied it though, he swore black and blue that he'd never been anywhere near her and yet now he was married to her. Harpur sucked hard on her fag. Bridget patted her arm softly. "Are you alright? I had to tell you because I didn't want him making a fool of you again."

Why had he never told her, he'd had many a chance to tell her about this? This was bad news. Wendy O'Malley had caused murders between them back in the day. She was a dirty no-good trollop who slept with anyone who'd give her the time of day. So, he risked the love he shared with Harpur for this skank. "Thanks for telling me Bridget. You have saved me a lot of heartache. And here's me giving it all up for him. He's just the same lying womaniser he's always been. Thank fuck I never left with him." Harpur opened her phone and typed him a message. She was angry, oh yes, raging inside.

"Dessie, meet me now. I just need to talk to you before I leave with you. Be there in half an hour."

There was no kiss at the end of the message this time. Harpur sat down and held her head in her hands. "I need you to help me find Maddie. I'll give it until tonight and if she's not come home, I'm going to the police. Will you ring Neil and tell him what has gone on?"

"Don't you think it might be better coming from you?"

"No, I don't want to speak to him. Just tell him what you know. Let him worry like I have. I just need to put this to bed once and for all. I'll be back soon."

Harpur grabbed her coat and hurried to the door.

"Sam, I'll be back soon" she shouted up the stairs. "If Maddie comes back here let me know."

Harpur was gone. Sam stood at the top of the stairs and nodded his head slowly. He whispered under his breath. "It's showtime mother, nobody messes with my sister and gets away with it."

The bar was quiet as Harpur walked inside. Where was he? Where was he hiding the little rat? From the corner of her eye she spotted him, stood at the other end of the bar. She was a woman on a mission and she was saying what she had to say and leaving. What an utter plonker she'd been. How had she allowed herself to get involved with him again? He was trouble and always would be.

"Hi babes, do you want a drink?"

Harpur stared at him. Her words were stuck in the back of her throat. Swallowing hard, she answered him. "Can you get me something stiff, maybe a Bacardi and coke, a double."

She turned her back on him and made her way to a corner nearby. This was private what she had to say, not for all the world to hear. Dessie bounced up to where she was sat and leaned in to kiss her, she turned her cheek away from him. "What's up, I only wanted a quick peck?" Harpur banged her fingers on the edge of the table with force. She wanted to see his face change when she told him what she knew, watch his arse fall out.

"So when were you going to tell me that you married Wendy O'Malley? The same girl who you denied cheating on me with. The same one you said you would never go near?"

Dessie went white, there was pain in his eyes, the truth was out. "It's not like you think Harpur and I was going to tell you. I've tried a few times but the time was never right."

"What were you going to do? Wait until I was sat on the plane with you before you shed some light on your life?"

"No, I was going to tell you as soon as I had the chance. Harpur, let me explain some stuff to you."

"No, fuck off. I don't want to hear your bullshit. You can save it for someone who gives a fuck because I don't. God, I was really going to give it all up and come with you. What the hell was I thinking. Phew, a lucky escape for me I think?"

Dessie dropped his head into his hands. "Harpur, just listen for a minute while I explain a few things." She swigged a mouthful of her drink and growled at him. This had better be good because she was ready to walk. "Okay, I did sleep with her once when we were together. I was at a party and she was all over me. You know what she was like."

"Yeah, a bleeding dirty cow. Is that what it was, sex? You risked everything we had to please your male ego and get a shag?"

Dessie hung his head in shame, she was right. Well, he wasn't getting anything from her was he and all his mates were having sex. He just needed to have a go, lose his virginity. He was pissed, off his head, not really knowing what he was doing until it was too late. Harpur's eyes clouded over, she'd been right all along. She hated him with a passion now. Her words were spoken softly, from the heart. "We were in love, so what if we were young, we both said we would love each other forever."

"Harpur, she told me she was pregnant a few weeks later. How could I have told you that? She told me straight that she was keeping the baby and she even brought her parents round to our house to see my mam and dad. I was devastated. I didn't want any children with her, I wanted them with you."

People in the pub were looking over at them now. They needed to calm down. Harpur gripped her drink in her hand and flung the remainder of it in his face. "There you go you bastard. It's what you deserve after the lies you've told me. I knew I was right all along. Once a liar, always a liar. A leopard never changes his spots."

Harpur stood up ready to leave. Dessie had to pull something out of the bag, otherwise she'd be gone forever. "I came looking for you Harpur. It might have been too late, but I did try. Did Andrew tell you how I confronted him one night and told him that he ever hurt you I would kill him?"

Harpur froze, Andrew was Sam's dad. What did he know about him? "No, why would you say anything to him about me?"

"Because I still loved you. I twatted him you know, did he tell you that?"

Harpur was confused, she was feeling light-headed, she needed some fresh air. Her head was all over the place now and she was so mixed up she didn't know if she was coming or going. "It makes no difference now does it? We should never have met again. The past is in the past for a reason."

Dessie had one last shot at this, he had to pour his heart out, make her believe that this love was real, forever. "Harpur, I made one mistake and I've paid for it for years.

I married a woman I never really loved and I've been living in misery for years. Don't you think I've been punished enough?" Her head tilted to the side. He was right in a way. And she'd been punished too for her mistakes. But how would these two ever work, they were both hotheads, sensitive, stubborn. Harpur's feet seemed glued to the floor. She said she was going, why was she still stood there? Should she leave while she still had the chance?

"Goodbye Dessie, it would never have worked out anyway."

Dessie stood up and shouted after her, so what if everyone could see him upset, he loved her, he loved her so much. "Harpur, don't do this. I love you like I've never loved anyone else. I promise I'll make you happy, don't give up on us please." Harpur heard every word but she carried on walking. She was heartbroken.

Harpur sat by her brother's grave, swigging a bottle of vodka. Bridget had just rung her and told her Maddie was home and safe. "I want to hate you Brady but I can't. I want to dig you up and throttle you. You could have just come to me and spoken to me about it. You know that don't you? I've lost it all now, I've got nothing left. You're gone, Neil's gone and the only man I've ever really loved has gone too. What's the point ay, I knew it was all too good to be true. There is no such thing as a happy ending in my life is there. And you made my mam lie too, you brought her into your dark, dirty world. My poor baby, Maddie. You told me you would always protect her and you never did." Harpur looked at the photograph of her brother on his headstone. "I can't come here anymore Brady. It just breaks my heart too much. I need to get on with my life, to look after my family. I'll never, ever, forget you our kid. You'll always have a place in my heart as long as I live. I'll keep your memory alive, I promise you. Even though my heart is broken, it just keeps breaking every day without you. You took my heart with you Brady, you did, you took it." Her head bent slowly towards his grave. She kissed his photograph with her cold lips and whispered her last goodbye. Harpur took a last gulp of vodka from the bottle and placed it on her brother's grave. "There you go Brady. I've left you a drink. We still share all we have. Be waiting for me when I take my last breath our kid. Until we meet again. I love you, I always will." Harpur walked away from the graveside. She would never come here again.

Sheila sat in Brady's bedroom holding her cushion tightly in her arms. She was talking to the cupboard where her son hung himself. Her tears were flowing and she was struggling to talk. "It's all over now Brady. The truth is out," she paused and choked up. "All but one secret though. There is only me who knows what went on in this room the day you died isn't there?" Sheila wiped the tears with the corner of the cushion. "I loved you son with all my heart but I couldn't do it anymore, you were destroying everything you touched. It needed to stop. Somehow, you had to be stopped." Sheila lay back on the bed and turned her head to the side. "Will you forgive me son? I saw you hanging there and I knew you wanted me to help you. You spoke to me and pleaded with me but I just couldn't do it anymore. I'm sorry son. I just walked away and closed the door and left you to die. Maybe one day you will understand why

I did what I did. I loved you that much, that I had to let you go, to stop you suffering." What was she saying here? Did she really turn and walk away when he needed her most? Sheila closed her eyes with the cushion held close to her chest. She was still whispering under her breath as she drifted off to sleep. "Nobody knows a mother's pain, to watch her child suffering. I loved you that much that I had to let you go, son." The room was quiet now, the curtain moved about slightly as a small draft from the window seeped inside. Was it really the wind or could it have been Brady finally at peace, knowing all his lies were out and everybody knew what he had tried to cover up? The shame he'd felt inside, the torment, it was all now over.

★

Harpur listened as her phone rang and rang, it was Dessie. She marched into the living room and as soon as she spotted her daughter, she flung her arms around her. There were no more lies in this house, it was like the family had been cleansed. Maddie sobbed her heart out. "Mam, I'm so sorry. I wanted to tell you but I was scared that I'd let you down."

"Ssshhhhh, don't say a word. It's over now." Bridget was an emotional wreck; she'd been crying for hours with Maddie before Harpur came home. Every detail she'd told her had stabbed at her heart, it was heart-breaking listening to everything this young girl had been through.

"Where's Sam?" Harpur asked. Bridget shrugged her shoulders.

Maddie dried her eyes and sat back in her chair. "He was the one who brought me home Mam. He came and found me and told me everything was going to be alright."

Harpur looked at the clock. It was late now, where the hell was he? Maddie was edgy, fidgeting, trying to change the subject.

There was a knock at the front door. Bridget lifted the curtain slightly and gasped her breath. "Bleeding hell, that's all we fucking need."

They all looked over at her. "Who is it?" Harpur asked curiously.

"It's erm, Neil."

Maddie choked up, she'd had enough heartbreak for one day and couldn't take anymore. "Mam, I'm going to bed. Please don't let my dad go on at me. I've not slept properly for days. Just keep him down here for now ."

Harpur nodded. She knew she'd have to face her husband sooner or later and there was no running away from it. Bridget stood up and placed her hand on her shoulder. "I'm just going to nip home and then I'll come back. You two need to speak love, even if it is to say it's over. I'll go now and give you some space."

Bridget left and Harpur could hear her talking to Neil in the hallway. Harpur looked like she could drop at any second, she'd had so much stress, her head was battered. All she needed right now was two loving arms to hold her and tell her everything was going to be alright. Neil opened the door slowly and entered the room. His eyes were red raw and you could see he wasn't in a good way. "Harpur, where's Maddie? Is she alright?"

"She's fine Neil, just a bit teary but what else can you expect?"

Neil edged closer to her. "Harpur, I love you so much. I can never say how sorry I am for what I've put you through. Please love, don't give up on us. Let's work it out.

We can't just throw away our marriage just like that can we?"

Harpur stared at him. If she was being honest with herself she had her own guilty secret too. Could she forgive him though, make things work out? Neil put his arms around her neck and sobbed his heart out. "Please babe, just give me one more chance. I'll never hurt you again. I swear, name it, I'll do anything." His arms around her neck made her feel loved again, somebody who cared about her, would be with her through thick and thin.

"Neil, I'm not sure anymore."

He didn't let her get the rest of her words out. "Just let me sleep here tonight and then I'll give you some space. I just need you near me again, just for one night then I'll leave in the morning I promise you. We can take it as slow as you want. I won't pressure you."

Harpur let out a laboured breath. It was sad to see him like this, so desperate, so full of remorse. "Go and get in bed Neil. I'll be up soon. I just need to clear my head and I need to be alone." Neil had an overnight pass, a start, a way back into her life. He kissed her cold hands and looked deep into her eyes. "I'll never let you down again. I'm going to make you the happiest woman ever. You just watch Harpur, you'll want for nothing. I'll talk with Maddie in the morning if that's alright. I just need to get my head around it all." Neil left the room and headed upstairs. Harpur was alone with her thoughts.

The midnight hour fell and Harpur lay wide awake next to her husband. He was sound asleep and snoring. She heard someone come into the house. Sneaking out of bed, she crept out of the bedroom and headed down the stairs. "Mam, what are you doing up, go back to bed."

Harpur shot a look at her son's hands. They were covered in blood. He could see her looking at them and placed his hands into his pocket quickly. "Come on, let's have a brew. It feels good to be home Mam."

Harpur was confused, where was his other half, they went out together? "Where's Joanne, is she not with you?"

Sam sniggered and shook his head. "Did you really think I didn't know what was going on with her? The lads in the jail talk and I know everything that dirty slut has been up to while I've been banged up. Come on, give me some credit?"

Harpur's eyes were wide open. "Oh, you've not killed her have you? Please Sam, is she alright?"

"Yeah, course she is. She's back at her mam's. I've told her I will look after Joseph but as for me and her, well, it's over isn't it?"

Harpur sucked hard on her lips. She was glad he knew the truth, she hated hiding anything from him. But where was the blood from on his hands, there was something he wasn't telling her? Mother and son sat in the living room slurping on hot cups of tea. Sam looked over at her and shook his head. "What's up Mam?"

"Nothing love, it's just you realise what's important in life don't you when things like this happen."

"Yes, it takes a trauma to see what really matters in your life. And sometimes you have to do what makes you happy, not everyone else." Harpur lifted her head and stared directly at her son. Did he know about Dessie? No, surely not, how could he? "So, you can't stay fallen out with Nana and Auntie Diane forever can you?"

"I'm still too angry with them both at the moment to even think about it. It will sort itself out, it always does."

There was a text alert on Harpur's phone. Sam shot a look over at her and nodded his head. "It's your phone that not mine, see who it is then, what you waiting for?" Sam's mother had to act cool. Pretend everything was normal. Her eyes shot down to the screen and a lump formed at the back of her throat.

"I'll always love you no matter what. I'm leaving in the morning and you will be rid of me forever. Please don't hate me. Love Dessie X"

This was it, the end, it was finally over. The whirlwind romance had hit a brick wall. "Who's the message from?" Sam enquired.

"Oh, it's just Bridget. She was checking if I was alright. She wanted to come back over here earlier but I told her I was fine. She's been my rock through all this Sam. Honest, without her I would have crumbled."

"She's a top girl Bridget is. Mam, are you sure you want Neil here? Maddie text me and told me he's in bed upstairs, if you want I'll drag the cunt out and kick fuck out of him."

Harpur smiled, he was such a hothead. But you could see in his eyes he was serious. Oh yes, he would have done him in proper if he had the go-ahead. His mother was his world and if anyone hurt her, they would have him to deal with. "No son, there has been enough trouble in this house to last a lifetime. It's a wonder I'm not six feet under. I swear to you, it's a wonder I'm still breathing." Harpur stood and kissed her son on his head as she stood over him. "I'm going back to bed Sam. I'm exhausted."

"Yes, I'm coming to bed soon myself. I'm just getting my head around being out of nick. I'll be up soon. See you in the morning Mam and remember, nobody can make you happy but yourself. All you've done is run about after us lot for years. Do something that makes you happy for a change."

His words were heartfelt and she dabbed a single finger in the corner of her eye to stop the tears from flowing. "I know love, I know. Goodnight, see you in the morning."

Sam stretched out on the sofa and looped his hands over his head. "Night Mam," he whispered as she left the room.

Sam was just drifting off to sleep when he opened his eyes in a panic. "Maddie, what the fuck?"

His sister moved his legs from the sofa and sat down next to him. "I couldn't sleep. Every time I close my eyes I can still see his face," she made sure they were alone and spoke in a low voice. "Did you get rid of him like you said you would? Please, tell me it's done. You said you would help me."

Sam chewed on his bottom lip and nodded. "I've told you no one will see sight or sound of that cunt again. Paul Burton is history. We have a bond me and you, like my mam had with Brady, and your pain is my pain."

Maddie reached over and patted his leg. "I had to deal with this mess. He was laughing at me, at our family. I only meant to scare him but before I knew it, I stuck the knife in him. His eyes, I can still see them." Sam could see she was about to go hysterical.

"Ssshhh. This is our secret, not a word about it to anyone. If we get caught for this we will both be jailed for life, you know that don't you?"

Maddie was shaking, twitching. "He told everyone I was just a bang. I loved him Sam. But I was just a bit of fun for him, nothing more. I was such a fool."

"Live and learn sister, live and learn." Sam eased her down to lie at the side of him. He stroked his hand across her forehead. "Big brother is home now, you're safe. Remember that always." Maddie lay with her eyes wide open. She would never breathe a word of this again. She would take it to the grave.

Harpur stood at her bedroom door looking at her husband. She'd already been outside to the car and put something in the boot. The morning light was breaking now and the house was in complete silence. She crept over to the bed and placed a letter quietly at Neil's side. With one look behind her, she sneaked down the stairs. Harpur popped her head inside the living room and looked at her children who were sound asleep on the sofa. Under her breath, she whispered, "I love you both so much. Look after each other. Goodbye now."

Where was she going at this time of the morning?

Harpur sat in the car and rested her head on the steering wheel. Slowly, her hands moved and the key flicked the ignition. Before she started to drive off, she sent two text messages.

★

Harpur walked up the street. The birds were tweeting and dawn was breaking. She flicked her hair over her shoulder and raised her eyes up towards the sky. "This is it our kid, wish me luck." The sound of feet coming towards her, pounding the pavement, heavy breathing. He gripped her tightly in his arms and choked up. "I love you so much. I promise, I will never let you down again. We'll be happy together forever I swear. Thank you so much for giving me a second chance." The two of them shared a passionate kiss and walked away together holding hands. Harpur was on a new journey now with the man she had never stopped loving. Just before the two of them got into the taxi, Dessie took her suitcase from her and placed it on the floor. He held her head in his hands and a single bulky tear ran down the side of his cheek. "Me and thee. You and I. Who'd have thought it, ay. Come on lovely. We have a plane to catch."

Harpur smiled as the taxi pulled away from the street. She reached over and held Dessie's hand tightly. "This is forever. You know that don't you?"

Dessie smirked and nodded his head. "You better believe it is, always."

THE END

Other books by this author